My Daughter

lou zitnik

My Daughter is a work of fiction.

The works cited list in Entry 11 is incorrectly formatted by the narrator, but the titles and authors are correct. Readers are encouraged to consult them as important sources of information about Hawai'i.

Cover design by lou zitnik. Based on an oil painting by Barbara Nichols, in the private collection of the author.

First Edition: The People's Edition

ISBN-13: 978-0-9985504-0-4

DEDICATED TO HER MEMORY

CONTENTS

Before you take another step:

    This manuscript was discovered during the search for three patients who had escaped from the state's high-security hospital in Kaneohe, Hawaii. Since then, two of the patients have been returned to the hospital. The third, the narrator of this manuscript, remains at large

Entry 1: FAMILY MATTERS

I shouldn't be the one telling you this, about Papa Joe and his daughter.

Words like to play hide and seek with me, and trying to write them down only prolongs the agony. But the Doc says it could help, so it's me who has to write the report.

You can call me Manny. Most people do. Only Ms. Song up at the college used the official version. "Manual," she'd say, making my name sound like a book of instructions, "write like you talk, from your heart."

She was a good-looking woman, that Ms. Song, like a painting in a museum or a foldout in a glossy magazine. Just thinking about her leaning over my shoulder to see another blank page makes me want to paint my masterpiece. But back then I didn't have any words in my heart, and whenever I tried to talk people looked at me like I was trying to talk a foreign language. "Manual," Ms. Song would say, "never mind all that. Get to the point."

The point is, the night Papa Joe disappeared I was reaching into the dark. Joe's .22 felt cold and oily, his Zippo lighter worn around the edges, but his fifth of Sauza felt smooth and new, in perfect working condition. I was twisting off the cap, when Joe reached across the desk, picked up his lighter, and flipped it open.

Joe's a big guy, and the flickering light made him look even bigger. "You got any kids?" he asked.

"Not that I remember." That's what I said, but I said lots of stuff like that when I was talking to Joe. It wouldn't be much of a conversation if I didn't toss in a noun or two.

"You'd remember a kid."

"I can't remember yesterday." That's what I told him, and it was true.

He lifted the lid off his hurricane lamp and held the lighter to the wick. When the flame caught, he snapped the Zippo shut, pushed it across the desk at me, and said, "Keep it."

That's Joe. His birthday was five minutes away, and he was giving me presents. Then he broke the news. "Sometimes," he said, "a man needs a family."

This from a guy we called Papa because he took care of stray cats. "I got plenty of family," I told him. Counting Joe, I had Doc Trina up at the hospital, my cat Steamer, Rayzah the waitress, Frankie the lawyer, and in a pinch, as a last resort, the Golden Madonna, profession unknown. "Besides," I told him, "no matter. I can take care of myself."

As soon as I said it, I knew it was a mistake. When people in Hawaii get to feeling sentimental, usually after a six pack of Bud Lite or a couple chunks of birthday cake, they like to talk about family, ohana, like it's some kind of magical glue that holds the world together, a cure-all for every disease from cancer to assault with a deadly weapon.

On cue, like lightning in an old monster movie, Joe's grandfather clock chimed midnight. If that wasn't enough, a siren kicked in down by the ocean, rushed at us, and hung in the air as I lifted the bottle of tequila to my lips.

"To life," Joe said.

"Sure. Life." I tilted my head back, and let gravity do its work. I slammed the bottle down and reached into my shirt pocket. The tequila needed reinforcements. The withered joint I dug out had survived a month of near misses. Saved for an emergency. Joe's birthday fit the description. I brushed the lint off its brown skin and said, "Happy 70."

"72."

"Really? So soon?"

Joe laughed but it didn't stop him from picking up the .22. It wasn't much of a gun, just an old target pistol, with a six-inch barrel and a cracked grip. Even so, me and guns are like me and words. We don't get along, so I pushed my chair back, taking the zippo with me. The joint caught fire on the first try. It smelled of musty books and tangerines, and burned my throat almost as much as the tequila.

Joe waited for me to stop coughing. When I slid his lighter at him, he pushed it back. "I said to keep it. An early Christmas present." I rubbed my finger over the block letters engraved in the worn brass: VIETNAM.

He asked if I remembered my promise.

"Sure," I said, remembering to inhale. Him asking didn't bother me. The truth is, in those days I had a little problem with my memory. Still do. And it's not getting better. "How could I forget?" I said, holding the smoke in where it could do its best work.

Joe smiled and pointed the .22 at his grandfather clock. It didn't stop ticking. "I haven't fired this thing since Nixon resigned."

I didn't ask for details.

He flicked open the cylinder and looked at me through the holes meant for bullets, nine of them. "We were drinking wine," he said. "A buck-fifty a gallon. Nasty stuff. Life can feel pretty damned good when you're young and drunk."

For Joe that was a speech, the most I had heard him say in a month. He reached into his desk drawer, dug out a handful of stray bullets mixed with paperclips, and said, "We were shooting at stars."

For the record, I should note that while Joe played the part of Chatty Kathy separating bullets from paperclips, I was big gulping tequila. A couple of times, and in between I worked on the joint. So maybe I wasn't exactly sober when he pointed the .22 at the clock and pulled the trigger.

Nothing happened.

3

"Cheap ammo," he said. He stood up, straightened his arm, and pulled the trigger. The shot ripped open the night, tore a hole in the clock's face. "Time's up," he said.

I should have said something, but my ears were ringing. The clock's little hand was pointing straight down, the big hand was blown off. I took another puff.

"Traveling time," Joe said.

It sounded funny coming from a guy who hadn't been off the island for as long as I could remember, not even to Honolulu, not even back in the day when it only cost $25 for the fifty-minute flight. Holding down a cough, I managed to say, "I'm going with you." But when I tried to stand up, my legs went numb.

Joe walked by me, slapped me hard on the shoulder. "Stay here," he said. "You're in charge now."

Searching for words, "Sure" was all I found. The rest were hiding somewhere. That's the truth.

Papa Joe stopped next to his chest-style freezer, another one of his garage-sale purchases, and turned to me. "When the Judge gets here, tell her I was working on deadline. She'll understand. You help her, Manny. And don't forget your promise." Before I could say anything, he disappeared into the Empire.

I took a few more hits off the bottle, a couple more off the joint, thinking I could handle the Judge with my eyes closed. To test the theory, I leaned back, took a deep breath of smoky air, and closed my eyes. In a second I was dreaming about the Judge stealing my boat and throwing me in jail for thirty days.

When I woke up, the hurricane lamp was sipping the last drop of kerosene, giving off just enough light for me to see the empty tequila bottle. When the light flickered out, I stood up and shouted into the dark. "Hey, Joe."

Following his trail, I tripped over a 50-pound bag of rice and crashed into the freezer. Navigating Joe's thirty-year collection of stuff should've made me turn on the lights, except I didn't want to see anything. I wanted to be in the dark.

I squeezed through a narrow canyon made of bookshelves, found the stairs, felt for the banister, caught hold, and climbed to the projection booth. "Joe," I whispered, pushing open the door.

A battery-powered candle was burning on the old projector. Joe's letterman's jacket was lying on the cot. I dug into the pocket and found a smashed package of Girl Scout cookies dating back to WWII. Chocolate mints, still crunchy. Not an easy task staying crunchy in Hilo. It's a small town by a river, in a rain forest, in the middle of the ocean. Sidewalks and asphalt are the only things that stay hard longer than a week.

To cover the sound of my chewing, I leaned out the window. The wind off the ocean was a sweet whisper, like Ms. Song's breath on my neck. In the sky, the stars were struggling to stay alive. If what the science guys said on TV was true, some of those stars were already dead. They just didn't know it.

I was going to leave the next part out, but Doc Trina says the point of this report is to write down everything and tell the truth no matter how crazy it might seem. The truth is, I was leaning out the window. When I looked down a naked woman climbed out of a dumpster.

"Looking for something?" I shouted.

"You," she shouted back. "What are you waiting for?"

When I didn't move, she leaped up, grabbed the fire escape, and started climbing. Somewhere between the ground and Joe's window she managed to wrap herself in a terry cloth robe and gold slippers. The uniform matched her flaming red hair, splash of freckles, and nametag from the 1972 Democratic National Convention: G. Madonna. My faded jeans and ragged Obama t-shirt made us look like a couple.

"I'm worried about you," she said, snagging a cookie from my hand. She pushed me out of the way and climbed through the window. "Mints! Oh, no, we need something stronger than mints." She found the box of Girl Scouts, shook it once, and handed it to me. "Try these. Guaranteed vitamins."

5

I bit into a Peanut Butter Surprise. My favorite. If she wanted to, the Golden Madonna could work miracles. But it was a good idea to keep an eye on the tab.

"It's going to be a tough week," she said.

"Who told you?"

"Try more cookies," she said. "They'll take the edge off."

We sat next to each other on the cot, shoulders touching, her smelling of patchouli oil. She rested her hand on my knee, and the radio came to life, jumping from Joe's favorite, NPR, to Mick Jagger and the Rolling Stones. They were singing about having sympathy for the devil. The Madonna smiled. She liked a heavy beat. "I haven't heard from you lately, Manny."

"I thought it was the other way around."

Me and her were in the middle of a little spat dating back to her not showing up to stop the Judge from throwing me in jail. Papa Joe said I should forget it. He said I should accept life for what it was, a rollercoaster ride on an exploding universe with no madonnas. Get used to it, that's what he said. That's what he always said when asked for advice. Me, I knew better. The Madonna had connections. She could change things, if she wanted to.

She dug her fingernails into my knee. The pain made me think of better days. "I'm worried about you, Manny."

"I can take care of myself."

"Doubtful."

We crunched more cookies.

"It's not the worst thing, Manny." She pointed a half-eaten Peanut Butter Surprise at the ceiling. "No matter what they tell you."

"Who?"

"Them. Up there. I don't make the rules, Manny."

I didn't argue. My tongue was too busy trying to unstick fifty-year-old peanut butter from the roof of my mouth. I listened to the Stones beg to introduce themselves, until she said, "I'm going to help you."

A cat screeched, like in the old movies again. Thinking it was a warning or my pal Steamer in a fight, I looked out the window. Down in the alley, next to his old Datsun pickup, Papa Joe was lying face up.

"Joe," I shouted.

A hefty black rat materialized out of the drainpipe and sniffed at the pool of blood next to Joe's head. From the same dumpster that the Madonna had made her appearance, Steamer jumped into the moonlight, claws sparkling, and landed on the rat's back. They rolled together a couple times, hissing and spitting, then ran off toward the ocean, Steamer in hot pursuit.

Fueled by peanut butter and sugar, I dropped down the fire escape, into a heavy silence. The air was clear and still and smelled of cruise ship exhaust and coffee grinds.

Ms. Song used to tell me that people read to discover what she called insights. Here's one for you: Don't drink tequila and smoke weed after midnight. If you do, you'll end up like me, looking down at your best pal on his 72nd birthday.

Joe had changed into his best khaki shorts and a dark blue T-shirt. His blood was spreading slowly over the plastic tarp. The .22 was still in his hand, and a note was pinned to his chest. It was Joe's idea of a birthday card. Now all I had to do was wrap him up and send him on his way.

Entry 2: BLUE RAVEN

I woke up to a tap, tap, tapping at Joe's door. At first I thought it was in my head. Tequila can do that, create spatial problems, so I squeezed my eyes shut, stayed in Joe's chair, and tried to forget I was alive.

"I see you, Manny."

I saw the back of my lids and a bloodstained note.

"Manny!"

When I opened my eyes, Bobbie Marta was standing outside, sweating in her dark blue polyester uniform. The disguise was supposed to make Big Island cops look like the cops on television. She hadn't taken hers off since graduating from cop school. Me, I don't like polyester. I was wearing cotton: a black t-shirt and black board shorts, both a couple sizes too big. The web belt was from Joe's war surplus stock.

Officer Marta shifted her attack. With two knuckles she tapped gently on Joe's ancient window. "Wake up, Manny. We need to talk."

The Empire, held together by termites old enough to remember the territorial days, trembled under the pressure. I figured I had slept a day or two. Maybe Marta could fill in the details. She was a responsible adult with a couple of kids and a cheap watch. I stood up, waded through the sunlight, and slid back the deadbolt. Before I could step out of the way, Marta

8

pushed open the door and squeezed by me, asking, "Where's Papa Joe?"

I looked at the freezer.

"Hey," she grabbed my shoulder and turned me around so she could see my face. "You in there?"

"Not me."

"What?" She stepped back and gave me the cop eye, a stink-eye with an extra doses of stink. "You don't look so good."

"Kinda sleepy." Like I had been kicked in the gonads. I stuck my head outside. The air smelled of gardenias, harbor crud and burning tires. In place of stars, the sun was bright and smiley faced, ready to burn a hole in me. "Nice day," I said, closing the door.

"Where's Joe?"

"What day is it?"

"You been smoking?" she asked.

"I got medical."

"Smells like you've been over medicating."

"That's the lava," I told her. Back then our contribution to global warming and regional disaster was a river of molten rock. Moving at the blazing speed of 15-yards per hour, its target was Pahoa, an old plantation town made of dry wood that looked like a movie set airlifted from a spaghetti western. A few feet out of Pahoa, we could walk in front of the lava. We could even lead tourists to it. But we couldn't stop it. If it crossed the road, it would burn down Pahoa and twenty thousand people would be cutoff from Walmart. Even worse, when the wind was blowing out of the south, the air smelled like burning rubber.

"Never mind the lava." Officer Marta stopped at Joe's desk and picked up his empty bottle of tequila. "What's with the tokillya?" she asked.

"It's Papa Joe's birthday. If it's still Monday."

"Stop that. You know what day it is. How much did you drink?"

9

My stomach was hurting, like Steamer the cat and that drainpipe rat were still in my gut, chasing each other in circles, so I said, "Why don't you and me go out to Blaines, get something to eat?"

"Where's Papa?"

At Blanes we could find shoyu chicken with two scoops rice, two scoops mac salad, and a big Coke with plenty ice, so I said, "I can't remember the last time I ate. Except, maybe, cookies. I think I ate some cookies last night."

"Where's Papa?" That's how cops work. They keep asking.

"Gone."

"Gone where?"

"Traveling."

"Joe doesn't travel."

"I told him it was a good idea."

"And he listened to you?"

"Why not?"

She was looking around Joe's office, checking all the shadows. There were plenty of them to keep her busy. The Empire used to be a movie house, called the Empire, before it was a dance studio called The Empire Dance Studio. Then Papa Joe bought it and turned it into "The Empire of Used Antiques!" That's what the hand-painted sign on the window said. The name was my idea, so was the hand-painting. I like working with a brush. Joe liked collecting stuff.

Marta stepped over a 50-pound bag of rice and leaned her butt against the freezer. "When did he leave?"

"If it's Monday, last night. If it is Tuesday, the night before."

"Jeez, Manny." She hoisted herself onto the freezer, sat there, rocking back and forth with her hands on her knees. "It's Monday, okay. And there's a bullet hole in Joe's clock."

She had good eyes, that Marta. "Joe was celebrating his birthday," I said.

"Jeez! Already." She shook her head. "You have any alcohol? Or did you two drink it all?"

Joe had a walk-in safe behind his desk. It was a leftover from back in the day when people remembered that tsunamis liked to rip through Hilo whenever people forgot that tsunamis liked to rip through Hilo. And if tidal waves and lava flows aren't enough to scare you, we have hurricanes, earthquakes, and hundred-year floods that come every other year. Living in Hilo is enough to make buying a twenty-ton safe big enough to be a bomb shelter look like a good investment.

To keep Marta guessing, I fumbled with the combination like Joe did when he was trying to convince me the lock worked. The heavy door swung open and revealed Joe's .22 and two fresh bottles of Sauza on the top shelf. The tequila looked dangerous. The .22 looked clean and innocent, except for the bloody note pinned under its cracked grip.

"Quit stalling, Manny. Bring the drink."

I closed the door and poured a couple shots of tequila into coffee cups, the chipped ones Joe bought from the tourists who had jumped ship when the SS Dependence went down in a sea of rust. The chips didn't bother Marta. "Happy birthday," she said, and tossed back her morning smoothie.

For the record, while she sat there drinking and tapping the heels of her sensible work boots against the freezer, I should tell you that Marta was a good cop. On duty she stayed sober, most of the time, but ever since her twisted watch commander had her assigned permanently to the graveyard shift, sunrise was her happy hour. Just because the rest of the world wasn't drinking didn't mean she had to suffer.

Me, I left my cup on the desk.

"What?" she said. "Not drinking?"

"Not yet."

"You still seeing things?"

"I see you. Does that count?"

"Didn't the Judge help you with those problems?"

"She gave me thirty days."

"And?"

"I survived." I tried the cup again, but my hand wouldn't cooperate. Instead, I dug a stale cookie out of my shirt pocket.

11

My stomach shuddered at the scent of oily peanut butter, so I dropped the nugget back in place. Waste not, want not.

"Joe's truck is out back," Marta said, setting her cup on the freezer. "I checked."

Like I said, she was a good cop.

"If his truck's there," she asked, "how did Joe get where he was going?"

I had to think about that for a second. "I was drinking. Joe said he was going. I fell asleep. When I woke up, he was gone." I poured her another shot, proud of myself for telling the truth.

"Mahalos." She downed the Sauza. "Mind if I have a look around?"

She didn't wait for an answer. While she made her way down the hall and up the stairs, I navigated my way out of the office and into the snack bar. To give life meaning, I dropped a slab of butter in Joe's iron skillet, tossed in six eggs, a fistful of salt, and five slices of Portuguese sausage. In case Marta wanted to eat, I tossed in three more eggs. Then I turned the gas to high and waited for the sizzle.

Marta came down the stairs and went out the swinging doors to the auditorium. I dipped a chunk of Punaluu sweat bread into the spattering butter. Like a sponge, it soaked up the salty grease. The bread tasted like cotton candy from heaven. Not from the Madonna's heaven, where you had to strip down to a halo and live in the clouds without food. My heaven was a happy place, a vacation rental in Bangkok, with wood floors, extra-strong AC, plenty of bed space, and free tickets to all the latest Broadway shows.

The back door slammed shut, the swinging doors swung open, and Marta's footsteps headed my way. I dipped more bread in the butter, stuck it in my mouth, and chewed while watching her march into the snack bar.

"When the Judge didn't show up for court this morning," she said, "they sent me up to her place. To check on her."

"The Judge is always late."

"She's never late."

I thought about snapping back with a description of the Judge missing our midnight rendezvous, but she beat me to it. "I found this on her desk." She showed me a sheet of lined paper torn from a day planner:

Dec. 8, 2013: Empire at midnight. Talk to Joe.

"Her car's gone," Marta said. "Maybe her and Joe went somewhere, together?" She folded the evidence and slipped it inside her shirt, where only her husband would be brave enough to look.

"Sure," I said. "It could happen." As long as the Judge did the driving.

"You were here all night? You didn't hear or see anything?"

"I heard lots of stuff. I didn't see the Judge."

She stepped toward me. I gripped the spatula, ready to protect my honor. Her cellphone rang. She grabbed it off her belt and listened to it squawk. "Now?" she shouted. "No way. My shift is over."

I followed her through the hall, past the freezer, and out the front door. A line of cars drove by headed up the mountain. Exhaust fumes mixed with the salty smell of dead fish. "Where?" she shouted. "Fine!"

As she holstered the phone, I slipped back inside. I was about to jam the deadbolt into place, when she gently opened the door. "Sorry," she said, half in, half out. "If Joe comes back, ask him to call me."

"Sure."

She glanced at the desk, the clock, and the safe. "Got any more of that tokillyah?"

I handed her the bottle in a brown paper bag.

"Nasty times," she said. In her hand, the bottle looked right at home. "Tell Joe that we're looking for him. You know what I mean? He'll have to talk to them sooner or later."

"Who?"

She pointed up. "You know. Them."

"Sure." Them sounded familiar, but sooner was out. I was betting on later, much later.

After the door was locked, I opened the safe. Joe's note was stuck between his .22 and a hardback book. The book was worn around the edges, the spine cracked, like someone had been working it over pretty good. Using two fingers, I slipped the note free. Checked behind me. Sniffed the air. And read Joe's birthday card.

"Sorry for the mess. Remember your promise. Bury me at sea. Joe."

When it came to words, Joe was a lot like me, but I got the point. I was heading for the back door when I smelled eggs burning and saw smoke coming from the snack bar.

Entry 3: THE MANILA ENVELOPE

I eased out the clutch, what was left of it, and pointed Papa Joe's Datsun up the mountain. It ran pretty good for a piece-of-tin pressed into service back in '62. The brakes worked, the gas tank was full, and the paint was almost fresh, a gallon of flat blue brushed on by Joe.

It took me less than a minute to reach Blanes, where the smell of frying Spam shifted my thoughts from lava flows to images of starving diners digging into mountains of rice, eggs and Spam. Which meant I was looking left at the crowded picnic tables in front of Blanes when I should have been looking right, at Mr. Library Jaywalker. As usual, he saw me coming and jumped. I swerved, missed him by an inch, stepped on the gas, and watched him and my second try at breakfast fade into the rearview mirror.

The Datsun lumbered across the bridge to Reed's Island. Tourists go there to see a big house built in 1899. A famous writer slept there, twice. I think it was Alfred Hitchcock when he was doing research for The Birds, the movie version. It's called a Victorian mansion, which means it has three stories, eighteen bedrooms, sixteen columns and a wraparound porch, all painted bright white. As I passed it, I checked to see if Frankie was working on the yard. His truck was parked at the end of the driveway but there was no sign of its owner.

A few houses up, the Judge had her place, a two-bedroom bungalow built in a modern-retro-craftsman style. A blue-and-white police car was parked in the driveway, with a cop sitting behind the wheel, his head back, streaming his snoring into the quiet neighborhood.

I kept going, and since I'm supposed to be telling the truth, I should note that Reed's Island isn't really an island. It's a peninsula, a chunk of rock in the middle of the Wailuku River, with one road. It starts at the bridge and goes upriver, narrowing until it turns into an escape hatch wide enough for a small car or a big motorcycle. If it isn't blocked by a fallen tree or a chain-link cable.

When I was near the top, I cranked a three-point U-turn, scraping only one palm tree in the process. I shifted into neutral, turned off the engine, and let off the brake. The Datsun coasted downhill past houses surrounded by trees and covered by jungle vines. While they hugged the edge of steep drops to the river, I glided by the snoring cop, turned into the house of seven gables, and glided to a gentle stop behind Frankie's Ford F-100.

In the back of the truck, a Crapsman P900 lawn tractor was waiting. Pointed down a ramp made of two sagging 2x10s, it would take a brave man to ride that ramp. Frankie was the man.

Like every other retired guy in Hilo, Frankie mowed lawns for a little extra cash. Grass in Hilo can't get higher than an inch before a swarm of old guys arrive in a fleet of pickup trucks overloaded with lawn tractors and weed whackers. That was Frankie's competition, all of them eager to trim greens.

Behind the house, near the cliff that dropped down to the river, Frankie was meeting the challenge. With his back propped against a giant lychee tree and a baseball cap pulled over his eyes, he was sleeping in the shade.

"Working hard?" I asked.

He pushed back the cap, revealing the sparkling yellow teeth of someone who drinks coffee and smokes cigarettes with every meal. "Who's that?" He blinked. "Oh, you. Manny." Once he had me identified, he stood up, tall and thin in crusty work boots, faded jeans, and a long-sleeve t-shirt. That's the standard uniform for a Hilo yard guy. The more skin yard-guys cover, the more chances they have of surviving insects. We've got lots of biting insects on the Big Island.

"Manny, you mad man, I had a good dream going. I was driving my VW van..."

"You're supposed to be working."

"What do you know about work?"

Frankie used to be a tough-ass county prosecutor, so he knows how to ask the tough questions. I watched him dig a joint out of his pocket and stick it in his mouth. Without thinking, I whipped out Joe's Zippo and sparked the flame. He inhaled, held the smoke in, and asked, "Where'd you get the lighter?"

"Joe gave it to me. For his birthday."

He offered me the joint. I waved it away. "Not today."

"What?" He coughed smoke into the gardenia-scented air.

"I got business."

"Good for you." As his coughing faded, he inhaled again, trapping a massive buzz cloud in his chest. "You've been running away from your responsibilities for too long."

He said stuff like that to everyone. It was a habit leftover from his courtroom days, so I didn't give him cracks. His old lines would pop out like numbers at a Bingo game. My favorite was "There's no get-out-of-jail-free card in Hilo!" That's what he said the day he picked me up from getting out of jail. Anyway, what's the point in hitting a guy on Social Security, especially one strong enough to strangle a pig? I kept my hands in my pockets and said, "I've come for my boat."

"Did you see the cop up there?"

"They're looking for the Judge."

"They'll come for me next." He exhaled through a smile, a wink and a nod.

Frankie was a tiny bit paranoid, and he had good reason to be. Along with all the guys he had stuck in jail, the cops were waiting in line to break his neck. Right after he was fired for prosecuting a twisted liquor commissioner, he tried his hand at public defending and won so many cases that the county jail almost closed due to lack of business.

He held the joint out to me, again. I waved it away, again. He glanced across the lawn at the cop car, and asked, "Joe's birthday? What's he? 70?"

"72."

"Already?" He hit the joint again. "Where's he now?"

A puff off that joint would've helped me find the right words, but I had work to do, so I gave him the party line. "He's traveling."

"Joe? Traveling?" He shifted his eyes from me to the cop car, to the road, and back to me.

"People get older," I said, "they do crazy stuff."

Frankie sucked the life out of his joint. I was sorry to see it go.

"Wherever he is," Frankie said, "you're in charge now." He searched his pockets for another joint. When he came up empty, he walked to his truck, leaned on the hood, and looked up the road at the Judge's place. Standing next to him, I could hear the cop snoring. Certain parts of Hilo are like that. Sound carries.

"Frankie," I said, "you know anything about burying people at sea?"

"What people?"

"Not people. One person. If there was a person."

"But there isn't."

"That's true," I said.

"A hypothetical person. Buried at sea."

"That's it."

"Like a Viking? With fire and a burning boat?"

I didn't know much about Vikings or burning boats, except that in movies Vikings had red beards, wore hats with horns, and went around stabbing people. That didn't sound like Joe. He didn't wear hats. He didn't like beards because of all the scratching involved. And he only stabbed one person that I know, and that person recovered, eventually.

Frankie jabbed his green thumb into my chest. "Hey, the Hilo High School mascot is a Viking. You're not talking about that kid, are you?"

"No, not him."

"I think he's a kid. No regular person would be caught dead in that costume. Unless he was stoned. A stoned guy would do it."

I was wishing I hadn't turned away Frankie's joint. "My imaginary guy doesn't want anything special," I said. "Just something simple, the way the navy guys do in the movies. You know, push a body bag over the side."

"It's illegal," Frankie said. "This isn't a war, not yet. You can't just dump a body in the ocean. You need a death certificate and someone to do the cremation, and then maybe you could spread the ashes and say a few words."

"He didn't say anything about words."

Frankie brushed the dirt off the back of his jeans. "You're supposed to say a few words. It's the law."

The frigging law. "What kine words?"

"Final words."

"How many?"

"Some. It's not important how many. They have to mean something." He patted his pockets, making sure his first search hadn't been a fluke. "Like in normal funerals. You been to one of those, right?

"Plenty," I said. A few. Some. Maybe one. One was enough.

We listened to the river and looked up at the sky. For a moment we were floating in a beautiful sunny Hilo day. Frankie broke the spell. "If I were giving you any advice, which I'm not, I'd tell you to relax and quit thinking about filling up the ocean with body bags." He pointed that green thumb of his at the Judge's house. "Besides, looks like you're grounded. Wherever the Judge is, she's not giving up your boat."

A digital device in Frankie's chest kept his heart ticking but his eyes were still good as new if you didn't count the bloodshot parts. My boat, a 26-foot Radon with twin 250

Evinrude E-techs, was hidden under a blue tarp, dry-docked in the Judge's carport. The cop was still guarding the driveway.

"Don't get any ideas." Frankie said.

"Ideas? You mean, like, if the Judge is missing she doesn't need my boat."

I studied the strip of grass running along the river. A dim light struggled for life in my head, trying to be a bulb. "You look tired, Frankie. Maybe I can do some mowing for you."

"Fine with me." He climbed into the back of the pickup. "That last joint took a lot out of me, and the owners will be back soon." He hopped on the tractor, turned the key, listened to the engine sputter, and gassed it once. "Nice!" he shouted over the choking roar. He drove that Sears special straight down the 2X10's, like he was Evil Kneivel at Indy. When he stopped, the front end was pointing at the river. "I'm going to take a nap," he said, climbing off the tractor. "I'll think some more about that Viking thing while you drive."

When Frankie was back under the Lychee tree, sitting with his hat pulled down over his eyes, I climbed onto the tractor and prepared to launch at the Judge's house. It was an older tractor with a lever on the right that acted as a gas pedal. I pushed the gas to maximum and let my foot off the brake. In a roar of ragged engine noise, worn belts, and bent blades, the tractor jumped forward. My head jerked back. I thought about testing the brakes, left that for later, and made a sharp right toward the Judge's house. Looking over my shoulder, I saw a tractor-wide strip of grass cut flat. For a retiree, Frankie kept a nice set of sharp blades.

Looking official, I mowed along the river, staying well back from the road, and heading for the Judge's house. It was a small bungalow, a two-bedroom built in the 1920s with wood floors and high ceilings. As far as I can remember, no famous author has ever slept there. The Judge didn't like visitors.

She bought it for $200,000 a few years back, when the market was down and the bungalow was threatening to collapse. That's cheap for Hawaii. Before she moved in, she cut away the junk trees and filled in the holes with Hapu ferns and ti leaf, before patching the worn out lawn with centipede grass. Then she gassed the termites and nuked the mold, added a blue tile roof, new wiring, and copper pipes. Then she sanded the hardwood floors and added a screened-in porch to keep out the bugs. On Reed's Peninsula the mosquitoes are killers. I've seen them suck the life out of small dogs. After listening to Frankie, she added deadbolts to all the windows and doors.

I'm telling you this because of what people said later, about the Judge having money and a big place out on Reed's Island. The truth is her place was the smallest house out there, and for someone who was supposed to be rolling in bribe money, she never spent any of it when I was around. And I never saw her lie, not even when she was throwing me in jail, which now that I think about it I guess I deserved.

Enough said.

I glanced down at the river. It was a long drop, but the Crapmaster stayed strong and shredded grass as the tractor S-turned uphill through a long row of scraggly Rose bushes. I parked it behind the Judge's house, and in case the snoozing cop woke up, I left the engine running.

Staying low, I slipped along the back of the house, into the carport, and stepped over the Judge's surfboard, a ten-foot tanker. The Judge was no expert but she had been surfing all her life. That longboard of hers had cut me off plenty times. She liked to catch waves way outside and plow through anyone crazy enough to get in her way, which was only me because who else wanted a 10-foot Aipa and a 150-pound judge stuck in his back? To make the ocean a safer place, I thought about tossing the board in my boat and taking it with me once I had figured out how to get rid of the cop and hook the trailer to Joe's truck. But something inside me wouldn't let me touch that board. Not even the Judge deserved to have her board stolen. I've done some bad stuff in my life but I'm no surfboard thief.

Instead, I concentrated on stealing my boat. I ducked under the tarp and climbed up the dive ladder, over the transom, and dropped down to the deck. The air stunk of moldy nylon, peanut butter and dried beer. The peanut butter was me. The dried beer and mold belonged to the Judge. I pushed two duffel bags out of the way and knee-crawled to the forward hatch. Sweat dripped down my face as the lawn mower kept chugging.

The hatch to the cabin was unlocked. There was enough light to feel my way forward, through the galley, and into the bow. I slipped my hand under the forward cushion, my extra-secret hiding place, and found my spare key, my emergency joints, and a manila envelope. The key and joints fit easily into my pocket. Back on deck, I sat next to the ladder. The blue light filtering through the tarp let me have a closer look at the envelope. It was one of those 10x12 manila types with a metal clasp. Someone had written Joe's name in block letters where the address should have been. JOE.

I opened the clasp and pulled out a stack of papers. The top one caught my attention. Like a poke in the eye, the handwriting in red ink brought back fond memories. It was dated a couple days before Joe's birthday.

> *Dear friend,*
> *Do you know of anyone who can help? The police have been contacted, but the student has dropped out of school and nothing is being done to help her. Please, we need you. If we don't hear from you, we're going out there as soon as finals are over. Ms. K. Song.*

On the back of the note someone had drawn a crude map, with a thick black line heading toward the top of the page and the word PUNA. Crossing that line, another thick line bore right, ending at a stick-figure girl standing next to stick-figure house. An arrow pointed at one word squeezed in at the edge of the page: PRISON.

I knew the road to Puna, the land that time forgot. I knew the road to the island's only prison. And I knew someone who lived out that way. I was trying to remember who when I heard Frankie's lawn mower moving away from the Judge's house.

Peeking out from under the tarp, I saw Frankie driving his tractor up the driveway, headed for a blue uniform walking toward the house. I gave the rest of the papers a quick look: A typed letter addressed to "Your Honor" and what looked like a student's essay scribbled on lined paper. I stuffed everything back into the envelope, folded it in half, and jammed the thick wad in the back of my shorts.

Abandoning ship, I jumped off the transom, ran across the back lawn to the ledge that dropped down to the river, and crawled along the slippery path to the Big House. When I looked back, Frankie and the cop were laughing it up like old drinking buddies, which was a possibility. Frankie had gone out drinking with pretty much everyone in town, even with the two people who didn't drink.

Entry 4: GRAVY STAINS

On the picnic table, the Judge's manila envelope was hidden under a plate of hamburger steak, two scoops rice, and one scoop mac salad, heavy on the mayo. A tall coke with plenty ice steadied my hand.

I was sitting in Blaines, which happened to be Ms. Song's least-favorite restaurant. She claimed the lack of anything green on the menu had turned her against the local favorite, but the truth is she never got over the owner's refusal to use what I called a "high-comma" in the restaurant's name.

It was 11:30am, and I was trying to eat breakfast. On my left, three teenage girls were manning the counter window. Behind them, a couple of older gals were basking in the glow of the flaming grill. Teresa, aka Rayzah, was running the show. One second she was standing next to the deep fryer, shoveling fries out of the bubbling crude, the next second standing up front, counting cash into the register.

Across from me, at the next table over, an old couple was dipping plastic spoons into miso soup. Behind them, a table of thick, heavy contractors in yellow t-shirts and blue jeans were crowded around plates of rice and eggs, Portuguese sausage, pancakes, sweet bread, kalbee, and hamburger steak. One of them leaned back and laughed with his mouth full.

To start my day, I took a sip of sweet icy coke. The sugar helped.

At the table on my right, an office guy in blue slacks and a store-faded aloha shirt poked his chopsticks at an extra-large pile of ketchup-covered onion rings. A smile spread across his face as he speared a fat ring.

It was a nice, peaceful scene. Watching people eat, as long as I'm eating too, always reminds me that people are just people, not the nasty robots they appear to be. Eaters just want to get through the morning on a full stomach so they can enjoy lunch and a light snack in the afternoon before they rush home to dinner and a steady stream of lite-beer sucked in while watching a couple hours of TV.

Joe always said that people who like to eat make the best neighbors as long as they get enough to eat. There was no shortage of food that morning in Blanes, and all the happiness bubbling up from people eating their fill got me to thinking that Hilo wasn't such a bad town. Sure, it was buried under layers of mold and mildew, clinging to a couple of active volcanoes in the middle of the ocean, but it had its good points. Blanes and Reuben's were two of them. I was trying to think of a third as I lifted a plastic forkful of juicy hamburger meat toward my mouth. The first taste of gravy inspired the Judge's manila envelope to open and let the student's essay seep out, spreading words onto the picnic table.

Title: A significant person in my life

He was my best friend to me. He took me to the movies and to the beach. My parents don't like him. They are hanai parents. My auntie and uncle. I love them. They taken care of me since I was girl. My boyfriend told me he would take care of me.

Three reasons why I think my boyfriend is significant. 1. I love my boyfriend. 2) My boy friend is *repairing himself. For example he was in the army and came back and got in trouble. Now he's going to school and he wants to be a fireman.*

3. At first my boyfriend holds my hand and gave me a ring for my birthday. That was the last reeson. Now he doesn't want to let me go anywhere. He says I'm a cheater. He wants to know everywhere I'm going.

My boyfriend told me to get out. It was dark. He flicked his cigarette at me. He hit me and pushed me down the steps. He slapped me. He called me a pig and kicked me. I tried to run. He locked me in the shed.

Misses Song I am pregnant and I'm going to have his baby. Her name will be melody. I don't know what to do. I'm afraid. He said he was going kill me. I know he only says that when he's mad. He doesn't mean it. I'm scared. Please help me.

I stuck my plastic fork in the mac salad. It stood straight. Nothing on my plate looked good enough to eat. That's when the Madonna sat down across from me and asked, "What are you waiting for?"

No one but me noticed her arrival, maybe because the glorious glow of her flaming red hair was hidden under a black hoodie, and her skin-tight yoga pants were printed with the army's new camouflage print. Only her orange crocs spoiled her stealthy look. Even under the table they cried out for attention. She reached for the manila envelope.

"That's private," I said, pulling it away from her. The vog from the volcano was making my eyes water.

She grabbed my plate and picked out my fork. "When," she whispered, using the fork to tap Joe's name, "are you going to get off your ass and get moving?"

"After breakfast. Or is it lunch?" I picked up a pair of chopsticks. Sticks work good for mac salad. No skill involved. Just jab a scoop like you'd jab a meatball, lift and insert. It's simple, unless the Madonna is using your fork to shovel your mac salad and hamburger steak into her mouth, chewing like she was on deadline. Between swallows, she said, "I'm worried about you."

"Worry about Joe."

She dropped the fork and took the sticks from my hand. After she had them balanced between her thumb and middle finger, she found a slippery piece of shoyu chicken hidden under a scoop of white rice. "My favorite," she said. The chunk of thigh meat disappeared between her frosted red lips. "Hmmmmm, salty." She picked up a grain of rice and dropped it onto her tongue. "I love salt."

"Don't eat all my food," I told her. The Madonna didn't need to eat. She did it for fun. I did it for love.

"You've got a job to do." She jammed in more meat. "Too many carbs slow you down. They're not good for your heart."

I told her not to talk with her mouth full of my burger.

"You know what a heart is, right, Manny?"

I knew she didn't have one. She didn't need one. She was spirit powered.

Between bites, she said I looked a little flabby, said I needed some physical work, maybe a mixed-martial-arts class. "You need to get in shape. Exercise. Stay frosty, as they say in the movies."

At the rate she was eating my brunch, she was the one who'd need to work off flab. She'd eat herself to sleep by noon, which as far as I could tell was two minutes away. Under the table, her knee brushed against my knee, sparking an electrical surge, another one of her minor miracles. Watching her rosy cheeks glow, I said, "I've been thinking."

"It's not the worst thing." She shoveled in another pound of hamburger and shoyu chicken and starchy sweet mayo, and chased it down with three gulps of my coke.

"I've been thinking that I need my boat. You're going to help me get it."

With a sticky chopstick, she tapped the edge of the envelope. "Aren't you supposed to help the Judge?"

"After I bury Joe."

"Joe can wait."

"Until the cops find him?"

"You'll be arrested. No doubt." She said that back then even before it happened. That's why I call her the Madonna. She can see things. She said, "I need you to do me a favor."

I kept my mouth shut.

She smiled. "I'm a little busy these days, Manny." Apparently, she wasn't too busy to have detailed her nails with bright pink polish. They matched her frosty pink lips. "Listen to me. I need you to keep an eye on Ms. Song and Twyla. That's what the Judge wanted Joe to do."

I mention this conversation because 1) it really happened, maybe not word for word but as close as I can remember, and 2) it was the first time I heard of anyone named Twyla. Back then I thought the Madonna was talking about the student who had written the essay.

"Where's the Judge?" I asked.

She shrugged. "I can't see everything. It's a big world. Well, are you going to help?"

Maybe if she didn't spend so much time eating my food she'd have more time to do her job. When I didn't volunteer, she said, "No man is an island."

That was obvious. No man can live on an island forever would have made more sense. After reading that kid's essay I was one man who needed to get off an island. Joe was another one.

"You should feel for that young woman," the Madonna said, poking her sticks into my stomach. "Don't you feel her?"

My gut was feeling empty. So was my plate. The Madonna was chewing my last grain of rice. She wiped a drop of mayo off her chin and said, "Sorry about your lunch. This happens to me all the time at Blanes. It's like I can't stop. It's the original

28

Garden of Eatin." She laughed like that was supposed to be a joke.

"Without the fruit or vegetables," I said.

"No chance of biting into anything dangerous." She got a big laugh out that one, too. "Tell you what, Manny. You help Song and I'll send someone to help you. Give me a few hours to find a suitable candidate."

I should have known that meant trouble, and I was about to say so, but I couldn't stop staring at my empty plate smeared with brown grease and white mayo. It was one of those metaphors that Ms. Song liked to talk about in class, a gravy-stained metaphor for my lost hopes of breakfast.

When I looked up, Rayzah was sitting in the Madonna's place. That didn't surprise me. The Madonna had a way of slipping in and out of reality, and Rayzah, even for a big girl, could move pretty quick.

"Finished already?" she asked. She had plenty long black hair, wide shoulders, and a thick hips balanced on sturdy legs. That morning her hair was in a bun, and she was wearing a black t-shirt, a white apron, and black yoga pants. Unlike the Madonna, she knew the dangers of bright colors. Her crocs were black.

Her real name was Teresa, pronounced TeRAYsa, but Bobbie Marta called her Street Racer because back in the day TeRAYsa lived out of town, out on Stainback Highway, and she was always rushing around to raise five kids, three of them her own, getting them to school, soccer and dance lessons, and getting herself to three jobs, which wasn't easy on a motorcycle. And she liked to drive fast. That's why I called her Rayzah.

Anyway, that morning we were both looking down at the same empty plate. "Want more?" she asked. Rayzah didn't care much for lingering metaphors. To her, an empty plate had to be refilled with food or hauled away for washing.

"It won't help," I said.

"Food always helps."

29

"Sure." Single moms know all the secrets. Rayzah knew more than most. She was Mexican-food buddies with Papa Joe, so I didn't know what to say when she asked, "Where's Joe?"

I figured she didn't need the details this early in the morning. Instead, I gave her the line about Papa Joe gone traveling and leaving me in charge.

She dug a pint of Gogi Berry Super Juice from under her apron. "Sometimes you have to get off this rock," she said, twisting the cap.

"That's what I was thinking."

She gave me a hard stare. "You going somewhere, Manny?"

"Me? I could go to Kona."

"Have a few beers and watch the sunset with the tourists?"

"Sure." And catch a flight to Manila.

"Screw that. Let's drink to Joe." She tipped her head back and poured a stream of Gogi juice down her throat, avoiding the label's recommendation for two teaspoons at meals. I didn't have anything to drink, so I was sober when she stopped guzzling and said, "Joe was a good man."

Not the last time I saw him. But I didn't tell her that.

"You're going to have a hard time filling his shoes," she said.

We sat there, me looking down at my double-wides. They were spreading out from my cheap rubber slippers.

"What's this?" she asked.

When I looked up, she was brushing crumbs off the Judge's envelope. Her long fingers settled on Joe's block-letter name. To keep her from thinking about Joe, I broke open the clasp, pulled out the student's essay and Song's note, and pushed them across the table.

She started reading, covered her mouth with her hand, but kept going. She was a tough gal. When she was through, she wiped her eyes with a crumpled napkin and said, "This crap never ends. I know a hundred girls like her."

She offered me the Gogi. I shook my head. "Nope," I said, "I got problems." I meant stomach problems. No sane person pours Gogi into an empty stomach, but Rayzah fires up faster than gasoline tossed in a nuclear reactor.

"You got problems?" She emptied the rest of the Gogi into my Coke ice. "Jezzus, Manny. Did you read this kid's essay?" She pushed the wrinkled papers back at me. "Where's the Judge?"

"Missing." As I stuffed everything inside the envelope, I told her about Bobbie Marta's visit to the Empire and me going up to the Judge's place and finding the envelope in my boat. I told her there was more stuff in the envelope we could read but she shook her head. She had seen enough. She said, "That Ms. Song is a good gal."

"Nice looking," I said.

Rayzah sipped her Gogi-Coke as we talked about the old days, about living off college loans and Ms. Song helping Rayzah's boys pass their English classes, and me flunking both of those classes.

"Papa Joe's gone," Rayzah said. She licked her Gogi-stained teeth. "You're in charge. When are you going up there to the college?"

"After I get my boat back."

"Your boat?"

"The Judge doesn't need it."

"You know what you need," she said, loud enough to turn heads. "You need a woman." All of the customers, even the construction workers, even the old miso-couple, stopped in mid-chew to look at me. "A good woman," Rayzah said. "Not one of your Honolulu girls. You need to find someone who can keep your feet on the ground."

The construction workers smiled, the miso couple nodded, and I looked down at my feet. They were still planted firmly on greasy concrete.

Rayzah leaned in close, whispering. "A family. That's what you need, Manny. The Ten Commandments say so. A man should have a family. I think its number one or maybe number five. My kids know the specifics. That's what it says. A man should have a family and a home."

She was a regular churchgoer, every Easter, and she had put five kids through St. Joe's with waitress money, so I

31

figured she knew what she was talking about. She was the Madonna without all the flash, so I whispered, "Do those commandments say anything about suicide?"

She kicked me in the shin. "Quit wasting my time, Manny. You want to end up like Joe? Living alone?"

There were worst things.

She reached over and poked me in the chest. "This is your chance, Manny. Get up to the college, help somebody." She tapped the envelope. "Ask Ms. Song, she'll tell you. Who knows. Things happen."

I started walking toward Joe's truck, wondering what I'd do. I was halfway there when Rayzah stood up and shouted at me, "Forget about Joe. He's gone. Find yourself a good woman."

The construction workers got a major long-lasting laugh out of that. Come to think of it, everyone in the place did. Three blocks away heading for the university in the old Datsun, I could still hear them laughing.

Entry 5: NEVER TWO LATE

The security guard said, "It's never too late."

His white dress shirt and black slacks made him look like a door-to-door Mormon, but Tony Marta was no missionary. He was an ex-con who had spent two years in Lompoc Federal before coming home to marry Bobbie "The Cop" Marta. That made him a two-time loser. His real name was Antony, but he didn't like Tony so I called him Ant, or AntMan on more formal occasions.

"Did you hear me, Manny?"

I pointed at the gate, hoping that keeping my mouth shut would piss him off enough to make me turn around. All the way across town I had been thinking about a run to the other side of the island, where I could drink beer and catch a ride on a fishing boat. Ant's quarter-ton body on a six-foot frame was making me wish I had taken that option. His Joe-type fingers, more like ropes than digits, were resting on the gate switch, refusing to move. Him and Bobbie made a nice couple if you liked the bulging-bicep look.

"Never too late, Manny. Even for you."

Tell that to Joe. That's what I wanted to say but I figured it would go in one ear and stay there, making him ask more questions, so I tried, "For drugs."

"What?"

"Never too late for drugs."

33

"What are you doing with Joe's truck?"

"He's on vacation."

"Joe? He never goes on vacation."

"I told him it was never too late."

"Good for you."

"He left me in charge."

"That's funny." But the gate stayed down. Instead of doing his job, he changed the subject to his kids. He said that in no time his would be on the honor roll at St. Joe's and playing soccer and football and maybe the piano. As far as I knew his kids were still in diapers but he didn't give me a chance to set him straight. He said the lava was still flowing and explained how working the day shift while his wife worked the night shift was bad for making more kids. "You know what I mean?"

Sure, I knew, but I didn't ask for details. He was a good example of how getting anywhere in Hilo was like swimming in oatmeal. In Hilo everyone was like Ant. They liked to talk. To stop him I tried a scare tactic. "Saw your wife this morning. She was drinking."

"So what?"

"Tequila. Lots of it."

He jumped out of the booth and grabbed my arm. "I'm worried about her, Manny. They got her working late all the time. She's stressing out."

It didn't feel good seeing him all worried, so I said, "Just kiddin about the drinking. Never saw it. She's looking for the Judge. I'm helping her."

He let go of my arm. "Thanks, Manny. Thanks. You keep an eye on her and if something comes up, you call me. Too bad Joe isn't here. He'd know what to do."

What about me? I was going to ask but my reputation was a lost cause so why bother? Anyway, he was already back in his tiny box, working the control panel. The gate went up. As I drove into the university parking lot, he shouted, "Be careful. It's finals week. The kids get big time freaky."

"I can take care of myself."

"Sure you can."

I circled the lot two times and finally found the only open space, a reserved spot for someone called the Chancellor. Since it was past noon and too late for anyone to be coming to work, I figured this Chancellor person wouldn't need the space. Joe's Datsun fit perfectly between two sparkling white Honda sedans. Here's another insight about Hilo: Ninety percent of the cars are white. Per capita we have more white cars than anywhere else in the known world.

Joe's blue truck was an exception, one of the 10%.

I took the essay and the note with me, left the manila envelope under the seat for safekeeping with Joe's collection of smashed aluminum cans and spare change. I slammed the truck's door twice to make sure it locked tight.

The stale air of higher education smelled of success and unpaid bills, kinda like wet feet. When the sun popped out of the clouds, I ran for the nearest covered walkway. In Hilo, it's best to stay undercover. Rain or sunshine can give you third-degree burns.

The walkway blended into a construction site. Jackhammers clashed with the coffee-fueled chatter of students rushing by, going both ways, idealistic little go-getters hurrying off to a future filled with pizza and student loan payments.

Downhill, past the library, I walked into an intersection that offered a choice between two parallel lines of cinderblock buildings. When I saw a sign for "The Final Exam!" taped to a door, I figured it was an omen, so I poked my head inside. A pudgy professor wearing a lauhala hat, a dull green aloha shirt and grey slacks was standing behind a podium, staring down at two rows of students squirming in their seats. What was going through their sixteen brains? From their faces I figured it had something to do ripping the professor's hat to shreds and making him eat it for lunch.

"When I say go," Professor Hat smiled, "start writing. When I say stop, stop writing." He reached for the pack of cigarettes in his shirt pocket, stopped when he saw me, and snapped, "Who are you?"

"I'm looking..."

"Who are you?"

"Manny."

"The last name. Speak."

"Datsun."

I like to keep the crazy ones guessing, just in case they're thinking of following me home. He stepped to a podium and ran his finger down his roll sheet. "You're not on this list. Therefore, you're not in this room."

I have to admit, the first time I saw him I wanted to slap him. Twice. Maybe three times. That's true. I guess it was intuition.

"Are you still here?" he asked.

"I'm looking for..."

"Maybe a song will help. It certainly helps my students concentrate." From next to the podium, he picked up a 12-string guitar, broke into a smoker's cough, recovered and managed to sing a few too many lines of what he called his latest creation of Jamaican-Hawaiian beat: "Did you take Psychology 400? Hear me? Did you take Mind Games this semester? If not, get out. This is the Final Exam for Psych 400. Modern Mind Games. If you're here for Mind Games, stay put. If not, get out."

I couldn't move. I had never heard a professor in a lauhala hat singing instructions. It reminded me of the first time I had seen a two-headed goat. I couldn't stop looking, trying to see and forget at the same time. Weird. One difference, though. The goat had better voices, both of them.

When the Singing Professor coughed out that the second verse was the same as the first, I gave into my fears and backed out of the door. If I had stayed longer, maybe things would have turned out different. Maybe I would've beat him to a pulp then and saved all of us a lot of trouble.

In the next room, I found another two rows of students, another podium, and another hat. This one was dark blue, a wool watch cap, like the kine sailors in old movies wear. The gal wearing it was a lot better looking than the Singing Professor. In her tight black jeans and tight black t-shirt, the stretchy kind that breathes for its wearer, she looked a tiny bit young for me and little on the thin side, but when she smiled, I stopped thinking about bad singing.

"What room are you looking for?" she asked, moving out from behind the podium. Her clunky Danceskin shoes tip-tapped on the linoleum tile. For a small gal she had sturdy legs and long strides, like a dancer. All her students looked springy and happy and smiley, so I was hoping it was a dance class. I like dancers.

"Ms. Song?" I said. "You know her?"

"Are you one of her students?" Her eyes searched me. They felt a little bit like x-ray machines, only more human. "Sure," I mumbled. "Me and her go a long way back."

"Your eyes are bloodshot. Have you been drinking?"

"Not since last night."

"Finals are always difficult." She touched my shoulder, left her hand there. "You'll be fine." She pointed behind me, across a narrow stretch of grass. "Over there," she said, "The big room on the left. Room 139. You can't miss it."

I couldn't miss her sweet smell, like cinnamon and whipped cream, like a chai latte spiked with moonshine. I was drinking her in, the soft skin on her neck, the hints of black hair from under her cap as she guided me out. The door closed between us. Through it, I heard her ask the students to put away their cellphones.

In the direction the cute professor of dance had pointed, I found a drinking fountain. The water tasted clear and cool and full of mossy knowledge. Being on campus was making me feel optimistic, almost young again. When I looked up, I was standing before a handwritten sign on a metal door:

Room 139.
Professor Song
English 105 final exam

Through the tiny window in the door, I saw Ms. Song sitting at a metal desk, keeping her eyes on ten rows of students, about fifty of them hunkered over sheets of white paper, scribbling, looking up, trying to think, and scribbling again. Song could handle fifty students, no problem. She liked the big jobs.

Even so, something about her didn't look right. Her black slacks and classy white blouse were pure Song, but she looked smaller than back in the day. And the sock cap, the same kine the dance teacher was wearing, didn't help. It looked like it was pushing her down.

I was wondering what to do next, when the door swung open, and one of the students escaped past me, saying, "Sorry, excuse me. Got to go." Right behind her, the heat hit me. Then Ms. Song hit me. She pushed me out of the way and shouted at the escapee, "Don't give up. Come back."

Did I mention that Ms. Song was quick on her feet? Like a cat hyped up on milk and coffee, she squinted up at me. "You!" she said. "What are you doing here?" She snapped her fingers. "Manual! Right?"

"Manny."

She stepped outside and closed the door behind her. "We have to be quiet. They're taking a test. Are you here to complain about your grade?"

"I got a grade?"

"You disappeared, so I gave you an incomplete. When you didn't respond after one semester, it turned into an F."

"Something came up."

"Something?" She blinked. "Do you remember the rules?"

"Rules?"

"The 10 Commandments of Writing?"

I was wishing Rayzah was there. Or the Madonna. They knew more about commandments. They'd know what to say. I didn't, so I kept my mouth shut. My return to school was going exactly like my first two tries at college life.

"Be specific," she whispered. "Specificity." She patted my shoulder. "The reason you left? Be specific. A new baby? A death in the family? Arrested? It's usually one of those."

"The last one. The jail thing."

"I should have known."

I wasn't pissed. Plenty people say that I look like someone who should be jail.

"I apologize for saying that," she said. She opened the door and pointed at the metal chair next to her metal desk. "Sit. And please keep your voice down. The students are under stress."

Most of them were stripped down to shorts and t-shirts, a few of the women going one step further, peeled down to bathing suit tops to avoid the heat. Under their desks all of them had piled sweaters and jackets, even a couple of blankets in case the AC came back from the dead. While sweat dripped out of their brains, they strained to put words on paper.

I knew how they felt. Back in the day, I had tried to get words on paper before drops of my own sweat could blot them out. And on other days, I had tried to unstick my frozen fingers so I could hold my pen steady enough to doodle words on the lines.

"Sit down, Manny, please."

It was easy to take orders from Ms. Song. I sat down and waited for knowledge to seep into me.

"The AC is broken," she said, and slipped into her chair. "As usual."

She had a UH hoodie hung over the back of her chair. A sign on the wall said it was against the rules to open the windows because it could ruin the air-conditioning. The windows were too high to reach. The admin guys at UH had a great sense of humor. Sweat was dripping down my forehead and I was dreaming about a cold beer. To be specific, an ex-large pitcher of Bikini Blonde imported from Maui.

"The new semester is just around the corner," Ms. Song whispered. "You'll have to catch up." She shifted a stack of papers from one side of her desk to the other. "Still, it's never too late."

"That's what I hear."

The heat was pressing my jeans into my crotch, and I was trying to remember how many days I had worn my t-shirt, the black one from the Brooklyn Institute of Technology. It's my favorite, a present from the Golden Madonna. She liked to claim she was from the East Coast. In the UH heat, the Institute's cheap cotton would soon start producing smelly memories of her trips to Brooklyn.

Ms. Song leaned toward me so I could hear her say, "All of these young people have problems, challenges like yours."

I doubted that.

"For most," she said, pushing her sock cap off her forehead, "college is difficult."

I couldn't argue with that, especially if she had to wear a watch cap in an overheated classroom. I wanted to see her long hair again, so I asked, "What's with the wool cap?"

"Medical." She lifted the hat off and held it above her head, ready to drop it back in place. "It'll grow back, eventually."

She had a nice skull without any bumps. That's what I was thinking. My mind is like that. You might as well know the truth about me from the beginning.

She pressed the cap back into place. "I get tired sometimes. That's all. It's not important."

Tired, like Joe? It crossed my mind.

"Besides, I like looking like a sailor."

"Sure." She didn't look like any sailor I knew.

"Manual, listen, I can help you. Lots of people get out of jail and make a good life for themselves. Truthfully, not a lot of people but some people." She lowered her voice again. "There are two of them in this class."

Two big guys in the back row, in dark glasses, tank tops, and board shorts looked tough enough to fight their way out of prison and come to terms with an English class.

"Not them," Ms Song said. "Stop looking. You'd never guess." From a bulging canvas bag under her chair she dug out a Subway foot-long and asked, "Are you hungry?"

The sandwich almost looked like food.

"In a rush this morning," she said. "No time for breakfast. Have to keep up my strength." She unwrapped the sandwich, tore it in half, and pushed a six-inch veggie at me. "We all have to help each other."

No wonder she was tired. Giving away her food. Not even a small gal like Song can live on six inches of airy bread, limp lettuce, and fake cheese. I pushed it back at her. She reached into her bag again and produced a package of Girl Scout cookies. Peanut Butter Surprises!

I reached for the cookies. She held them away from me. "First, tell me why you're here, Manual."

"The Judge sent me."

She sat up straight and almost shouted, "Why didn't you tell me?"

The students kept writing. At least they weren't complainers. I dug the essay and her note out my pocket, slid them across the desk. On the way back, my hand snatched the package of cookies. Before I could dig out my breakfast, Ms. Song grabbed my wrist. "Is the Judge coming?"

"Not exactly."

"But she gave you this?"

"Not exactly."

She folded up the essay and note and slipped them gently into her goodie bag. It didn't feel good lying to her, so I told her the truth, how the Judge was supposed to meet Papa Joe and me at midnight but never showed up. How I found the essay stuff when I was looking for the Judge. The last part was only a small lie.

"Is Joe going to help us?" she asked.

"He's traveling. He left me in charge."

"You?" She looked at me, then the clock on the wall, then back at me. "Good," she whispered. "We have to hurry." Then she announced to the students: "You have sixty minutes. Don't forget to leave yourself time to proofread."

One of the bruisers groaned.

She took a big bite of sandwich. As the food moved around in her mouth, I could hear her mind working. That's what professors do. Multitask. Me, I try not to think when I eat. I

41

was about to toss a cookie in my mouth, when she said, "You're in pretty good shape for someone your age. How old are you?"

"Not that old." Not as old as Joe or the Judge. Maybe the same age as Ms. Song, and I knew I was in better shape than she was. At least I outweighed her. She needed to lay off those air sandwiches and pack on a few pounds with the Madonna's diet.

"You look, well..." She reached across the desk and touched my cheek, "...weather beaten." Then she shifted her hand to my bicep, squeezed it, and said, "Although, you do look durable."

The students kept writing. And sweating.

"Maybe a little heavy for your height," she said.

"190."

"At least 220."

"At most 200."

"Five ten?"

"Six feet."

"Five eleven. Heavy is good," she said. "The Judge trusts you?"

"We're friends from way back." My stomach didn't feel right, maybe hunger pains, so I said, "Maybe not exactly friends. Not way back."

"You look like you can defend yourself." She touched my cheek again. "I always wondered about this scar. How did it happen?"

I was trying to remember.

"You've been in fights?"

"A few." The ones I couldn't run from. "Maybe one or two."

"Bar fights?"

"Sure." Bar fights? Those professors in their ivory and cement towers got some goofy ideas.

"Do you mind if I ask you a question?" She didn't wait for my answer. A frightened face had appeared at the door's window. "Wait here." Ms. Song stood up and hurried out the door. I stared at the students. They stared at me. A few minutes later, Ms. Song came back with the gal who had tried to escape. Song led her to an empty desk, picked up a pen, and put it in her hands. "Write, young lady."

I was still holding the cookie. Ms. Song sat down next to me and leaned in close to whisper, "Will we need a gun?"

It sounded crazy coming from a gal as soft as Ms. Song, in a classroom full of sweaty dreams. "For what?" I asked.

"I'm sorry. In the movies they always have guns. This fellow, he's made me so angry." She covered her face with her hands, took a deep breath, and looked up at me with her dreamy eyes. "Will you come with us?"

I wish I could say I was smart enough to say no, but I was still too hungry to be smart. Ms. Song looked like she would go no matter what, and I didn't want anything bad to happen to her. "Maybe," I said, stalling for time, thinking I could slip out and call Bobbie Marta. It wouldn't exactly be snitching, so I asked her, "When?"

"Tonight." She grabbed her stomach. "Oh, God," she whispered.

The students kept writing.

She stood up, a little wobbly on her feet. "Please, could you watch the classroom? I'll be back in a few minutes. I just need some rest." She touched the top of my head. "Don't get up. It's terrible how tired I feel some days. Please. Stay here. If anyone finishes early, collect the essay. If anybody asks, I went out for water."

Before I could stop her, she was out the door.

A couple of the students looked at me. I smiled. They went back to scribbling. On the wall clock, the hands slowed to a dead stop. I was wishing Joe was there to shoot a hole in it. A student came up and asked for permission to use the bathroom, another to get a smoke, another to make a call. Never much for saying no, I let all of them go.

When I noticed the hands of the clock had started moving again, I said, "Thirty minutes." The two big guys in the back whispered to each other, and I tried Song's style, down low, "Quiet, please. For your fellow students."

43

"Then stop talking," one of them snapped back, just loud enough to cause a ripple of giggles.

They were still rippling when a knock at the door made me look up. The Singing Professor stuck his head into my sauna and asked, "Where is Professor Song?"

"She's coming back," I said.

"No doubt. Who are you? What are you doing here?"

"Teaching."

"Wait. I know you."

"Don't think so."

With his guitar strapped to his back, he walked in and took up a position beside my desk. The stink of cheap cigarette smoke rolled off him and made the students squirm for nicotine. "Give me a minute," he said. "I will remember. I have perfect memory."

One of the gangsters in the back shouted, "Keep it down. We're trying to write."

The Singing Professor's face flushed. "Who said that?"

I should have kept my mouth shut, but my love of music and lack of breakfast made me whisper, "Ms. Song told me to keep on eye on those two in the back."

Professor Sing-Along straightened up, pushed his shoulders back, and swung his guitar around front. "You two back there, keep it down."

"Oh my gosh," a student in the front row gasped. "He's going to sing."

She was right. He did start to sing.

A half hour later, two ambulance attendants were hauling him away. One of them, a fellow named Miles, stopped to pick up the professor's broken guitar and toss it on the gurney. He rolled his eyes at me and said, "Him again."

AntMan came in later, as the students were escaping out the door, leaving their essays piled on my desk. He had to make a report. I explained to him the same stuff I had told the first guards on the scene, that it was all a misunderstanding. The professor had slipped, concerned students had tried to catch him, and he had hit the ground, accidentally. "Ironic," Ant said, shaking his head.

I wasn't sure what that meant but I figured it was inspired by being in Ms. Song's classroom.

By the time Ms. Song returned, all the students were gone except for the escapist scribbling the finishing touches to her mangled masterpiece. When she handed in her paper, Ms. Song hugged her good-bye. It felt good to have touched a few young minds for the better. Seeing the screwy professor hauled off to the hospital felt even better. All in a day's work!

"I feel fine now," Ms. Song said, patting me on the back. "I just needed some rest."

She did look better. Her hat was on straight and her face had a bit of color. Not rosy but not see-through. "Sorry to put you on the spot, Manual." She picked up the pile of essay exams and stuffed them in her goodie bag. "You didn't eat your sandwich."

"I couldn't." It was on the floor, next to the desk. In the scuffle, someone had smashed it flat. "I got distracted." I scraped it up and tossed it in the rubbish as she lifted her tote bag onto her shoulder. Bright red letters against a tan background announced, "Love is an active verb!"

"Did you have any problems?" she asked.

"Problems?"

"With the students?"

"Not that I remember."

The Singing Professor was easy to forget.

She pulled me by the arm, and we stepped out the door into a stream of students fleeing classrooms. She turned sideways, accelerated, slowed and sped up to thread her way through the log jam. Me, I lowered my shoulder and put one foot in front of the other, shoving like Frankenstein going through the scrum. The sea of cellphones parted down the middle. Students are not built for power plays.

"Wait a moment," Song said, stopping in midstream.

Up ahead, from the doorway next to the Singing Disaster's classroom, the cute professor who had given me directions was

45

waving a stack of papers at us. Song waved back and rushed forward into her arms. The two of them blended into each other, a couple in watch caps, hugging, and kissing on cheeks. No doubt that was stuff they had learned while vacationing in Europe. Professors are like that, they do a lot of learning. I caught up with them and held out my hand to the younger babe. "Manny," I said.

"Oh, yes, yes, I remember you." She shook my hand. She had a tough grip, starting soft and gentle going to strong and rough, like her hands had worked for a living. "Twyla," she said. "Professor Twyla Sunn."

ENTRY 6: GRAMMAR POSSE

Ms. Song pushed her shoulders back and said, "Twyla is doing her first year of teaching."

I liked the name. It reminded me of dreamy gals singing dreamy songs in dreamy bars. Her and Ms. Song looked like they could be proud mother and prouder daughter, which got me to thinking, and it wasn't good thinking, nothing to be proud of, just what popped into my head. Anyway, Ms. Song saved me from my dreams by asking Twyla, "What happened to our friend the psychology professor?"

That brought me back to earth, earth being the crowded hallways of the university. Professor Twyla pretended to spit on the ground, before saying, "That fool." She shook her head and explained how the professor who had promised to help them was a no show. Again! "The last I saw of him, he was headed to your classroom. Later, his students came by and told me that he left in the middle of the exam and never returned. I had to collect their final exams for him." She shook a flimsy stack of papers at us. "Not surprisingly, the students didn't seem to mind. They were absolutely happy."

Ms. Song turned to me. "Did you see him?"

"Who?"

"Evil looking fellow in a lauhala hat," Twyla said.

"Lauhala hat," Ms. Song said. She described him as a pale fellow with nicotine-stained fingers, brown teeth and weak knees, who carried a guitar. I wasn't as fast on my thinking feet as them, but I was putting two and two together. Details do help even when overshadowed by the silky skin on Ms. Twyla's neck. "Oh him," I said. "Sure." I told them how the singing professor had tripped over his own feet, hit his head on a desk, and been hauled away in an ambulance.

They looked at each other like they knew something I didn't know, which was possible. Most people knew more than I did.

"He was supposed to come with us," Twyla said.

"Him? The twisted guy with the guitar?" That didn't sound right, even back then.

"We were desperate. He said he could help. He even said he knew the area." Twyla headed for a rubbish can. "Now, as usual, he's found a way to shirk his responsibilities."

"Never mind him," Ms. Song said. "Manual is here."

"Manny," I said.

Ms. Song caught my friend Twyla as she was about to chuck the Singing Professor's stack of tests in the rubbish can. Song took the tests into safekeeping and patted Twyla on the cheek. "We'll give the Professor these later. For his poor students, not him. Please, Manual, follow me."

As we worked our way toward the parking lot, the students flowed around us. We made a nice threesome, even if Ms. Song wasn't that quick on her feet. All I needed was a matching sock cap, a loaf of French bread, and a bottle of wine to help us pass for tourists in Paris.

"Are you feeling better?" Twyla asked.

Ms. Song nodded. Feeling guilty, I grabbed her goodie bag and her stacks of exams. Twyla tried to support her by the elbow, but Ms. Song shook her off and picked up the pace a little, saying, "Fine. Much better. We have to hurry."

We reached the spot where I had parked Joe's truck. Instead of his blue Datsun, the space was filled with a black Lexus.

"Isn't this the chancellor's spot?" Twyla asked.

"You parked here?" Song asked.

I looked around. "Maybe."

"You've been towed," Twyla said.

Back then I didn't think much about it because whenever I parked at UH bad things happened. I was used to it.

Twyla's car was a few rows down, a VW bug, one of the real bugs, old enough to be made in Germany. Under a ragged moon roof, it was covered with rust. According to Ms. Song, for the last few months Twyla had been doing all the driving. She didn't say why, but I didn't have to ask. I've had enough DUI stops to understand why it's important to keep your driving record a secret.

I squeezed into the back seat, and Ms. Song sat up front, trying to roll down her window. Twyla didn't bother trying. She tossed her watch cap in the back, shook out her shoulder length hair, and went to work on the ignition. After a couple hundred tries, the starter kicked the engine to life. "The windows stick," the little prof shouted over the chugging, missing, wheezing engine noise that sounded worse than Frankie's lawn tractor. With a straight face, she said, "They'll fall down after we hit enough potholes."

The three of us managed to tug and pull and drag the canvas moon roof far enough back so we could breathe. Almost. At the security gate, Antony jumped in front of the car. Twyla pumped the brakes three times. Lucky for the Ant, she had a fast foot. The brakes worked an inch before they reached him.

Pumping himself up to full size, Ant slapped the hood and shouted, "Open your window."

"We're in a hurry," Twyla shouted through the moon roof.

AntMan stood on the running board and looked down into our world. "Where are you going?" He reached for me, but Ms. Song slapped his arm, and before he could crawl inside, Twyla stepped on the gas.

"Where's Joe's truck?" I shouted as we pulled away and Ant rolled to the curb.

A cloud of moldy-upholstery dirt invaded my nose while three springs poked me in the ass. Through a rust hole in the floor, I saw a blur of speeding asphalt. Behind us, Ant was standing in the middle of the road, waving his hands over his head and shouting something, but I couldn't hear him over the exhaust.

Ms. Song rested her head against the window while Twyla worked the steering wheel. She drove like a younger version of Rayzah. We were headed downhill fast toward the main road when she cranked a hard right turn that threw me against rusty metal. We were aimed at Puna, the land that time forgot, a demilitarized zone populated by people who had moved there because Alaska had too many rules.

Ms. Song rested her head against the window, saying, "We have to help her. No matter what."

"Don't worry," the young speedster said. "We'll make it."

After that, Ms. Song closed her eyes, and a few minutes later she started snoring. Twyla held the steering wheel with her knees while she poked her fingers at her cellphone. "No connection," she said, and then stepped hard on the gas. The VW picked up a mile or two of speed.

We were chugging out of town in a rusty VW weighed down by stacks of essays, two lightweight professors, and me. Two lanes spotted with potholes were leading us toward the lava flow.

Song looked up long enough to ask, "Where are we?"

There was nothing much to see except trees and more trees, mostly Albizia, African Tulip and Ohia. Something else was out there, lurking in the shadows, sneaking up on me, trying to tell me something. Ms. Song must have felt it, too. She was sweating.

"I think we should go back," Twyla said. "You look worse."

"No. I'm fine."

As we passed the sign for Stainback Highway, Twyla said, "Here we are." She dropped from fourth to second gear and twisted the steering wheel hard right.

"Good," Ms. Song groaned. As the car turned uphill, she leaned her head against the window and closed her eyes. She was looking smaller every second. I reached over and touched her forehead. Her skin was hot.

"We should turn around," I said. "Get her home. Or to a hospital."

"No," Song whispered. "I'm just tired. I need to rest a bit and I'll be fine. We have to keep going. I'm not turning back."

Twyla took her hand off the wheel long enough to gently touch Song's forehead. "You're burning up."

"Please," Ms. Song whispered. She had dug out her note to the Judge and the kid's essay and was squeezing them to death in her hand. "Not now," she said. "Please, Manny"

The headlights caught a hand-painted sign nailed to an Albizia: "Smile more. Life is good." Funny, isn't it, how odd stuff like that can make a brain fire on all its cylinders. It looked like my handiwork, which got me to thinking about food being the good thing about life, which got me to thinking about Rayzah and Blanes and those papers being strangled by Ms. Song's fingers, which made me reach between the two gals and point at a dirt road leading into the jungle. "Turn there. Go. Now. I know a place!"

Twyla didn't hesitate. Me and Ms. Song were thrown left, and the VW skidded onto a cinder driveway. It squeezed between walls of trees before the driveway opened up and turned into a muddy yard in front of a single-story structure with a tin roof and wide front porch. The house was surrounded by tomato plants, goats, wild dogs, chickens, papaya trees, a giant lychee tree, and an even more bigger avocado tree that reached over a storage shed, a chicken coup, and back to the house. Twyla parked under the avocado's deepening shade, next to a beat-up Yamaha dirt bike leaning against the tree's massive trunk. From the porch, two barking baritones came running. The biggest one, some kine collie mix, jumped on the hood and poked its snout in through the moon roof. Twyla tried to shoo him away, and he took the opportunity to blast her with more howling and growling and scratching at rusted metal.

"Pele," I shouted, "Get back."

The dogs kept barking until Rayzah, wearing her green terrycloth robe, the one Papa Joe found at a garage sale in Sunrise Ridge, busted out of the house, ran down the steps and across the yard. On her way, she snatched a broom out of the soggy air. Swinging it like an axe, she swatted Pele off the VW.

"What are you doing here?" She stared at me through the front window.

I stuck my head out the sunroof, touched a finger to my lips. Rayzah got the idea. She pressed her face to the glass. "Is that Ms. Song?" Song's eyes were closed, her head against the window. "Oh, my dear." Rayzah dropped the broom and reached for the door handle. "What are you doing to her, Manny?"

"Me?"

"You're in charge, right?" She tried to yank the door off its hinges.

Ms. Song opened her eyes. "I'm fine," she whispered. "Manual is a good boy."

It was easy to like Ms. Song.

Rayzah tugged at the door while I climbed out of the sunroof, slid down the backside of the VW, and landed in red cinder. It crunched under my feet as I wrapped my hands around Rayzah's big boney fingers and helped her wrestle Song's door open. Twyla pulled Song out of the car and supported her under the arms.

"Honey, you don't look fine," Rayzah said.

I scooped her up like a bride and headed for the house. As I climbed the steps to the porch, I was hoping that the future Ms. Manual would be as light as Ms. Song. Then I started thinking of the odds of there ever being a Ms. Manual. They weren't good.

Ms. Song fit real nice on the porch, in one of the rocking chairs. Twyla shooed away three stray cats while Rayzah disappeared into the house and came back with a glass of water and a pitcher clinking with ice cubes. Ms. Song managed to sip a little water from the glass, enough to make her smile and lean back, saying, "Are we there yet?"

We all got a smile out of that one. "Rest a moment," Twyla said, standing behind Ms. Song, gently massaging the older woman's neck.

Rayzah held the pitcher out to me. Up close I could see ice cubes mixed with slices of oranges, lemons, and limes floating on what smelled like pineapple juice. I waved it away. Me, I was hoping for a pitcher of tequila, but I guess Rayzah had considered my past record.

"It's good for you, Manny." Rayzah handed the pitcher to Twyla, who sniffed it, smiled and asked for a glass. Rayzah disappeared inside, letting the screen door snap shut behind her.

While she was gone, I had a moment to look around. Like I told you, that Rayzah was a worker. Since my last time at her place, she had patched her hog-wire fence to help keep the pigs out. If you can keep the pigs, weeds and bugs out, everything grows in Hawaii. For the bugs and weeds, poison works until they turn drug-resistant and come back bigger and meaner, which means its time to buy bigger and meaner poison. Nothing works on pigs, not even poison. They're like armored rototillers eating everything down to the roots and then eating the roots, the worms, and the dirt. The fence was a good start. Her herd of barking dogs helped. Now, if she threw in some claymore mines and electrified barbed wire, she'd have a fighting chance.

That's life on the Big Island.

At least her place smelled good. Kinda musty and hoppy, like the inside of a brewer's vat. I inhaled, hoping to detect a hint of marijuana in the air. Nothing. Her kids must've been out for the night.

Rayzah came back with two glasses, one for her and one for Twyla. They went to work on the pitcher, pouring and drinking, exchanging chit-chat, and checking on Ms. Song. I walked over to the VW and dug around until I found Ms. Song's note and essay crumpled up on the floor. After flipping the note over and giving the map a second look, I waved for Rayzah.

She came down the steps, and both of us leaned our butts against the VW, looking down at the stick-figure map. As darkness settled on our shoulders, she pointed at the stick-figure house, at the stick-figure girl next to it, and then looked up the mountain. "Three miles up on the left. That's her. I bet. I seen her."

How she knew that from looking at stick figures I wasn't sure, but she was Rayzah. That's all I needed to know. "When are we going up there?" she asked.

"We?" I figured if she ran into the beater, she'd probably get ten years for assault with a deadly motorcycle. I stuffed the note in my pocket.

"You're right," she said. "We can't take them. Those professors don't know squat about kicking the crap out of a sicko. They'll get themselves hurt."

Like I said, Rayzah fired up pretty quick.

She looked up at the porch. Twyla was standing behind Ms. Song, gently massaging her sick friend's shoulders. The disappearing light made them look like they were wearing halos. There's nothing like Big Island light. In the late afternoon early evening, it softens the rain and turns everything into a velvety glow. If you're lucky, someone will be playing slack key guitar as you reach into a cooler for an icy bottle of beer.

"Maybe the girl should go with me," I said. "Twyla. She's wiry and knows who we're looking for."

"She's a child," Rayzah said.

Twyla came down the steps and butted in between us, nice and cozy with our backs to the car. She didn't look like a child to me. "When do we leave?" she asked.

Rayzah gave her one of her hard looks, then passed it on to me. "You don't want to go up there, young lady."

"I can take care of myself," Twyla said. Two big dogs came up and parked their butts in front of her, ready to back her up in a fight. I was beginning to like that little professor. She reminded me of Joe in a smaller package, and not the same sex.

Rayzah shook her head and said, "Wait here." She ran up the steps and into her house. Twyla and me stayed resting against the VW. Ms. Song was napping. The evening tasted like the first drink at happy hour. My shoulder touched Twyla's as we looked up the mountain.

"I'm a lot tougher than I look," she said. "I've been around."

"Sure you have."

She told me that she was twenty-five. She told me she worked out. "I have a few moves," she said, and jumped into a fighting stance, like a boxer working a bag, and threw jabs, leading with her left, following up with a short right uppercut. "Check my arms." She showed me her bicep, grabbed my hand and made me squeeze her muscle. It felt solid as a tennis ball.

I let go when Rayzah came out of the house carrying a shotgun. "Forgot where I hid it," she said, coming down the steps. She tried to hand it to me. It was a side-by-side double barrel with two exposed hammers and two triggers, an old coach gun that had been sawed-off for close-in work. "Not me," I told her. "Guns and me don't mix."

"It doesn't kick much," Rayzah said, still pointing the double-barrel cannon at me. "My old boyfriend gave it to me."

I didn't ask why, or where he was now. At least he had good taste. I liked the UH Rainbow decal on the stock. The new logo without the rainbow is junk. That's what I was thinking.

Rayzah showed me two fat slugs. "Public Defenders," she said. "No buckshot. Lead slugs. Just in case."

Twyla nodded and took the gun.

"In case what?" I asked.

The two gangsters looked at me. They weren't smiling. With Twyla holding a shotgun twice her weight and Rayzah playing with tank-buster rounds, I figured I was caught in a heavy current. "What's the plan?" I asked.

Twyla had it all figured. "Teresa stays here with Ms. Song. We drive up there, you and I. You knock on the door. If the guy gives us any trouble, I step up with this." She pointed the shotgun at me. "Pop, pop," she said, pointing the gun at my crotch. "We take the woman."

All figured out.

Rayzah gave me a quick wink and tossed me the ammo. "I'll heat laulau to get your strength up." She motioned to Twyla. "Can you help?"

"Sure." Twyla dropped the shotgun through the sunroof into the back seat and followed her into the house.

With the two of them banging around in the kitchen, as quick as I could I tossed the ammo in the glove compartment and dug an emergency joint out of my shirt pocket. How it got there I wasn't sure. It wasn't there the last time I looked. Even so, you might ask, who would be stupid enough to smoke weed and play with a shotgun? Good question. I figured that lighting the pin joint might give me the answer. I inhaled gently, then hard, like my life depended on it. Maybe it did. A little paranoia never hurt anyone on a lonely country road.

Don't get me wrong. I can be tough if I want to be. If the guy up the road deserved a beating, and I'm sure he did, I could handle. I took a hit off the joint and held the smoke in. The night was shaping up to be a Clint Eastwood revenge movie. Me and Joe had watched plenty. I exhaled a cloud of wisdom and inhaled another drag of inspiration. If that little professor started waving a shotgun someone was going to get hurt. That's what I told myself. After the next exhale, I knew that would be me.

In the cool mountain air, an owl flew over the driveway. It circled me once before disappearing up the mountain. I couldn't remember if the Hawaiians thought it was a good sign or a bad sign to see an owl. I think it was good, but I get those cultural things mixed up.

Whatever, it got me to thinking that if Twyla went up there and beater boy got hurt, his family would come after her. She was hard to forget. The same went for Rayzah. They'd know her for sure. When things went bad on the Big Island, it turned into a family feud. Rayzah knew that. That's why she had a shotgun in her house.

Just when thinking was getting too much for me, Rayzah stuck her head out the front door and waved at me to go. She pointed up the mountain, shook her fist at me, and then disappeared inside. I took three more drags, quick as I could. My heart thanked me for the extra jolt. I tossed the joint on the cinder, stomped it dead, and made a promise to lay off the weed at least until I could get rid of that double barrel. I swear I was serious. At the time.

Without saying anything to Ms. Song, I squeezed into the driver's seat. It wasn't easy. My knees were jammed in against the metal dash, my chest up against the steering wheel. I had forgotten how small those VWs were. I backed out of the driveway and pointed the VW up the mountain. Like Joe, I worked better alone. Easier that way. And safer. No shooting involved.

As Twyla stepped out of the house, I popped the clutch and stepped on the gas.

Entry 7: THE HUNTING PARTY

No matter what other people say, here's how it happened. Where it happened, that's a different story.

I drove the VW uphill, tapping the speedometer to steady its nerves. The needle jumped from 20 to 40, then dropped to 30. One headlight worked, throwing a soft circle of yellow on the narrow road. Its dim glow reached the edge of the ohia forest. I was keeping my eyes open to watch for pigs crossing or drunks swerving into town, or crazed prisoners stumbling toward short-lived freedom.

Somewhere further up on a misty plateau, the prison had been built to hold criminals near their release dates. People used to ask me why a babooze with only a month left on his sentence would try to escape. To that I'd say, Why ask me? Maybe the lack of barbed wire fences and the miles of Ohia forest were too tempting. Maybe prisoners cracked just like real people, without warning, like when a politician tells the truth.

Anyway, sometimes the prison was closed, sometimes open, depending on the last election. I think it was open back then when I drove up the mountain looking for the stick-figure house, because the road had been resurfaced recently. No doubt, so the guards could reach the prison without breaking an axle.

Twyla's bald tires hummed over the smooth asphalt with no centerline. As cool air rushed in through the moon roof, the speedometer dropped from 40 to 30, to 20. Tapping the glass didn't help. The gas pedal was all the way to the floor when I saw something move up ahead on the right, on the dark side, away from Twyla's one good headlight.

Wild pigs? Like I said, we got plenty of them on the Big Island, and the only thing worse than finding them chewing up your backyard is driving through one of them in the middle of the night. A few months back a friend of mine, Jerry Finger, the Jerry with a green thumb, was driving downhill from Volcano going 60 when he broadsided a pig with his F-150. The 80-pounder ricocheted off the front end, blew into pieces, flew over the hood and smashed through the windshield, landing headfirst in Jerry's lap.

No lie. And as the dead pig's friends disappeared into the forest, without even a sorry here's my insurance card, they stopped to snack on stray pieces of their unlucky friend. No lie. Pinned behind the steering wheel, Jerry saw them eating bloody guts. His truck was totaled, and after that he gave up eating pig, went vegan on us. Which got me to thinking about him eating veggie burritos, when a line of pigs charged into the middle of the road.

I slammed on the brake, pumped it a couple times, a couple more times. The VW kept gliding uphill. I pulled the parking brake, turned off the engine, and the old bug coasted to a stop, a few inches from a hog blockade. A 200-pounder with a nasty Mohawk of spikey pig hair stepped out of the pack, sniffed the VW, and shot me the stink-eye.

I revved the engine, honked the horn.

Fat ass and his 20 buddies stood their ground, forming a wall of stinking, snorting hog flesh. Flies buzzed in a cloud of pig stink, tagging along with the pigs, like remora fish on sharks. Rayzah's dogs would've helped. Local boys hunt pigs with knives, and to keep the party from turning nasty they bring along a pack of dogs. A pig can't do much with a knife at its throat and a dog snapped onto its gonads.

I stuck my head out the moon roof and shouted, "Get lost."
More stink-eye. No movement.

I doubted that Twyla's VW could survive a ramming run at the pig platoon. Instead of the Ford 150's steel front end, it had a gasoline tank and a spare tire. Instead of a pigdozer, it was more Molotov pigtail.

No way was I getting out of the car. Pigs are sneaky. They got tusks. A few years back, one gouged Joe in the thigh, nearly killed him. Fifty stitches from Doc Trina saved his leg. Gave him a couple more years of life so he could reach his 72nd birthday. Even in the fading headlight I could see that a few of them were old enough and big enough to be leg gougers. Even the skinny one hanging back behind the leader looked capable of taking off a knee. And all of them smelled guilty.

I honked the horn, blinked the one headlight, gunned the engine, edged a few inches forward and yelled, "Move it, assholes. I got work to do."

They stood their ground.

So be it. I dug the shells out of the glove compartment, reached behind me, and grabbed the shotgun. It broke open easy and the shells fit like they were made for the gun. I stood on the seat so I could aim out the moon roof, safari style.

With both barrels pointed at the team leader, I pulled back the hammers.

"What are you doing, Manny?" The Madonna was sitting in the passenger seat, looking up at me.

"You could've called ahead," I told her.

"You don't have a phone."

She had a point. At least this time she was wearing appropriate clothing: A green camouflage t-shirt, combat camouflage skinny jeans, and Desert Storm combat boots. "Well?" she asked.

My fingers were still on the two triggers. "I got a pig problem. Trying to scare them out of the road."

"You can't scare pigs."

She was right about that. "I'll shoot one. Maybe that skinny one behind the leader. Just nick him. The rest of them will get the idea. While the rest of them are snacking on him, I'll do an end-around. out flank them."

"Come down here." She tugged at my pants. "Those are my friends." The skinny pig in the back broke ranks, sniffed his way toward the VW. The Madonna, with her hand pulling at my back pocket, said, "Isn't he beautiful?"

Did I tell you that the Madonna had some strange ideas about beauty? I pointed the shotgun at Mr. Skinny as he sniffed the front end of the VW, no doubt checking to see if German tin was edible.

"He's very smart," she said.

"I like my pig roasted."

She nodded. "I like mines in chili verde at Reuben's. If I'm cooking, nowadays I buy my pig at the Sack and Save near St. Joe's Church. A good pork butt at $1.99 is a deal. No mess, no fuss. Of course, it has to be free range. No feeding pens for me."

I didn't buy that story. The Madonna never did any cooking. So I waved the shotgun at the skank smelling the front tires, and said, "If your friends don't move, I'm sending you to Sack and Save."

"There's no reason to be mean."

I could think of one. It had four legs.

"What are you going to do after you shoot it?" the Madonna said. "You're in a hurry, and you can't leave it here."

"Sure I can. Everyone else does." Drive any back road on the Big Island and you'll likely smell rotting pig. Lazy hunters take the meat and toss the guts. They rot out in a week. The guts, not the hunters. No mess, no bother, if you don't mind a week of stink.

"Don't be silly," the Madonna said. "The girl needs you. Let my friend in and everything will be fine. You'll see. He's yours now." She blew me a kiss and disappeared into the night.

I figured the Madonna was trying to tell me something. She wasn't the easiest to read but a roadblock made of hairy wild pigs seemed like an easy read. The Madonna's skinny friend had left a hole in the blockade. With a bit of nudging, maybe I could slip through the crack. I set the shotgun gently into the back seat and settled in behind the steering wheel. The engine started on the fifth try. The pigs were still squatting in line, sucking gas fumes and attracting flies. I pressed lightly on the gas. As the VW edged forward, I didn't hear any squealing. I was about to floor it when the skinny, stinky hairball of a spy pig climbed up the front end and peered down at me through the moon roof.

"Hey, get off there!"

I hit the brakes, and the giant ball of wet pig stink dropped through the roof, slammed into the metal dash, bounced back, and managed to arrange itself into a sitting position. It was sitting up straight, resting on its butt and gazing out the front window as if it was the most natural thing in the world to be a pig in a passenger seat.

With all its mud and hair and stink, I couldn't tell for sure, but I could see and smell enough to know at least part of it was pig. It had a pig nose, pig ears, and pig breath. When he turned sideways to look at me, his pig mouth was in my face, but the creature's eyes were soft and brown, more dog than pig. And its lanky body, except for the pigtail, definitely had a dog shape, some kind of black lab or mastiff or huge Pitbull. Due to the graphic nature of possible mating combinations, I opted to imagine a virgin birth.

"What are you?" I asked, waving away flies. "Pig or dog?"

The pig-dog kept its beady pig eyes on the rearview mirror, watching a small circle of light rushing toward us. As the light grew bigger, pig-dog's eyes became glowing diamonds.

"Watch my back," I said, squeezing out of the VW. The rapid beat of a big, single-cylinder engine was thumping up the mountain. The noise didn't bother the pig blockade. They held their ground with a fierce laziness, some of them even yawning as they stretched out for a nap. I stepped into the middle of road and waved my hands over my head, yelling, "Stop! Hey, stop!"

Pig-Dog stood on his hind legs and made noises out the moon roof. It sounded like a howl mixed with a squeal mixed with a bark, and it caused the oncoming motorcycle to brake hard, skid, and swing its tail, sending a cloud of exhaust and grit at me.

Twyla left the engine running and swung her leg over the gas tank. "Glad I caught you!" She was wearing an army surplus field jacket too big for her and a pair of goggles to match. The elastic strap was tied in a knot at the back of her head. Even in the dark, with the pigs, the pig-thing and the old cycle stinking up the place, it smelled good to be standing next to the little professor. Like smelling success.

"What's that?" she asked, peeling back her goggles to get a better look at pig-thing.

"Long story." It barked a dog-like hello. "I think it was raised by pigs. Like a wolf boy, only without the wolf."

Heading for the VW, Twyla gave it a long look, shook her head, then turned to me and said, "We have to hurry." She opened the passenger side door, pushed pig-thing out of her way, and pulled out the shotgun. She told us the phones weren't working and Rayzah didn't have a car. "You have to take Ms. Song to the hospital. Hurry."

Pig-thing tried to get by her, but Twyla pushed him back into the car. "Stay!" She pointed a finger at him. "I mean you, Pig-Thing." It sat back and kept its mouth shut. "Manny, take the car. Go back. I can handle the motorcycle."

I told her I was pretty good on a motorcycle. She broke open the shotgun, checked the load, and snapped it shut. "I'll ride up the road." I opened my mouth to say something but nothing came out. She climbed onto the motorcycle. It was an XT model with knobby tires, a 500cc single cylinder, and a bench seat. Maybe it was big enough for two people, two really small people. Over its rough idle, she shouted, "Rayzah's said I should go!"

I reached for her arm, but she was too quick. Before I could grab her, she tucked the shotgun under her right arm, pulled her goggles into place, and popped the clutch. The business end of the shotgun pointed back at me as the motorcycle shot straight at the wall of pigs.

Maybe she slipped through the gap between the leader and the pack. Maybe she popped a wheelie and used the gang leader as a ramp to jump the roadblock. The truth is, it happened too fast for me to see. One second she was about to collide with the pig bandits, the next second she was a tiny red taillight disappearing up the road.

"Jeezzuz, did you see that?"

Pig-Dog was looking in the same direction as me, sniffing the air, so I figured he had. Then he turned around and pointed his nose downhill. For a Pig-Dog covered in dirt and pig shit, he spoke good sign language.

I turned the car around, and we headed downhill, me glancing at the rearview mirror, Pig-Dog sticking his head out of the moon roof. I kept hoping to see Twyla and her single headlight. When I pulled into Rayzah's place, her dogs came running, took one look at Pig-Dog and scattered into the shadows.

Rayzah waved at me from under the porch light. "Hurry," she shouted. "We have to get her to the hospital."

I ran up to the steps and lifted Ms. Song from the rocker. Her breath felt warm on my neck. She felt light as a baby, like the only thing holding her together was the air around her.

"Did you see Twyla?" Rayzah asked as I carried Ms. Song gently down the steps.

"For a second."

"That little buggah is quick. I turned around to get my jacket, and she was gone. Stole my keys."

"She's got your shotgun."

"How'd that happen?"

"She's quick."

Pig-dog jumped out of the moon roof, landed neatly on the ground, like a cat, and shook itself. A ton of mud and crap flew into the air.

"What's that?" Rayzah said, opening the VW's door.

"That's a long story." Lack of food was making me weak. My arms were giving out while Rayzah did what she could to brush the pig dirt off the passenger seat. "Some kine pig-thing," I said, worried that I was about to drop Ms. Song. "Doesn't say much. His friends were blocking the road."

Rayzah pushed the passenger seat back as far as it would go, and turned around to take Song from my arms. She placed her gently onto the seat and closed the door. Song curled up like a cat and fell asleep. "You drive," Rayzah said. "I'll wait here for that girl."

After I was in the driver's seat, Pig-dog climbed up the back of the VW and jumped through the moon-roof. He landed in the back seat, sat up straight, and focused his attention on the driveway.

As we drove away, Rayzah yelled, "Don't stop for anything, Manny."

I didn't. Heck, even if I wanted to, I couldn't, not with Twyla's slippery brakes.

Entry 8: NO PLACE FOR DYING

From Song's room, we watched Twyla run into the crosswalk and dodge a speeding pickup truck. When she reached our side of the road, she turned and waved to Rayzah. Straddling her motorcycle, Rayzah waved back, twisted the gas, and shot downhill, aiming for the strip of bright morning wedged between black clouds and blue ocean.

"So, that's your little professor," Doc Trina said, standing next to me in her baggy black scrubs, the ones the hospital had stopped reminding her were not regulation blue.

Earlier that morning I had told her about the essay, my excursion to the university and our trip to Teresa's place, leaving out the part about Joe, the blockade of pigs, and the shotgun. Doc was a pal but she had enough to worry about without tossing in mystical pigs and a shotgun-waving professor. A professor on a motorcycle she could handle.

"She's going to get herself killed," the Doc said, "running like that in a crosswalk."

"She's from the big city."

The Doc brushed her hair back, rubbed the back of her neck, and looked down at Ms. Song. Our patient was enjoying a drug-induced sleep, dreaming about miracle cures and a world without papers to grade.

"You should have taken Papa Joe," the Doc told me. "He's better with violence."

"He's on vacation."

"Vacation? Joe?"

"Traveling."

The Doc looked at me like she was checking for signs of disease. "Right," she said. "Is it December already? Joe's Birthday?"

We heard the elevator door open, then running steps in the hallway. How Twyla got by the front desk and security, smelling like she did, covered in mud and pig shit, I don't know. But she did. The smell hit us first. She came next, rushing in just in time for the Doc to block her. Using her clipboard like a cop would use a nightstick, she poked it at Twyla's chest. "Get back, young lady. Take your dirt outside. Go."

Twyla tried crying and shaking, and telling the Doc how much Ms. Song meant to her. It didn't help. The Doc prodded her out of the room and down the hall toward the elevator. It was a good fight for sports fans. Black pajamas and soap smell versus skinny jeans and pig stink. Twyla was quicker on her feet. The Doc had a few inches of height and width advantage. Both were good with their hands. But the Doc had home-court advantage and sharper edges. Working in a hospital can do that, sharpen your edges.

"She needs rest." The Doc jabbed with the clipboard, threatened Twyla with nurses who would strap her to a wheelchair and shove her into a closet until the police arrived. The elevator doors opened, and Twyla fell back. Looking around the Doc at me, she pleaded, "Manny, tell her." The Doc prodded her deep inside the elevator. "There's nothing he can do. Go home and get cleaned up. Then come back."

The elevator doors closed, and I followed the Doc back to Song's room. She sat down gently on the edge of the bed, sighed, and looked at Song for a long time. She was thinking. That was a good sign because she was good at thinking. After burning a few brain cells, she said, "At least Joe doesn't have to see this." She crossed herself.

"Making crosses? You a believer now?"

She shrugged. "No, but why take chances?"

It was a strange thing for a doctor to say, but the Doc spent more time at the hospital than I did, so I kept my mouth shut. She knew the ropes. She took Song's hand and placed it gently in her lap. Seeing them like that, I half expected the Doc to tell her everything was going to be okay, not to worry. It didn't happen. After a few minutes of silence, the Doc leaned over and kissed the sleeping woman on the forehead. "Dear, dear woman," she whispered. She stood up and waved for me to follow her into the hallway. The hall smelled of disinfectant and pig dirt. "That dirty professor, where'd she come from?"

"From Cali, I think. Ms. Song knows."

"Her and Ms. Song are close?"

I shrugged. "They're work buddies."

The Doc paced back and forth. She liked to keep moving. She wore people out with her moving. Me, I liked sitting still, getting low. I needed sleep and food, but I didn't want to try them at the hospital. If I sacked out now, they might wheel me off by mistake, and I'd wake up without my appendix, or something worse. And the food, well, do I need to say anything about hospital food? And it wasn't a real hospital because they don't serve wine. Enough said.

The Doc pulled me away from Song's door and whispered, "It's not going to get any better for Ms. Song. You understand?"

"Sure." I understood. More friggin good news. People were dropping faster than I could count. First Papa Joe, then the Judge disappears, now Ms. Song was getting ready to...make the transition. I told the Doc she had to be wrong, told her how just yesterday Ms. Song was running down students and hauling in essays. "She hasn't been eating right," I said. "What say we order in some Reuben's?"

The Doc grabbed my hand. "She's been fooling people, Manny." Her fingers pressed hard around mine. "You don't look so good yourself. Have you been drinking?"

"Not lately."

"You look like you need one. I know I do."

When it came to alcohol, her and the Madonna saw eye to mysterious eye on the benefits of serious drinking. They both liked Knob Creek. The Doc headed for the elevator, talking to me over her shoulder. "Go home. Talk to your little professor. Get her cleaned up, and then bring her back so she can see Ms. Song. We don't have much time. Stand back, I'm going up."

She disappeared into the elevator, the doors closed, and a second later the door to the stairwell flew open and Twyla stepped out. It was like watching a magic show.

Twyla ran by me into Song's room, leaned over her, and kissed her forehead. She turned to me, a tear working its way down her mud-splattered cheek. "I can't stand it," she said, "doing nothing."

I looked around inside my head for something to say. In the movies, I'd give her a big hug and say something about prayers and going to a better place. I stood there with my mouth closed.

"Thank you for taking care of her," she said, holding out her hand. "I can't believe I left her."

To keep the place tidy, I kicked a couple of stray dirt clods under the bed. I gave her hand a weak shake. What else could I do? My hand came away covered with dirt. "Thank me? For what?"

"For going back to help her. I was crazy. All I could think about was that poor girl, up there, with him."

That's when she told me about finding the house. Its lights were out. She knocked on the front door. It was locked. No one answered. There were dogs barking but they were in cages, so she went behind the house and tried the back door. It was unlocked. "It was so simple," she said. "I don't know why I was scared. I walked in and found the girl hiding in her bedroom. When she saw me she started crying, and we walked out the front door." She snapped her fingers. "Easy."

Right. Easy. "Where is she now?"

"Out! Both of you!" Doc Trina busted into the room and grabbed Twyla by the shoulder. How she had snuck up on us, without a sound, I don't know. Maybe it was the black pajamas. "Christ," she shouted, "you two are filthy." She pulled Twyla away from the bed and pushed her out the door. "Out. I can't trust either of you."

While she was roughing up Twyla, I managed to lean over and kiss Ms. Song on the forehead. "Take care," I said. "We'll be back. I got work to do." Weak fingers touched my hand. Without opening her eyes, Ms. Song whispered, "Be careful, Manual."

I was rubbing water out of my eye when a couple of heavy hands locked onto my elbows. Doc Trina had brought along two heavies in blue scrubs to wrestle me and Twyla into the real world. The one towing me had been lifting weights.

"Shame on you," the Doc shouted, right behind us.

If I had been myself, with some food in my belly, I could have busted free, made quick work of the nurses. That's what I told myself. I mean, how tough could nurses be?

The two heavies shoved us into the elevator and backed in to block our escape. Before the doors closed, the Doc shouted over the nurses, "Take her home, Manny. And you, young lady, come talk to me when you've cleaned yourself up. And don't let Manny talk you into sharing a shower to save water. That's not an experience you'll want to remember."

That's the Doc. If a meteor was going to crack the world in half tomorrow, she'd find a way to joke about it today. Just to lighten things up, right? The elevator doors closed, pushing all of us closer together. It was a tight squeeze. That's when I noticed our two captors were male nurses in running shoes. Nurse Thug #1 was as tall as me. Nurse Thug #2 a few inches shorter. Both of them were yards wide and weighed enough to make the elevator strain its cables as we dropped to the first floor.

Twyla glanced at me, then at the backs of the two heavies. "We can take these two," she said, loud enough for them to hear.

"She's always joking," I said. "Be nice, Professor."

"You want to hear a real joke?" Thug #1 one said, glancing over his shoulder at me.

Twyla was about to say something but I covered her mouth with my hand. Her lips were wet.

"We had a professor in here yesterday who cried like a baby," Thug #1 said.

"Did he do any singing?" I asked.

"How did you know?"

"Finals," I said. "Professors always get a little spooky."

"Is he still here?" Twyla asked. "The singing one?"

"He didn't stay long. Nothing serious. Fake back injury syndrome. That's what Doc Trina called it. We kicked him out as soon as we could. Couldn't stand his whining. Kept crying about all the papers he had to grade."

The elevator doors opened, and the nurses guided us through the lobby and into the sunlight.

"Don't you worry about Ms. Song," Thug #1 said.

"We'll take good care of her," #2 said. "We had her for English 100."

"Me, too," I said.

It was a class reunion. Out front, they waved goodbye to us like we were old buddies leaving Auntie Sally's Luau House after a night of eating and dancing and talking about back in the day.

The breeze off the ocean felt fresh and new and full of life, as long as I stayed upwind of Twyla. As we ran across the street, she told me, "I don't want to die in a hospital."

When I was safe on the other side of the road, I turned and looked at the Hilo Hospital, four stories of industrial strength concrete. It was an office building for dying. At least Joe saw the sky when he went out. "No place is good for dying," I said, as a pickup truck whizzed by us.

"I'm not going to leave her there."

"The Doc knows what she's doing."

"I'd rather die in the street."

If she kept using the crosswalks in Hilo, she'd get her wish. We found her VW in the back of the lot, behind a dumpster. "What were you hiding from?" she asked.

I kicked the driver's side door to loosen up the rust. The keys were in my hand, so I was going to drive. "I figured he'd scare people."

"Who?" She went around to the passenger side, looked inside, and stopped with her hand on the door. "You brought him?"

Pig-Dog was waiting for us in the passenger seat. When he saw Twyla, he jumped into the back. He stunk but he had good manners.

"It wouldn't leave. Wouldn't go inside. Kept barking at the hospital."

Pig-Dog gave me stink-eye while Twyla reached over the seat and rubbed its muddy head. "It has potential." She rubbed its chest, its belly, and lower down, ending with, "He's a boy."

That professor was braver than me. No telling where her hands had been. Pig-Dog agreed by barking twice. Apparently he could read minds. After the introductions were over, the three of us sat up straight and looked out the front window.

"Where to?" I asked.

Twyla shook her head. "I don't know." She told me that she was renting a room at Ms. Song's place, up in Volcano, but she didn't want to go there. "It's too far," she said. "I don't want to see her things. I can shower at the gym. Buy a clean sweatshirt and pants at the bookstore."

"What about him?" I glared at Pig-Dog. "We could set him free over there in the trees." There were plenty of trees in Hilo. People kept cutting them down and they kept growing back. The jungle by the hospital covered a hundred acres and doubled as a rubbish dump. The trick was to find a spot where you could pull over, stop, make a quick drop of a TV or refrigerator or pig-thing, and speed away before the jungle grew over you.

"Don't be silly," Twyla said, rubbing Pig-Dog's head.

Girls and their dogs. She said that we could go to my place, drop me off, and she'd take the dog-thing with her to the university.

We rode downhill, past the jail, the high school, and Kosmic Cone. "They got gravy burgers in there," I said. "And dipped cones."

Pig-Dog gave Kosmic a long look, like he was memorizing the address. He did the same when we passed Blanes. Twyla kept her eyes closed, not saying anything, which was okay because I was talked out and I didn't want to discuss apostrophes with an English teacher. Both of us were going down fast. Only Pig-Dog seemed alive.

He stuck his head between us. I elbowed him back. He stuck his head between us. I pointed at the empty parking space behind the Empire where Joe's truck had lived for twenty years. "We're home."

*** (Pause for sigh of relief.) ***

I made the mistake of closing the moon roof before we piled out. All of us, even Pig-Dog, were gasping for air before we managed to force the doors open. Twyla found a chunk of cinderblock and shoved it behind the back tire. Pig-Dog sniffed the ground where Joe had checked out. He bared his teeth and tusks and growled. For a mutant hybrid he had a good nose, one that could smell memories. I looked in the shed, found the bucket, sponge and dish detergent that Joe used for scraping crud off his truck.

"You two, over there." I pointed them at the middle of the alley. Twyla was too tired to argue. She raised her arms over her head and said, "Hit me." Pig-Dog sniffed his way to her foot, sat down beside her. A hybrid couple. I hosed them down pretty good, starting with Twyla's head and working my way down. Whenever the spray got close to Pig-Dog, he snapped at it. I figured he was asking for more, so I kept blasting him in the mug.

I push-kicked the bucket at Twyla, saying "More soap." She squirted in a long jet of dish detergent, and I worked up the suds with a blast of hose water. That got the party going.

Twyla picked up the sponge and went to work. As she rubbed Pig's scraggly fur, he took on the shape of a medium-size dog with an Airedale head, the short, stocky body of a pit bull, and the nose and tail of a pig.

A lot of local guys liked Airedales for hunting pigs. My guess was his mother had walked away from the job, gone over to fraternize with the pig enemy, and after some hard partying in the enchanted forest popped out a pig-dog.

While I was rinsing him off, Twyla stripped down, first the shirt, then the jeans. Not that easy for skinny jeans. The black bra and panties came off easy. She bent over, picked up the bucket, and poured it over her head. It was a masterpiece: Nude standing under a soapy waterfall. She worked the sponge head to hips. When she bent over to sponge her calves and knees, morning sunlight flashed off her soapy skin. As she rubbed the sponge over the hard-to-get-at spots, Pig-dog looked at me, and I blasted him with the hose. Sometimes life is good.

"Towels?" Twyla shouted.

I shut off the water, unlocked the back door.

"Hurry," she said, following me into the darkness. When I turned on the lights, Pig-Dog shoved by me and nosed his way into the theater, moving fast, tail slapping back and forth.

In the war surplus section, I found a stack of old towels, small as napkins and rough as sandpaper. Hilo Hotel surplus. Twyla used three of them to dry her nooks and crannies. When she was through, she said, "Clothes?"

Papa Joe didn't have any regular girl clothes, but he had shelves full of war surplus uniforms. I showed her the way. She stepped onto a footlocker and stretched to reach stacks of white, sailor caps, what Joe called Dixie cups. "Wow," she said, on her tiptoes, "where did he find these?"

Me and Pig-Dog kept our eyes on the floor. I figured it was easier for him than me. When I looked up, she was wearing a pair of navy blue bell-bottoms, a navy blue work shirt, a web belt with a brass buckle, and a Dixie cup hat. She tucked most of her hair under the cap, rolled up the bell-bottoms and tied a knot in the extra foot of web belt. Her and Pig-Dog looked like they belonged on a box of Cracker Jacks, a slightly twisted demented box.

"This is quite a place," she said, picking up a foot-long bayonet.

"Papa Joe was a collector." Pig-Dog faded into the shadows. We followed his wet footprints through the main auditorium, past the freezer, and into the office. We found him parked next to the safe, ripping open a package of frozen red dogs. The only red dogs I remembered were stored in the freezer.

"Do you have anything to drink?" Twyla asked.

"Alcohol?"

"Sounds good."

Marta's cup was still on Joe's desk. I handed it to her and found another bottle of tequila in the safe.

"Is this cup clean?" she asked.

"Cleaner than most." Except for cop cooties.

Pig-Dog had the red dogs strung out on the floor and was inhaling them like they were lines of coke. Me, I was trying to remember where I kept my stash of emergency weed. Twyla snatched the bottle from my hand and sat down in my chair.

"You're not drinking?" Before I could answer, she poured tequila in the cup, gulped it down, and poured another.

I dropped into Joe's chair. My stomach was shrunk down to walnut size. It needed food. "I guess not."

"But you smoke?"

"The Doc says it's good for me."

"Sounds reasonable." She downed a shot and poured another. "What about Papa Joe? The fellow who owns this place? Does he smoke? What's he like?"

I scratched my ear, hoping to spark an idea, wondering how to describe a guy who sets his 72nd birthday as a deadline. The Sauza looked clear and smooth and full of promise. Pig-dog finished inhaling hot dogs, collapsed next to the freezer, and was doing his imitation of an 80-pound doorstop. He closed his eyes but kept his ears pointed at us.

"He's a nice guy," I said. In Hilo that's the highest compliment you can pay someone, man or woman -- being a nice guy.

She smiled, and it made her look even younger. "Why Papa? Did he have any children?"

That threw me off, made me see Joe in the flickering light, asking me the same question about kids. "Not that I remember." I didn't want to talk about Joe. He was still too close, so I said, "I can barely keep my eyes open."

"Wait," she said. "We still have work to do. The essays. There must be a hundred of them. We can't forget the students. They're depending on us."

I could forget plenty of things. No problem. But that girl had a good brain and plenty of energy, even with all that tequila in her. She hurried out and Pig-Dog went with her. When she came back hauling a stack of essays, he was right behind her. She dropped the essays on the desk, and he dropped by the freezer, went back to snoring.

The stack of essays was a couple feet tall. She split it in two. "One for you, one for me."

"I'm not good with words."

"Work will help us keep our minds off Ms. Song until I can drink enough to pass out."

Like I said, she was pretty tough for a professor.

"Read fast and make three stacks," she said. "One stack for the really bad ones, that's easy. Another for the really good ones, that's easy. And a stack for the betweens. That's the hard part."

She worked fast, and by the time Pig-Dog started snoring she had three piles in front of her. I was still trying to read my first essay. I'd read a line or two, get lost, start again, and get lost again. It must've been one of those in-between hard ones, so I tossed it on the table and tried a few more about babies being born, high school graduations, drug parties, and rotten teachers before I ran into some crazy talk about a book called Why People Fuck with Your Mind. I told her that the Singing Professor's stuff must've got mixed in with Song's stuff.

She checked my pile, shuffled out a small stack and said, "Give all those an A. They deserve it for lasting the whole semester with that creep. I never trusted him."

It felt good drawing an A at the top of each paper. I started with the three-line method and in no time was slapping on A's in one continuous movement. For the short essays, I tossed in a plus sign. For the long ones, a minus. On every other one, I added a short note on the last page: "Very good. Next time you see me, kick me in the ass, hard, really, for not recognizing your brilliance earlier."

Fueled by alcohol Twyla kept working seriously, scribbling in the margins, sipping from her teacup. "Do you have any pictures of him?" she asked without looking up.

"Who?"

"Papa Joe."

"Joe didn't like cameras."

"But this was his home, right?" She kept scribbling. "There must be a picture of him here somewhere."

"The Judge used to say he looked like a guy called Hemingway."

"The young one or the old one?"

"There were two of them?"

She stood up, stretched her arms over head, and held that pose while she said, "The old Hemingway had a beard and a comb-over, lots of kids and four wives. And he drank way too much." She did a couple of jumping jacks, a couple squats, and a slow neck twist.

"Joe could drink pretty good," I said. "But he didn't have wives or a comb-over, and no kids or beard. He took care of stray cats."

"So did Hemingway." She sat down and went back to reading and scribbling, before she said, "He killed himself with a shot gun."

I figured that Joe's way was better. Less mess.

Professor Twyla poured another shot and emptied it like someone headed for her first AA meeting or a chat with the old Hemingway. "How old is Joe?" she asked.

"Seventy-two."

"A person can't live to seventy-two and not have pictures. Does he drive?"

"Not anymore."

"What?"

"Not legally. No license."

"A rebel."

"Nope. He doesn't like taking tests. When he gets a ticket, the Judge fixes it for him."

"Was she his lover?"

It was hard to think of the Judge as a lover. I tried to imagine her without clothes, which I figured was a good starting point for being a lover. I couldn't get past the black robe and rubber slippers. It didn't work any better with Joe.

All the questions and grading were catching up to me. Stressful stuff. "Stay here," I said, and went out back to Joe's storage shed. I dug through a mountain of toilet paper until I found Joe's ammo box, another one of his secret hiding places. Inside it, under a stack of old photos, I found my freezer-lock baggie of emergency joints. I went outside and sat down with my back against the wall. After looking at the ground under the VW for signs of Papa Joe, I searched through the stack of old black-and-white photos until I found the picture of the young Papa Joe in his dress uniform. With his service hat pulled down over his eyes, it was hard to see his face. And the woman standing next him had so many flower leis piled around her neck that only her eyes were visible. But she was the right height for the Judge. Wearing one of those flat, black hats that college kids throw in the air at graduation to celebrate no more tuition, she had an arm around Joe's waist. I lit a joint, and stared at the two of them as long as I could. A couple of hits later, I closed my eyes.

When I woke up, the sun was disappearing behind the mountains. Someone had thrown an army blanket over my legs. The photos were still there, except for one.

I checked the auditorium, the dressing rooms, and the snack bar. No Twyla. She was gone, so was the bottle of tequila, and so was Pig-Dog. I climbed the stairs to the projection booth. A thin strip of light was escaping from the crack under the door. "Twyla?"

"In here."

She was lying on Joe's army cot, on her back, using Joe's leather bomber jacket like a pillow. The bottom half of her was hidden under a war surplus blanket. Her navy clothes were folded neatly on the floor, next to the half-empty tequila bottle. Her Dixie cup hat was sitting on top of Joe's Howdy Doodie lamp. The windows were open. A cool breeze caressed the back of my neck.

"I didn't want to wake you," she said, tapping at her phone. "I slept for five hours. Took a little tour of the place. The door was open."

"I'm surprised you found it." She must've done a lot of looking.

She glanced up at me, "This whole place is crazy. I love it. All the ..."

"Stuff."

"Yes, stuff." She smiled before adding, "I've been researching him." She pointed under the cot. Pig-dog stuck his head out and rested his chin on Twyla's pile of clothes. "I'm sure he's an Airedale." She sat up. The blanket settled in her lap as she flashed her phone screen at me. "See."

I stepped closer, watched her scroll by the Wikipedia logo, down a column of Airedale pictures.

"What about the pig parts?" I asked.

The phone rang and she answered it, listened, and said, "Yes, yes." She threw off the blanket and stood up. "That was the hospital. I can see Ms. Song."

I looked down at Pig-Dog, and he eyed the tequila bottle. When I looked up, she was tucking her shirt into her bell-

79

bottoms, tying it all together with the web belt. "Got to go," she said. She picked up Joe's leather jacket and found the cookies in the pocket. "I love peanut butter," she said, before tossing one in her mouth.

She tried on the jacket. Even though it was too big, she looked good in it, like a high school kid in her boyfriend's letterman jacket. She pulled the jacket tight across her chest. "Do you think he'd mind me wearing it?"

I tried to say something, but I was too busy imagining her riding that motorcycle with the shotgun under her arm, the girl clinging to her back as they flew down the mountain.

"I'm sorry," she said. "I shouldn't have asked."

I wanted to ask her where she had taken the girl and how she had managed to carry the shotgun and the girl on Rayzah's motorcycle. But I was too busy watching her stand on her tiptoes, feeling her kiss my cheek. "I'm going to the hospital," she said. "We can finish the papers tomorrow. Pig-Dog, you stay here with Manny."

Before I could say anything, she was out the door, shouting back at me, "Meet me at school tomorrow, at 1, for lunch. After that we can finish the papers and clean up around here. You know. Clean up."

Pig-Dog and me looked at each other as her footsteps faded down the stairs and out the back door. From the window we watched her climb into the VW. She was still wearing Papa Joe's jacket. As she drove away, I remembered Joe's photograph. It was still missing. So was the Judge.

Entry 9: FACE DOWN IN MUD

Something was bothering me, so I kicked the ammo box out of the way and pointed a flashlight into Joe's shed. A few years back, during the west-coast-dock-strike panic, Joe had bought enough war surplus toilet paper to supply the island for a week. Stacked it neatly in the shed. Then, a few months later, we watched an earthquake shake the paper mountain into a pile of rubble.

To get to Joe's motorcycle I had to dig through that pile. Until my lungs gave out, I picked up boxes of toilet paper and tossed them at Pig-Dog. He dragged them into the alley. While he worked, I caught my breath and promised myself to give up smoking. To make the point, I kicked a box into the alley. When I turned around, a handlebar surfaced from the sea of paper.

With me pushing at bars and Pig-Dog barking at the sidecar, we muscled the contraption out of the shed. The old Ural weighed as much as a bus. To stop it from rolling down the driveway, Pig-Dog dragged Twyla's piece of cinderblock under the back wheel. Joe had hidden a bottle of tequila in the sidecar, another of his secret hiding places. To keep it company, I tossed in a medium weight claw hammer and a flashlight. While I packed, Pig-Dog chewed through a carton of toilet paper. He had some nasty teeth. They looked bigger at night.

Everything about him looked bigger and stronger at night. Back then I thought it was the moonlight.

I used his toilet-paper trail to wipe the dirt off the motorcycle's metal seat. Like the rest of the Ruskie bike, it was built to last, not for comfort or speed but for cold-hearted strength. Joe had left a black hoodie hanging on a nail inside the shed. I pulled the moldy cotton over my head, brushed the dust off the Niners' logo, and asked Pig-Dog what he thought. He turned and disappeared into the Empire. Maybe he wasn't a Frisco fan. The keys to the bike were in the hoodie's kangaroo pouch. I didn't own any socks but I found a pair of Joe's jungle boots in the shed. They fit, maybe only a size too big. I tucked my jeans into the boots, and jumped up and down a couple of times to get my circulation going. It could be cold up the mountain, and I wanted to be ready. There was something up there I needed to see.

Pig-Dog was waiting for me in the Ural's sidecar. I checked the gas, climbed onto the motorcycle's tractor seat, and found Joe's goggles hanging on the handlebars. The world looked a little hazy through the scratched glass but the goggles fit. In the scratchy haze, Pig-Dog licked his lips, glanced at the engine, and hunkered down behind the tiny windshield. I didn't blame him. Riding in a sidecar is dangerous, especially if the driver has the shakes.

"Get ready to be impressed," I said. The bike started on my first try. Okay, the truth is, it wasn't on the first try. Joe had used a heavy dark pencil to write the starting instructions on the back of the shed door, and maybe I didn't get them right the first time and had to take a second and third look. But eventually I reached under the seat to turn the power switch on, waited for a second for volts to build, turned the key to on, checked the green light for neutral, reached under the gas tank to turn the fuel on, set the choke at half way, primed both the carburetors, nursed the kick starter a couple times until I felt the tension, and stomped down hard. After four or five more stomps, the engine stuttered to life. When I twisted the gas, the bike sounded like Frankie's lawn mower screaming into a bullhorn. Pig-Dog squeezed himself deeper into the sidecar.

"Ready?"

Pig-Dog nodded his head.

I wasn't. To make sure I knew what I was doing, I asked again. "Ready?" He showed me his tusks.

"Professor Twyla isn't the only one who knows how to ride like the wind."

He barked three times.

I let out the clutch and we flew down the alley, turned right at the ocean, and chugged along Bay Front. By the time we passed the soccer fields, I had made a list of things to do. First thing in the morning, I was going to check on Ms. Song. Second thing, I was going to find Joe's truck. Third, find something to eat. Fourth, get new shocks for the Ural. A few minutes more of wrestling the Ural over Hilo's potholes made me reconsider. I moved new shocks and finding Joe's truck to the top of the list.

The Ural was killing me. Frankie's tractor had better suspension. Anything had better suspension. You need good suspension on the Big Island, and good steering. Hilo's roads have more cracks and ruts and holes than they have asphalt, and the Ural wasn't good at dodging any of them. It only knew how to go in a straight line, no matter what, even when I tried to turn it. Normal motorcycles leaned into a turn. Urals with sidecars turn like a truck with a flat tire.

Pig-Dog didn't mind. After a few bumpy miles of hiding at the bottom of the sidecar, he sat up straight. The wind blew his curly dog hair and pig ears back, and his flashing tusks made him look almost happy. That freaky hybrid had some Ruskie in him. The Mongol part. And he certainly had some red in, including a patch of bright red flames running down his back.

I tightened my grip on the handlebar grips and drove into the night, concentrating on Ms. Twyla and her trip up the mountain. If she could do it, I could. Out by the Plaza, you know, the big mall on the edge of town, I looked in the rearview mirror and noticed a long line of headlights backed up behind me. The speedometer wasn't working. When I pulled over to the slow lane, twenty cars rushed by us. Pig-Dog snarled and snapped at all of them except a big pickup truck that refused to pass.

Its headlights were bright enough to blind me. I made a quick right turn, coasted into the Ginger Patch deli and gas station, and watched the big truck with jumbo-jet tires drive out of town on the back road. We waited five minutes. The Hilo Argonauts, a peewee soccer team trying to make airfare to the gaming tables in Vegas, had a truck-bed rotisserie setup in the parking lot. It was churning out Huli Huli chicken and huge clouds of smoke. Pig-Dog inhaled enough fumes to start him foaming at the mouth.

When he was about to jump out and charge the big kid manning the rotisserie, I headed out of town on the back road. Pig-Dog looked back lovingly at the roasting chickens. The moon disappeared behind clouds as he licked his chops and I kept an eye out for over-sized pickup trucks. The Ural's fat headlight swept across both lanes. The engine accelerated into a comfortable roar that vibrated through the metal seat, like a motel-bed administering a 25-cent massage. Life felt pretty good out there in the wind, so good I almost missed the turn.

As we pulled into Rayzah's driveway, a fat moth smashed into my forehead. Clouds of flying bugs swarmed the headlight. Pig-Dog snapped at them, snatching strays out of the air. I hung a slow U-turn, looking for Rayzah's dogs or motorcycle, or anything. Everything was dark. I parked the Ural under the trees with its front end pointed at the main road. My feet crunched on the red cinder as I headed for porch. Pig-Dog ran ahead, up the steps, and stopped at the front door.

"Rayzah," I called. Pig-Dog barked. I knocked three times, waited. Nothing. I tried peeking through the windows and tapping on the glass while Pig-Dog kept an eye on the road. I was bending over, feeling for the key under the mat when headlights stopped at the driveway. Maybe it was the same truck that had followed us out of town. All I could see was a splash of light, so I stayed down, feeling for the key, pressing myself into the porch. It smelled of musty feet and dog hair.

Pig-Dog was tougher. Instead of hiding, he ran down the steps and threw himself into a fit of wild barking and snorting as he ran toward the headlights. They backed up into a U-turn and headed up the mountain.

Pig-Dog ran back and hopped into the sidecar. If the rescued girl was in Rayzah's house, I figured she was hiding in the dark and trying to break in would only make things worse, so I followed Pig-Dog's lead and ran down to the Ural, hopped on, grinded it into gear, and headed up the mountain, with the headlight turned off. Hitting every bump and crack, we kept climbing, watching for brake lights and stray pigs. Pig-Dog saw the driveway first, announcing his sighting by sticking his slimy snout in my ear and barking.

Instead of listening to his advice, I shoved him back into his seat and drove a mile or two up before I hooked left and made a sweeping U-turn off the asphalt and into the wet mud. A heavy black shadow turned out to be a clearing in the trees. I shifted into reverse and backed the Ural into hiding. Branches poked me in the ribs, slapped my face. When I turned off the engine, the night wrapped around us like a wet blanket. If we could ever find it again, the Ural was ready for a quick getaway.

Pig-Dog jumped out. His seat cushion looked like it had been used for home plate in a slow-pitch softball game. I found the hammer on the floor. It was a Stanley, 16-ounce FatMax Xtreemee with an easy grip handle. Mob guys in the movies like baseball bats. I like a good hammer. There's nothing like a hammer for fighting in close, and what cop can blame a guy for having a hammer in his WWII motorcycle? A baseball bat will get you handcuffed. A hammer will get you a knowing nod.

The moon slipped out of the clouds. With the Stanley in my belt, I felt around in the bottom of the sidecar for the flashlight. My hand bumped into the bottle of tequila, and I remembered reaching into the dark for a bottle that night with

Joe. I took a long hit off the tequila and offered a shot to Pig-Dog. He shook his head. Me, I needed another hit. To stay warm. I took two, wiped my mouth, and left the bottle on Pig-Dog's seat cushion.

I dug deeper for the flashlight. The sidecar felt like it went on for forever. "What's this?" I said, pulling Joe's .22 out of the dark. Pig-Dog looked away so I couldn't see the guilt on his face. "Your idea?" I asked. "Or the Madonna's?" When he didn't say anything, I stuck it under the seat cushion. Maybe sitting on it would help his memory.

Giving up, I was walking away from the motorcycle when Pig-Dog stuck his head into the sidecar. A second later, he surfaced with a flashlight in his mouth. In my short time with the army, I didn't learn much about guns. Mostly they taught me how to mop floors, haul trash, and use a hammer when duct tape didn't work. But I knew how to use a flashlight.

Following its narrow beam of light, I moved along the edge of the woods, close enough to duck into the shadows at the first hint of car noise or headlights. None came. The air was damp and fresh and cool, and for someone scared crazy I was feeling pretty good by the time we reached the driveway. That's when the flashlight failed. I tossed it into the woods and stumbled into the driveway.

I couldn't see but I could smell Pig-Dog. Following him was like following the trail of a burning cabbage. When I lost the stink in a gust of fresh wind, I could still hear him sniffing his way along the narrow driveway, inhaling cinder and gravel. My eyes adjusted to the dark, and I saw him with his head down, tacking and angling his way toward the house, like a hound searching for... a friend. The house was set back from the driveway, a one-story ranch, with a small plastic storage shed off to the side and a pen made of chain-link for dogs.

Pig-Dog ran back to me, licked my hand, and pointed his nose at the house. My hand felt sticky. I wiped it on the back of my pants, slipped the hammer from my belt, and pointed it at the house. "Go check it out," I whispered. He disappeared into the shadows.

I took a few steps, stopped, and looked behind me first and then every shadow, no matter where it was. Pig-Dog busted out of the darkness and came running to me. He wanted me to follow him around back, but I didn't trust him. Not in those days. I still don't. Instead I stumbled my way to the front door and knocked three times. Nothing. Pig-Dog barked twice and ran around back. I followed him into the shadows so he wouldn't wake up the neighborhood, what there was of it. I was heading for the back door when my foot hit something hard, and I fell forward onto my hands and knees.

Barking like a madman, Pig-Dog ran in circles around me. I told him to shut up but he wouldn't listen. He kept barking until I felt around under my legs. The body was face down in the mud. He was barefoot and his jeans were rolled up above his ankles. His hair was greasy wet but that wasn't his main problem. There was a hole in his back and plenty of blood on his shirt. I rolled him over to get a better look, but I didn't see much before flashing blue-and-red lights turned into the driveway.

Pig-Dog ran in circles around me. That was his normal response to police cars. Without thinking, I lifted the body onto my shoulders, stood up, and ran into the woods, fireman style.

Why? My main excuse is lack of experience. Back then I had been spending most of my nights inside bars, not out in the woods playing sneak around. And we were a long way from a bar. It was dark. I was stoned. It was my first day on the job, and I hadn't seen a body in a couple of days. Maybe most, I was thinking what would happen to Twyla if the cops found that body.

The good thing is, it started raining. In the trees, it wasn't too bad. Out in the open, the cops would be getting most of it, and there wouldn't be much of a trail to follow. I kept moving, digging my way through mud, climbing over fallen trees, dropping the body and stopping to rest. It took a while going uphill, but I kept going until I bumped into the Ural.

A couple of feet inside the tree line, I dumped the body, and rolled him over so he could look up at the sky. I offered

87

my apologies for the rough treatment, kicked him once for being a turd, and left him to rot. Pig-Dog was waiting for me, sitting up straight in the sidecar, the .22 clenched in his teeth and tusks.

Instead of heading down the mountain, I pointed the Ural uphill, wondering what Twyla did with the shotgun.

Entry 10: LOVE IN THE SHELVES

We spent all night on the road. I figured it was safer than going back to Hilo. Instead, we drove up the mountain toward the prison, turned left, spent twenty minutes sneaking along dark asphalt, and connected to the only road that circled the island.

I was still looking over my shoulder when we stopped for gas at Volcano Village and Pig-Dog stole a jar of pickled eggs from next to the cash register. Maybe I should have sent him back inside with an apology, but I was in a hurry. I kept my hoodie tied tight and my eyes on the road while he gorged himself. To the sound of his chewing, we drove along the fault line that was threatening to drop a thirty-mile chunk of island into the sea. We buzzed through Ocean View, slipping by houses built on crushed lava rock, and added a trail of rotten egg and Ural exhaust to the volcano's fumes.

Three hours later, when we stopped in Keahou, Pig-Dog howled at the stars until him and his bloated pig belly fell asleep under a kiawe tree. I sat with my feet in the water, staring at the stars, trying to think. Back then I was trying to image the little professor using that shotgun on the wife beater. It didn't fit. Nothing came to me, except that Kona was a long way from Hilo. It was warmer. And it never rained. Deep down, though, I couldn't shake the feeling that it didn't make much difference where I was on the Big Island. If I turned over a few rocks, soon enough I'd find a body with a bullet hole in it.

When the morning broke open behind us, I kicked Pig-Dog, mostly to nudge out any leftover egg gas but also to get him up and moving. We drove through Kona with our eyes closed to avoid the temptation of Kona brewed pale ale on tap and deep fried mahi with garlic fries. Instead of scooting along the beach, we took the mountain road out of town, swerving through the black lava fields, inhaling vog and avoiding Waimea Town by turning onto the newly paved Senator Dan Highway.

With Pig-Dog playing tourist, eyes open wide and mouth barking at each sighting of wild turkeys, skinny goats or rampaging pigs, we rode the lunar landscape through the volcanoes. We passed the firing range, the telescopes, and the spot used to fake the moon landings. When Pig-Dog spotted a rubbish can filled with half-eaten hamburgers, we made a quick U-turn and a stopped for his breakfast. From there, our homecoming led downhill, a rapid descent into the middle of Hilo's ten-minute rush hour.

Up until then, my mind had been a blur, running on fear. Stuck in line behind a hundred cars waiting for a light to change, I started to think about my butt. The Judge's envelope was under the seat in Joe's truck. The UH had towed that truck. Maybe there was something in that envelope I needed to read, something about Twyla. More important, I needed to get off Joe's motorcycle. That's what I was thinking, so I steered onto the shoulder, drove by the line of cars, and turned into the backside of UH. I parked the Ural behind the dormitories and walked to UH Auxiliary Services.

I wasn't worried about leaving Joe's Ruskie contraption. Even if the Big Island was home to 1,893 motorcycle thieves, none of them would steal a Russian motorcycle painted military green with a matching sidecar. Where could they hide it? And if they stripped it for parts, who would buy them? The Ruskie three-wheeler was its own anti-theft device.

Behind the round hole in the window, the student worker checked his list three times. After each check, he said the same thing, smiling through his protective hole, "I'm sorry, sir, you must be mistaken. The university did not tow your truck."

"Could you check once more?"

From behind him, the student's supervisor appeared and pushed the under-paid worker out of the picture. He aimed his nicotine-stained teeth at me through the window. "The University did not tow your truck." He left out the "sir" and "sorry" and made his denial of any connection to Papa Joe's truck sound like the university had made a mistake by not shoving his truck and me off the nearest cliff.

Pig-Dog stood up, set his front paws on the counter, and growled at the teeth-filled window.

The supervisor mentioned something about the leash law, and then announced to the twenty sweating students waiting in line behind me: "On the other hand, you owe, according to our records, $250 in parking fines." A few of the students groaned, and one raised her voice enough to be heard from the back of the line, "Fascist bureaucrat!"

The bureaucrat patted his stiff grey hair into place before saying, "Obviously, a friend of yours." He was sporting the uniform worn by the male members of the UH administration: a bland, colorless aloha shirt neatly tucked into bland, grey slacks held up by a shiny new black belt. A nametag pinned to his shirt pocket announced, "Aloha, how I can not help you?"

The student behind me poked me in the ribs and said, "Be careful. That's Franz Kafka. Get it?"

"Sure."

"Please wait a moment," Franz said. "I'm gong to check my data base. You may have other outstanding accounts."

That drew a few more groans from the students and another squeaky shout from the back of the line, "Bloated fascist bureaucracy!" A more practical response bubbled up from the middle of the line, "Better get out the coolers. This is going to be a long one."

91

Pig-dog dropped to the ground, where he curled into a circle of sticky pig-hair and fell asleep. I spent a few minutes telling myself not to forget this Kafka fellow. He'd have to show his face around town some day.

He came back without the strained smile and said, "You also have $275 in fines from the library."

"For what?"

He shrugged. "Possibly you checked out a book."

"Not likely."

"My thoughts exactly."

"I never had a library card." The truth is I had forgotten that back in the day Papa Joe had borrowed my student ID from me in exchange for a five-pound bag of rice and a cold beer. When he was drinking, Joe liked a little lite reading. The Doc will probably tell me that someday I should apologize to that fellow Franz because him remembering me saved me a lot of trouble later on when I was trying to explain how Joe's truck ended up at the bottom of a cliff. Yes, someday I'll have to do that.

"Will you be paying with cash, check or credit card?"

I checked my pockets and Joe's. Mines were empty except for an emergency joint. Joe's hoodie had one cookie left in the kangaroo pouch. I placed the Peanut Butter Surprise on the counter. It looked like a fat, moldy poker chip. "How much will this cover?"

He brushed the cookie off the counter into Pig-Dog's waiting mouth. How that pig-thing saw it in his sleep I don't know. The students were impressed too. They had their phones out snapping pictures of what one of them called, "The amazing cookie-catching pig-thing."

"Cash, check or credit card?" Franz said.

For the record, Frankie paid those fines for me, eventually. You can check with UH to verify the facts. I hear they're very good at record keeping, as long as no one looks at the records of their recordkeeping. That morning though I stepped away from the window, saying, "I'll be back." My exit was accompanied by a collective sigh of relief from the waiting students. The anti-fascist at the end of the line gave me a pat on the back. When in doubt, keep moving.

In the old days, when me and Joe needed a quiet place to think or sleep, we'd walk up to St. Joe's Church. The UH Library wasn't as quiet as St. Joe's but it had high ceilings like a church, and the seating arrangements were better, with no pews for kneeling but plenty of couches for sleeping and three floors of nooks and crannies for secret meetings. That morning the air-conditioning was turned up to extreme high, cold enough to freeze a Ruskie.

As we pushed our way through the turnstile security screener, the young woman at the circulation desk gave Pig-Dog and me a quick smile, saying "What a beautiful service dog." Pig-Dog wanted to stop to say hello, but I kept moving, heading toward the reference desk situated in the middle of the cathedral.

The reference gal tapped at her keyboard a few times before she looked up. "Oh, my, well, I guess it's never too late."

Pig-dog showed his tusks, and she took it for a smile. "Cute," she said, reaching over to pat his head. He had a way of making women see what they wanted to see. While she was wiping pig grease off her hand, I slipped a pencil off her desk.

"Can I help you find something, Manny?"

Sure, she knew me, but you don't need to know her name. I always called her The Librarian because that's where she worked. She didn't have anything to do with what happened later, so never mind her. She helped everyone, not just me. That much I can tell you.

She had a soft voice and a way of touching my arm in the line of her duties that made me feel like the world was fine, like everything would be peachy, what Papa Joe used to call a false sense of security. She had thick grey hair and a boyfriend in his twenties who worked as a model for an Australian brand of surf clothes. He rode one of those 1000cc, race-replica Suzuki superbikes, packing her on the back, with her arms wrapped around his leather jacket.

That morning she was wearing a see-through silk blouse, partially hidden under a silk scarf that gave me a gauzy peek at her under-armor. I leaned over the desk and saw her knee-length black skirt leading down to cowboy boots. Very inspiring.

"Still the same old Manny," she said, touching my elbow.

Unlike Pig-Dog, I had a way of making women see what they didn't want to see. That didn't stop us from chatting about the old days while I watched her lips move and remembered her ponytail flying free in a motorcycle's jet stream.

"You look tired," she said, her deep green eyes researching my bloodshot browns. "Back for more sleep? I seem to remember you were very interested in sleep."

It felt good knowing she remembered me, even if it was for me using the library as a Motel 6. "Could you check something for me? That fellow up at Auxiliary Sucks said I have fines for overdue books."

"What guy?"

"The guy with the stiff hair. Franz Kafka."

She offered me a gentle smile. "Oh, Manny." The bulb in her beautiful head blinked on, creating a golden halo as she said, "However, now that you mention it, I do remember a long time ago seeing your name on the overdue list and thinking it must be some kind of mistake."

"Exactly. A mistake."

She tapped at her keyboard. "However, wait a moment. Here it is. Do you remember a book called Land and Power in Hawaii?"

It sounded familiar, at least the Hawaii part. She scribbled on a pink sticky note. "Go downstairs. Non-fiction. Try Aisle 6. See if it jogs your memory. Or makes you sleepy. I'll check for others."

Pig-Dog was already moving down the stairs. How he knew the way I'm not sure. In my college days, or my college day, I had spent many happy hours down there, sipping from a flask of tequila and dreaming of librarians on motorcycles. Now it seemed that Pig-Dog wanted to share in those dreams. He hurried down the stairs and zig-zagged through the deserted aisles until he found a desk and chair in the back corner of the non-fiction section. He curled up and fell asleep in the "Love-Nest of Ice," as us students liked to call it.

I stepped over him and sat down at the desk, zipped up Joe's hoodie. By then, Pig-Dog was already snoring in rhythm to the freezing hum of air-conditioning. Just being in there with those books was making me think. I was thinking that I needed a thicker jacket. I had a pencil but no paper. I reached for the nearest shelf, ran my finger along the spines of imprisoned books until it stopped on a small paperback that looked lost and lonely, stuck between all the hardbacks. Murder in Paradise. Its spine had never been cracked but the title seemed relevant to my situation. I pressed it open in the middle, softened it up by closing and opening it a few dozen times, turned to the last page, a nice blank page, and wrote in caps:

HONEY-DO LIST:

FIND JOE'S TRUCK AND JUDGES'S PAPERS.
TALK TO TWYLA, GRADE PAPERS.
CHECK ON SONG.
GET BOAT BACK.
BURY JOE. AT SEA?
FIND MY CAT STEAMER.
FIND A HOME 4 PIG-DOG.
KEEP HIM AWAY FROM HARDBOILED EGGS.
BUY A FAST MOTORCYCLE,
PREFERABLY A SUZUKI.

I leaned back and looked at the cover. Murder in Paradise. Three nasty looking suspects stared out from their mug shots. I needed a drink. I needed a smoke. Sorry to say, that's how my mind used to work. I'm not proud of it, but it's the truth. It wasn't long before I closed my eyes and started dreaming about librarians.

"Manny, wake up."

When I opened my eyes, AntMan was standing over me, hands on his hips, in his missionary uniform: same white shirt and black pants, same white socks and black shoes. As usual, he wanted to talk.

"Think you could hide from me?" he asked.

Pig-Dog raised his head and opened one eye.

"What's that thing?"

"He's a friend. Let him sleep."

"Okay," he said to Pig-Dog. "Go to sleep."

Pig-Dog closed his eyes.

"He stinks."

"He's been eating pickled eggs."

"Tough luck. You still looking for Joe's truck?"

"How did you know?"

"Your friend at Auxiliary Services called."

"Franz? That stiff ass."

AntMan jerked his thumb at the ceiling. "See that?"

"The ceiling?"

"The camera."

Sure, I saw it. The UH had cameras everywhere. Last I heard, some of them worked.

"Follow me," he said. "Leave the pig thing, or whatever it is. I don't trust him."

Pig-Dog kept his eyes closed and stayed in place. He always liked the cold. It reminded him of home. I stuffed Murder in Paradise in my kangaroo pocket and followed AntMan up two flights of stairs to a door with a security keypad. He punched in his code and the door opened into a tiny room crowded with dead computers, piles of wires, printers, motherboards, tank-size monitors, and cardboard boxes. One of the monitors worked. It was playing a shot of Pig-Dog asleep under a desk.

"He likes to sleep," I said, playing with the mouse. Two aisles over a couple of students were locked together in a cone of silence.

"Never mind them." AntMan pushed my hand away from the mouse and sat down in front of the monitor. He pressed a few keys, and the monitor switched to a view of the parking lot, where a black tow truck moved slowly between lines of cars. AntMan froze the action. "This is from a few days ago. Go ahead, have a seat."

There were no other chairs, so I leaned against the wall.

"You see it?" he asked.

"Yes."

"What? Do you see?"

Sometimes people, even my friends, look at me and think they need to talk real slow so I don't miss anything. "Don't bother with the plates," he said. "According to them, that tow truck is a 68 Cadillac." He pointed at the monitor. "Does that look like a Cadillac?"

"No."

"Look at it."

For the sake of keeping this report shorter than a life-sentence in a crowded prison, I'll summarize. Believe me, nothing is missing, only AntMan's wordiness. This way you get the important stuff without the repetition. It's still the truth.

According to AntMan for the last two semesters the students had been complaining about cars being stolen from the university's five lots. Due to budget cuts, the main gate was the only one with a guard so it was impossible to keep track of all the thieves coming and going. The UH had spent all its cash on constructing new buildings and paying AntMan his five bucks an hour. The monitor we were watching wasn't even his. His pal in audio-visual had lent him the equipment and the use of his locker-size office after someone stole his car. No wonder the UH was trying to collect on fake parking tickets.

"Call your wife," I said. "She's the cop."

"You know what it's like being married to a cop?"

I had a feeling, but I didn't want to explore it. "Don't tell me."

That didn't stop him. He dove in, telling me how he was sure his wife was catching crap at the station for being married to an ex-con. He wanted to make something of himself. He didn't want her to be stressed. "She's been drinking a lot."

"Who told you that?" I was wishing I had a lot to drink.

"If we can catch these guys, we'll show everyone, even the hard heads at the station house that I'm better than what they think."

Most people didn't think much of me either. But I didn't let it bother me.

"I want my kids to look up to me."

He was over six feet, and his kids were only a foot or two, so they already had to look up to him. What more could a parent ask for? That's what I was about to tell him when he said, "You haven't got it yet?"

"Got what?"

He pointed at the video monitor, pressed a couple of keys, and I saw Joe's truck being hooked to the counterfeit tow truck "That's from Monday. They stole Joe's truck, Manny. Not us, not the UH. Your truck, they got it."

I checked the monitor. "Joe's truck," I said. "They stole it."

"Now you're thinking."

I gave the truck another look. AntMan enlarged the shot to give me a close up of a fuzzy, grainy short fat guy hooking the tow-truck's winch to Joe's bumper. He looked familiar. His truck looked familiar. It's no secret that I've worked with people who the professors at the university might call "outsiders inhabiting the contested margins of the oppressor's culture." When you own a boat capable of inter-island shipping, you get to know people. They get to look familiar.

"Know him, Manny?"

I didn't say anything. I was trying to place that grainy belly.

AntMan smiled, stood up, and slapped me on the back. "You can't argue with logic. We'll go up there as soon as I get off work." He looked at the clock. "We got five hours."

"Up where?"

He told me that he had already done his "due diligence." Those were his exact words. He had followed the truck, on a student's moped. "Undercover" was how he explained it. I tried to picture an undercover moped chasing a tow truck.

"You know the road up by the caves? The Rancher's place?"

I knew it meant trouble. Some people are best left alone. I gave the monitor face another look. Maybe it was him.

"We can leave the kids with Teresa. They'll be safe there."

I saw the body with the hole in it. I saw the Judge's envelope. "Sure," I said, but only because I never say no.

We made plans to meet later. He said he'd work on specifics, and I hurried down the stairs to see the librarian. Her scarf was gone, exposing a wavy, Hawaiian-style tattoo peeking out from the neck of her silk blouse. I liked it, a jazzy take on fishhooks.

"Where did you get your dog?" she asked.

"Long story. You want him?"

I looked over the desk and saw Pig-Dog curled up next to her cowboy boots. With my other eye, I saw the librarian's thick grey hair fall over her ear, softly, to her shoulder and beyond.

Pig-Dog curled his lips into a smile.

"He's a flirt," the librarian said.

"How can you tell?" I leaned back into a relaxed pose.

"You found him on the mountain?"

"You could say that. More like he found me."

"He steals things," she said.

"Just red dogs. And pickled eggs. How did you know?"

"I bet he likes chickens."

We watched Pig-Dog walk out from behind the desk to a poster pinned on a nearby wall. In it, taro fields spread across a huge valley, growing thick and rich green. A small shack near a black river was surrounded by a herd of fat chickens. It was easy to see criminal intent in Pig-Dog's beady, staring eyes.

"Wait," the librarian said and went to work in the shelves behind her.

I stayed waiting, smelling her ginger perfume, managing to see a hint of her backside, and wondering how long it took librarians to fall out of love with Australian models. She placed a stack of books in front of me.

"Since you're going to start reading, I found a few more for you."

That's what happens in a library. Librarians, even the racy ones, try to stick you with you books. So I kept my mouth shut and pretended to be interested when she told me the first one was a thesis written by a very bright student.

Ms. Song had taught me something about a thesis. From what I could remember, it had something to do with being the first sentence in an essay before the writer tossed in evidence to fill up space. This thesis was an oversized hardback with a plain blue cover that was worn around the edges and looked as if someone had actually been reading it.

Acting like I would read it someday, I picked it up and was turning to leave when the librarian asked, "What about that book in your pocket?"

I dug out Murder in Paradise. I was thinking about tearing out the back page with my list on it when Pig-Dog growled and gave me enough stink-eye to start another murder in paradise. Sleeping in the library had turned him into the public defender of books.

The Librarian grabbed the paperback out of my hands and read the sub-title aloud: "A Christmas in Hawaii Turns to Tragedy." She scanned the spine and handed it back to me. "It's terrible," she said.

"The book?"

"The killing. Those creatures almost got away with it."

Across the paperback's cover, three mug shots dared me to open the book. They looked like yearbook shots from Prison High School. The back cover warned, "It can't happen here!"

"Nasty," I said.

The Librarian disappeared in a cloud of ginger and came back with two more books. Those babies were replicating. "You have to read these two if you want to understand crime in Hawaii." She handed me one called Rape in Paradise, saying, "It's all about the Massy case."

From a quick read of the back cover I could tell the book happened too long ago, back somewhere in the 1930s, for it to be important. Even though it was about rape, racism and murder, it was old style rape, racism, and murder, and we already had enough of the new stuff. That's what I figured back then, but I kept it to myself. The librarian was trying to do me a favor.

"And this," she said, pushing a shiny new hardback complete with glossy jacket cover at me. Land and Power in Hawaii. "You kept the original so long that the university purchased a new copy. It's about selling land and the power of real estate."

I wasn't interested in real estate, what Joe liked to call greasy-collar crime, but I had seen that book somewhere before, somewhere safe with a bottle of tequila.

"Stealing land can be worse than murder," she said.

Back then, I figured people could bounce back from almost anything except murder. I figured that lack of experience in the real world was making her book crazy. It's a common disease among college people. They start believing what they're reading.

She stacked all four books in a neat pile and told me to call her if I had any questions. "Questions about what you should be reading," she said, and gave me an encouraging smile.

I figured the books were too smart for me, but with a little sleep and some alcohol I might be able to finish reading the covers. Before I left, she was nice enough to zero out my fines. Don't bother trying to nail her for that crime. She's retired now and living somewhere in a paradise where land isn't power, pigs don't need to fly, and women aren't raped and beaten, and left on the side of the road to die.

Entry 11: ACADEMIC SENSATIONS

What happened between Twyla and the Singing Professor was nowhere near as bad as some people like to make it sound. I was there, so I should know. The same goes for what happened later with me and the priest. A lot of things sound worse when you hear about them happening in Hilo.

First, you have to understand that they do things different at the University. They call themselves goofy names like chancellor and dean and provost. They give speeches every fifty minutes, and then ask too many questions about what they said, like someone was supposed to be listening. And they argue all the time. It's in their job description. Professors are paid to argue about history, science, business practices and medical procedures, about the best way to build a telescope or the worst way to cook a turnip. And students pay to learn how to argue. That's why the U.H. offers BS and BA degrees (Bachelor of Bull Shit, Bachelor of Argument.)

Once in a while, a student or professor gets hurt feelings, or kicked in the butt, or stabbed in the back. But it's not a real-life butt kicking or stabbing. At the university all the howling in pain is a figure-of-speech. None of it stops anyone from dressing up in black robes and funny hats, and watching the grand wizard hand out pieces of paper that are supposed to be worth the price of admission, which in tuition and fees is roughly equivalent to the price of an aircraft carrier.

I got a good taste of that crazy world when I left the library that morning with my free books. After a few wrong turns, I found the note on Ms. Song's office door. Neatly typed and easy to read, it said that Professor Song was on sick leave and any questions should be directed to Assistant Professor Sunn or Mr. Manual, both of whom were currently at an emergency meeting of the Academic Senate in Room K-169.

"Mr. Manual?" I said to Pig-Dog.

He was sitting next to me, keeping his eyes on the few students left wandering the halls. He growled at the males and smiled at the females. "Did you hear that?" I asked him. "We're going to an Academic Sensation meeting." He pinned his ears back and straightened his tail.

I remember the sky was gray. Maybe it was going to rain, maybe it was going to shine. That's Hilo. The wind was blowing from the south. I could smell lava burning Ohia as I followed Pig-Dog across the grass to room K-169. Through the same shoebox-size window that I had watched Ms. Song a few days earlier, I watched Twyla sitting in the front row of a room packed with fifty professors. They were all stuffed into student desks except for the Singing Professor.

He was looking down at them from behind a lectern, hiding inside grey slacks, a colorless aloha shirt, and an orange smile. Balancing his lauhala hat atop a wad of leftover bandages, he set his guitar down next to the lectern, reached for the pack of cigarettes in his shirt pocket, gave up and tried to say something over the chattering professors.

Half of the profs were dressed like him, minus the moldy bandages. The other half looked too sane to be professors. Instead of crazy hats and bland suits of armor intended to encourage respect, they were wearing shorts, t-shirts, and slippers. Both sides looked tired, with sagging shoulders and drooping eyes. It's a tough profession, teaching people how to use words or remember facts, and I didn't blame any of them for being worn around the edges as they dragged themselves across the finish line. On a table at the back of the room they had piled sweaters, jackets, pink pastry boxes, three huge bags of M&Ms and a coffee maker the size of a nuclear reactor.

The Singing Professor reached for his cigarettes again, jerked his hand back and pointed at a column of numbers on the blackboard. Twyla, still wearing Joe's leather jacket, shook her head, but the Singing Professor kept talking, like he was in charge, until Twyla stood up and waved her hand. When the Singing Turd acted like he couldn't see her, she slammed her hand down hard and shouted loud enough for even me to hear, "Bullshit!"

The Singing Professor opened his mouth to say something, but his words were drowned out by a rippling explosion of shouting and arm waving that started at Twyla and worked its way to the back of the room where the teachers in shorts were smiling, biting into malasadas, and chewing until their lips were coated with a thick layer of powdered sugar. Twyla picked up a stapler and slammed it down. The Singing Professor pointed a piece of chalk at her. Twyla pointed a finger at him. He said something that made the malasada eaters stop chewing and go wide-eyed, and Twyla bolted for the door.

Just in time, I stepped out of the way.

"That man is crazy," she shouted, letting the door slam behind her. She spit at the grass. "Completely crazy." Pig-Dog dodged the spit bullet, but he got the message. He bared his teeth and growled at the door. "You know, don't you, boy," Twyla said, reaching down to pet his greasy head.

I figured it was as good a time as any to ask if she had seen any dead bodies at the wife beater's house, but before I could say anything she grabbed my arm, with Pig-Dog grease still on her fingers, and said, "Listen to me. I'm going to smack that singing jerk. I've heard things."

Apparently I had missed a few important points while watching the silent version of the "Singing Turd Plays Headmaster." Twyla provided the soundtrack. They had been discussing something called the adoption of common core standards and a vote to support the students in a drive for a moratorium on tuition increases. But the Singing Professor kept changing the agenda, bringing up crap like more parking for the professors and less grade inflation. "What bullshit," she said. "That's our academic Senate Chair. A lazy lunatic."

I looked through the window. The professors were still chattering away. No blood had been drawn yet. "Could be worse," I said. "At least there's plenty of snacks. And no one's throwing blows."

She stayed the course. "He's only the vice-chair, and he only got that job because Ms. Song is sick and he kisses administration ass."

The Singing Professor was looking worse every time she brought him on stage. Twyla rested her hands on her hips, faced the classroom door and shouted, "Sadist. Pedantic sadist."

Pig-Dog barked three times. I had to agree, even though I didn't know what pedantic meant. And I never did figure out Pig-Dog's barking code. But I had a pretty good idea what sadist meant. I had a girlfriend once who liked...but that's a different story.

Twyla pointed at the door. "Look at him. He's pure evil! The worst of the worst."

Strange but I didn't agree. There's always someone worse. It's a fact of life. Where she was pointing, I saw a little squirt with a nasty temper and a mean spirit. Back then I figured he was an irritant, like a mosquito bite, and Twyla was mad because he had bailed on her rescue mission. As for pure evil, there was a mean looking gal in the front row that fit the description. Bulging through a faded orange muumuu, she was nodding up at the Singing Turd, her eyes spinning in their sockets while she death-gripped a plastic fork and shouted, "Yes, yes, yes!" She was a likely candidate for the title. No doubt, a voting member of the howler monkeys.

Shoots, back then I had worked for plenty of bosses crazier than the Singing Professor. A couple years back I had a boss who came to work carrying a baseball bat, and he never played baseball. The Singing Professor was a chain-smoking fashion disaster who sang like a goat but he didn't use people for baseballs. At least that's what I thought back then.

I tried to calm Twyla by telling her that jobs in Hawaii didn't come easy. If people wanted to pay their rent, they kept their mouth shut and showed up for work. I told her that she and her buddies had it easy. Easier than the students. I was about to say she had it better than a guy with a shotgun hole in him, but the door swung open and the Singing Professor stuck his head out. "Are you coming in, Ms. Sunn? We have a vote on the parking issue."

"Certainly," Twyla said, smiling. Those academics can throw a smile on pretty quick. She introduced me as Mr. Manual. Apparently I had been fished out of something called the lecturer pool and would be teaching two of Ms. Song's classes in the spring. I was there to observe the Senate at work, to test the collegial atmosphere. That's what Twyla told him. It sounded almost believable coming from her.

"Good to meet you," he said, simmering under his day-old bandages. He reached out to shake my hand. "Aloha."

Pig Dog barked three times.

"I'm sorry," the quack professor said. "Dogs are not allowed on campus."

"He's a service dog," Twyla told him.

"He doesn't look like a dog."

To keep them from throwing blows, I grabbed his hand and shook it, saying, "Sure, aloha." I can't remember what his hand felt like. These days I'm tempted to say clammy.

"You look familiar," he said, giving me the pink eye.

"A lot of people say I look like Hemingway, the young one, without the beard and the combover."

That threw him for a couple of seconds of silence, before he recovered enough to say, "I see the resemblance." He stepped back to give me a long look, head to foot. "Certainly, yes."

Which made me think that pretty soon I'd have to check on this Hemingway fellow to see exactly what I looked like.

"Please excuse the bandages." He tapped his head as if it were a tender egg. "An incident during finals." He lifted his hat to show me more of the moldy bandages. "Quite disturbing. Two students. In this very room." He gave me a second long look.

"We don't want to scare Mr. Manual away," Twyla said. "Do we, Professor?"

"Of course not."

"It was an accident," she said.

"Yes. Possibly." He rubbed his temple. "Mr. Manuel should know the truth about our students. Know the types. What they are capable of or, more accurately, what they are incapable of." He jabbed his finger at me. "The UH is not Harvard or Yale, you understand, Mr. Manuel?"

Pig-Dog growled and Twyla held him by his pig ear to keep him from leaping at the Singing Professor's neck.

"I have considered the difference." That was something Joe used to say when talking about which beer to buy.

"Good for you, Mr. Manuel. The students are weak, believe me. Not at all top tier. But we must try." His breath reeked of nicotine and stale coffee. "You'll find yourself having to repeat key points, over and over. Patience, Mr. Manuel. Patience."

I was about to say that patience had done wonders for his head, but the more he talked, the redder Twyla turned, so I stepped between them, saying, "The time, Professor. We have work to do."

"Certainly. Yes, you are correct." He turned to Twyla. "Has this observation by Mr. Manuel been cleared with administration, with the Dean?"

"Certainly," Twyla said. "I spoke with the Dean this morning."

Maybe she had. I never found out.

"Well, if that's the case, welcome, Mr. Manuel. Strictly observing, correct? No voting rights." He smiled.

"Strictly," I crossed my heart.

"Please do not take part in the discussions. These are sensitive issues for us to decide."

"I have my books." I held them up so that the Singing Professor could see that I was the college-type.

"Well, good. Please sign the attendance sheet." Nodding, he led the way into the classroom. "Note yourself as a visitor."

Pig-Dog wouldn't go inside. I guess he didn't like classrooms, or maybe it was the Singing Professor's breath.

Twyla sat in the front row where she could lead the charge out of the trenches. I found a chair in the back, near the snack table, next to a cutie with short red hair and a black t-shirt that announced in gold letters "MLA in Las Vegas: Active Not Passive!" I'm still not sure what that meant but I did eventually find out that MLA stood for Modem Language Association, or something like that. The Las Vegas redhead whispered that much to me when she caught me trying to make sense of the message on her chest. I was asking her about the active and passive part when the Singing Professor commanded, "Quiet, please."

Twyla stood up and introduced me to the crew, saying I had been at Berkeley "many years ago" before teaching at San Francisco City College and then retiring to the Big Island.

The Las Vegas girl smiled and said that I looked too young to be retired. "I agree," I told her, and everyone except the Singing Professor got a laugh.

"Quiet, please!" The Singing Turd brought us all back in line.

While I nibbled a malasada and the Singing Professor droned on about parking places, Ms. MLA told me that she had grown up on Oahu, graduated from the UH, and come to work here, in Hilo, which she said was like stepping back in time. "You know, like being on a plantation. Colonialism? Marginalized. Paternalism?"

I kept chewing. She had an easy smile and a soft voice and wrote something she called slam poetry. "I rage against the machine!" she told me, and said the Academic Sensation meeting would go on forever if the howler monkeys had their way. She shouted, "Let's get to work." Then she rolled her eyes at me.

They were playing by something called Robert's Rules of Order, which involved raising your hand to get on a list of speakers and then waiting for the Singing Professor to stop talking about grade inflation so you could get in a word or two before someone shouted "Call the question!"

It seemed like a complicated game. I didn't bother learning the finer points since my tenure as a college professor was bound to end soon. The Vegas poetry slammer whispered in my ear, "There's rumor about him. You should see his wife. Po ting. A little mouse."

Her sideways wink helped me get the idea.

"Beautiful children," she said. "Two of them. I feel sorry for them." Her fingernails were painted two-tone, orange and white, like little Creamsicles.

"Are there any good guys here?" I asked.

"Your friend Ms. Sunn is. She's so naive. Too outspoken for someone in her first year of teaching. If Ms. Song doesn't come back, she will never get tenure."

While the rest of the professors played the arguing game, the Vegas babe showed me how how she could use her finger to write stuff on the glass surface, like it was paper. She wrote a blurry message in a dialogue bubble: "I want a sabbatical!"

The Singing Professor shouted, "Our grades don't mean anything. We're too concerned with self-esteem and not concerned about standards."

That threw everyone into a tizzy, which I avoided by flipping through the first couple of pages of Murder in Paradise. It started with "a faint voice" calling for help on a lonely road and turned into "a journalistic account of the actual murder investigation of Frank Pauline Jr., Albert Ian Schweitzer and Shawn Schweitzer for the 1991 killing of Dana Ireland in Hawaii." I can write that down word for word because where I'm staying now they bring me reading materials.

The Vegas slammer leaned over and ran her finger along the edge of my books. "That's a good one," she tapped my paperback. "But not as good as this one." She pushed Rape in

Paradise at me. "It's about a historically significant murder. It should be called The Rape of Paradise."

I asked her how one murder could be more significant than another, and she told me because one was about abuse of power by the government. That didn't help me. I figured that was the government's main job, abusing power. Now that I've had plenty of time to read both books I don't want to remember either of them. If I could, I would wash them out of my head with soap and bleach. If you read them, don't blame me if you can't stop seeing stuff, like a young man shot and stuffed in a car trunk, or a young woman alone on her bicycle in Puna, riding home to spend Christmas Eve with her parents, followed by three men in a VW.

"We have to stop this!" Twyla shouted.

"Ms. Sunn, please keep your voice down," the Singing Professor shouted.

"No!"

The Vegas girl with the classy fingernails tapped me on the shoulder. "I absolutely love this." She pointed at my big blue hardback.

"It's a thesis," I said.

"No kidding. I have it on my I-pad." She showed me the digital glow. I read a few lines before I thought about reaching into the last box of malasadas. As she scrolled down the page, I imagined sucking in coconut cream filling. She pointed at yellow highlighting and said, "See, rebellion against increasing western dominance."

"Interesting," I said, eyeing a fat malasada. Interesting is what those professors say whenever they're warming up for a speech or a punch out. Me, I was waiting for a chance to grab that malasada.

The Vegas Slammer asked if I had my e-mail account yet. I said no. She asked if I had a phone. I said no. While she went to work with pencil and paper, what she called "low tech," I leaned over, slipped the malasada out of the box, and sniffed it like it was a glass of wine. It smelled of powdered sugar and coconut. A good year.

The poet with the mostess handed me a piece of paper with two words at the top: "Works Cited." Under that was a coded message that looked like disjointed and scrambled sentence fragments. I asked her if it was a crossword puzzle. She pointed at her shirt. "MLA style." Then she tapped the paper with an extra-long Creamsicle nail. "I made it for you in less than two minutes." She pointed at her I-pad. "This is where we should be concentrating our efforts. Teaching these kids how to research important issues."

The original was lost somewhere up at the caves while me and Pig-Dog were dodging bullets, but it looked something like this:

Works Sited

George Cooper and Gavan Daws wrote *Land and Power in Hawaii: The Democratic Years*. Honolulu, HI: Benchmark, 1985. Print.

Dorton, Lili Kala wrote *A Lengendary Tradition of Kampua'a, The Hawaiian Pig-God*. A Thesis. Honolulu, HI: Bishop Museum Press, 1996.

Loos, Chris, and Rick Castberg. *Murder in Paradise: A Christmas in Hawaii Turns to Tragedy*. New York: Avon, 2003. Print.

Wright, Theon. *Rape in Paradise*. New York: Hawthorn, 1966. Print.

I was wondering what the student who escaped from the wife-beater could learn from a list like that, but before I could ask the Vegas Slammer for insights, she stood up, set the i-Pad down in front of me, and waved her fist at the Singing Professor. "No more tuition increases. No more. No more tuition increases!"

That made perfect sense to Twyla. She stood up and yelled stuff about lost culture, the need for teachers to nourish the community, not just earn a paycheck. Or something close to that. It was hard to keep track.

"Quiet!" The Singing Professor shouted. "You're out of order. Both of you. Please follow the agenda. This is not the place for theatrics."

"Screw you," I tossed in as I snatched another malasada.

The place went quiet. Heads turned my way and saw me with half a malasada in my mouth. Chocolate. Very good powdered sugar.

"What did you say?" the guitar hero spit at me.

"Screw you!" Twyla said and picked up her stack of papers. "That's what he said, and I'll say it again for him. Screw you. I'm finished. I'm going where I can do some actual work." She headed for the door. The Singing Professor grabbed her elbow. Twyla shook him off. He grabbed again. She elbowed his arm. "Get away from me."

"Ms. Zane, you can't leave!"

She turned and slapped him hard across the face. The room gasped, then went quiet. Twyla opened the door and stepped out. I figured that was my cue to slip the MLA paper in one of the murder books and snatch the last malasada.

"You all saw that," the Singing Turd shouted.

For a second I thought he was busting me for taking the last snack.

"I didn't see anything," the Vegas Slammer shouted.

I picked up my books, thanked the Slammer for my works sighted list, and headed for the door. As I walked outside, and just before the door snapped shut, I heard the Slammer shout, "Self defense, that's what I saw."

Pig-Dog was barking. Twyla was egging him on, walking in circles and shouting professor-type cuss words like ignorant, self-serving, and hypocrite. Nothing that I'd consider fighting words.

"I can't stand him," Twyla said. "I have to get out of this place."

I figured she meant the Singing Professor, not Pig-Dog, and the place was obvious, so I told her about St. Joe's Church and how Papa Joe liked to go there when he needed peace and quiet. As we walked I gave her directions, trying to keep pace with her, carried along in the wake of her righteous glow. Behind us, Pig-Dog played at rear guard, stopping, looking back, barking, and running after us. By the time we got to her car, he had disappeared and I was sucking wind, telling myself I had to get in shape if I wanted to spend any more time at college with young professors. Maybe I could handle the Vegas Slammer. Her training table was probably loaded with alcohol and lots of rest stops. But Twyla, she had speed and endurance.

Pointing over my shoulder, I asked her if all that was the usual.

"The usual bullshit. I'll probably get fired."

"For that?"

She smiled at me and held up her stack of papers. "I still have his final exams," she laughed. "Talk about grade inflation."

We climbed into her VW, and she drove me to Joe's Ural. Pig-Dog was waiting in the sidecar. Twyla was impressed. "Nice machine," she said, and drove off.

"We're going to church," I said, tossing my books in with Pig-Dog. He bared his teeth and growled. I figured he didn't like books, and shrugged it off. He stayed growling as I struggled through the ten or twenty steps needed to get the Ruskie tank moving. In all that time he never gave me a hint that it wasn't books or reading that had pissed him off. It was priests he couldn't stand.

Entry 12: GODLESS TURDS

Antman cupped his hand around his mouth and shouted over the engine noise, "They found a body up the road from Teresa's place."

I turned off the engine, and listened to the latest police gossip while a line of cars piled up behind us. According to Ant, the cops had found the body of a 30-something male at a place called the Dumping Grounds, a popular spot for dead bodies. He said that a couple months earlier they had found a body up there, a witness who had helped send three men to prison for life. "One of the Judge's cases," he said.

I knew the place.

AntMan kept talking, telling me how they were still trying to identify this new body. His wife told him they suspected a "criminal act."

The shotgun hole must've been a clue.

I started the engine. Pig-Dog was sitting on my books. The cars behind us were honking their horns, like waiting in line was something out of the ordinary. AntMan stepped down and petted Pig-Dog's ugly head. "What you got in there, big fella?" He wiped his hands on his missionary pants.

"Books."

"You reading now?"

"Pig-Dog likes to read himself to sleep."

"If you're not back by four, you know where to find me."

"Where?"

"Wake up, Manny."

I was trying.

"I'm going up there no matter what."

Ant was beginning to sound like the law firm of Song and Sunn. I reminded myself to keep him away from shotguns. I let the clutch out and headed across town to St. Joe's. It's the quietest place in Hilo, except on Sundays, and even then the services don't get louder than a whisper. The congregation doesn't go in for rock bands and shouting "Amen!" They prefer kneeling.

We took the long way, me and Pig-Dog, him smiling, face into the wind, with his tongue hanging out, and me thinking clutch, gear, throttle. We flashed by the health food store, the grade school, the back of the ponds, the pet store, the tire shop, the craft store, and the Hilo strip maul called Kilauea Ave. An empty police car, one of the official blue and whites, was parked across the street from the Empire. Leaning back against the Palace Theatre, a cop was talking into his cellphone. I figured he was still waiting for the Judge.

I parked near the abandoned McDonald's, behind a moldy statue of an orange clown wearing a coating of graffiti. Twyla hadn't taken the same precautions. As we walked uphill, I saw her VW parked in the lot next to the church. Pig-Dog followed me up the steps to the front doors, but he wouldn't go in. He plopped down on the top step, closed his eyes and started snoring. No amount of prodding with my foot could wake him, so I stepped over him and opened the door.

The inside was all high ceilings, wood beams, statues of saints, rows of pews, and colored light falling through stained-glass windows. It was the closest thing Hilo had to an art museum, and a good spot to enjoy the quiet life. Twyla was sitting in the front row, still wearing Joe's jacket, working on her stack of papers.

As I walked toward her, I tried bits and pieces of the stuff the nuns had taught me while trying to strangle the truth into me. I dipped my finger in the water, made a cross on my chest, and dropped a knee at the altar before slipping into Twyla's pew. Kneeling next to her, I felt eyes watching me. Not hers. She was too serious when grading essays. Maybe it was one of those statues. We were alone in the church.

"The priest lives next door," I whispered. "If he comes in, pretend like you're praying."

"I will not. Where's Pig-Dog?"

"Outside, sleeping on guard duty."

She scribbled at the end of an essay, slapped on a grade, and shoved it under the stack. She wouldn't give me any papers. She said it would go faster that way. That was fine with me. My knees were tired already, so I backed my butt onto the hardwood pew and took a look at my surroundings.

Twyla looked beautiful, not in a speedy, motorcycle-riding-librarian way, but in a glowing, churchy way, like one of those saints in stained glass, with a shotgun in her hands, a stack of essays under arm, and her foot pressed down on a serpent wearing a guitar.

Two women in polyester slacks and thick sweaters, with black scarves wrapped around their white hair, knelt down behind us. Two more, older babes dressed like the first two picked the pew across the aisle from us. Twyla leaned in close to say, "We're being surrounding by women in scarves."

An old guy, heavy set, in a black t-shirt, black shorts, and black rubber slippers, with no scarf, towed a kid a couple feet tall to the altar. He bent a knee, made his son do the same, and the two of them turned left, went to the far end of our pew. The squeaker scooted in and sat with his rubber slippers dangling. His dad pushed him deeper into the pew and knelt down. The black beads of a rosary dropped from his thick fingers.

Twyla was the only one grading papers.

"Come on," I said. "I want to show you something."

The confessionals were in the back, a three-door unit under the choir loft. I took the middle door and she took the right. My chair faced the door. It was a big chair with plenty of legroom but the lighting was no good, so I felt along the wall until I found the shutter to Twyla's cell. When I slid it back, through a dark screen I could see her kneeling, facing me. I tilted my ear toward her, and said, "Yes, my child. Speak freely. I'm a priest."

"That doesn't sound right," she said.

I tried to remember being in church when I was a kid. I couldn't remember much, except that it was a good idea to keep a few fake sins on hand so I wouldn't get stuck with a lot of rosary time. "Tell me the truth," I said. "Or there will be consequences."

"Never mind. Bless me father for I have sinned," she whispered.

That threw me off, but I was interested. "Really? Tell me about it."

"It's been a long time since my last confession."

"Me, too," I said. "Your sins, my child. Tell me. Have you shot anyone lately?"

She leaned in close, scratched at the screen, and asked, "Can you see me?"

I could see her lips. "No, my child."

She whispered, "It's you who should be confessing."

I figured she was right, but I had a job to do, so I went with another of Frankie's lines, "It's me who is asking the questions, young...lady."

"You let this crap go on," she said.

"Please, my child, your language."

"You and your so-called heavenly father."

"Tough talk for a professor."

"If I have to, I can kick some ass."

"Even thinking about violence can be a sin, my child. Have you let the devil in? Have you had violent thoughts, my child?"

"Plenty."

"But you control these thoughts, my child. Correct?"

"No."

I was about to ask for specifics when I heard shuffling outside, people going by. I figured they couldn't hear us.

Otherwise, the priests would be renting out the closest pews at ten bucks a shot.

"I want to strangle a man at work. He's terrible. I hate him."

"The Singing Professor?"

"Yes. How did you know, father?"

"That's quite all right, my child. Some people deserve to be strangled. Have you killed anybody else?"

"I didn't kill him."

That's when Pig-Dog started barking, and a second later my door flew open. A tall priest in a black cassock stood outlined against bright light. He raised a hand in the air and shouted, "What are you doing in there, you godless turd?"

I opened my mouth but he didn't wait for an answer. His fingers dug into my wrist. "Get out!" he shouted. Then his teeth flashed, his eyes bulged and he screamed. "Help!"

When the priest spun around, I saw that the Pig-Dog was biting down hard, through the thin black material, into the priest's fat butt. The priest screeched and twisted and kicked as Pig-Dog dragged him toward the door. They spun in circles, Pig-Dog growling and grunting while the priest shouted, "Get him off me. Get him off me."

Pig-Dog bit in, tightening his grip.

"Jesus, Mary and Joseph!" the priest yelped.

When Twyla stepped into the light, I grabbed her and ran for the front door. We passed the swirling ball of priest and Pig-Dog. "Pig-Dog!" Twyla shouted over the priest's screaming. "Leave that poor man alone. Come here."

Outside, a woman in black was yelling into her cellphone. "Please, come quick. It's a mad dog. It's trying to kill a priest."

Twyla shook free of me and ran back inside. I ran after her. Pig-Dog was dragging the priest toward the baptismal fountain. "Someone help me," the priest begged. "Call the police!" Get this beast off me!"

I grabbed Twyla's shirt, tried to pull her back. "Leave him. Pig will catch up."

She shook free. "You go. I can't leave."

The priest's mouth stretched open, screaming, "Please. Help!"

"Pig-Dog can handle," I told her, backing toward the door. The rest of the church was empty. The scarf people had escaped, even the little kid and his dad had run off.

"Get out of here," Twyla shouted, and shoved me hard, sending me backward out the door.

That's when I heard the sirens.

I held the door open long enough to see Twyla grab Pig-Dog's tail, what there was of it, and tug it as hard as she could with her mini-professor arms. The priest screamed. Pig-Dog howled, and in that second it took him to protest the tail pulling, Twyla yanked him free and shoved him toward the door. "Go!" she yelled at me.

I ran toward the Ural, thinking those two would be in the VW before I could even get the Ruskie's engine started. But when I jumped on the bike and looked over my shoulder, only Pig-Dog was running toward me. Twyla was half in and half out of the church, straddling the face-down priest, pressing down hard with both hands on his butt.

Entry 13: FLARE GUNS & ROTS

I have a theory about the police. If they're anywhere near me, my best bet is to go in the opposite direction. If I'm riding Joe's crazy Ruskie motorcycle with his .22 hidden under the sidecar cushion, running is my only bet.

Twyla preferred a different tactic. She liked to ride a priest bareback while waiting for the cops to arrest her. Later, she told me that she ran back into the church to find her backpack and the essays. But when she saw the priest bleeding through his cassock and trying to crawl out the door, she couldn't stop herself from bending over and applying direct-pressure to his wounded butt.

The ambulance driver told her that she had saved the priest's life. He'd never seen a butt wound bleed so much. He said the wound looked like a shark bite from a hammerhead. That's what he told the cops while he injected the priest with a massive dose of painkillers and antibiotics. Twyla told me he was quite good looking, the driver not the priest. Those were her words. "The ambulance driver was quite good looking."

She also told me that even the priest thanked her. As he was being hauled to the ambulance, no doubt. The cops gathered up the essays that had spilled onto the floor and stuffed them, still spotted with priest blood, into Twyla's backpack. They took her name and phone number without asking for identification, and asked the ambulance driver to check if she was well enough to drive. She said, "He had such a pleasant smile, a very nice young man, Miles. And all of them, even the police, waved to me when I drove away. I felt quite good about it, like a beauty queen in a parade."

In my defense, I should point out that the priest hadn't called her a godless turd. To him, she was just an innocent churchgoing bystander with excellent first-aid skills. I was the crazy godless turd. A turd driving a 2,000-pound Russian motorcycle. As I dug out from behind the orange clown, Pig-Dog added his prime suspect presence to the sidecar, jumping in and snapping at the wind, barking loud enough to wake a dead saint.

Trailing a smokescreen of black exhaust, we took the back roads, zoomed by two-story apartment buildings and one-story houses outlined with Christmas lights. We passed carports packed with rusting cars, stacks of cardboard boxes, sagging couches, and rusty refrigerators. On the sidewalk a big woman carrying a big kid on each big hip marched alongside us, smiling, making her kids wave to us as we passed in a cloud of black smoke.

Pig-Dog barked once.

"Keep your head down," I warned him. He leaned into the wind, hanging his tongue out the side of his mouth as we cruised into the back entrance of U.H. When he saw the planetarium and the school for pill-pushers, he jumped out and ran into the bushes.

The UH employees had a parking lot back there, back where the students smoked grass before sneaking into the planetarium for the Pink Floyd specials. Two rows deep, I found AntMan tossing a duffel bag into the back of his F-150 pickup. Dressed in jungle boots, camo pants, and a green t-shirt, he looked the part.

"Got enough equipment?" I shouted over the Ural's death rattle.

"Leave the bike," he shouted back.

"No kiddin." The Ural died in place. I left my books in the sidecar but took the .22 and the wounded bottle of tequila, stuck them under the front seat of the pickup. When dealing with car thieves, the worst scum on the earth, one should always carry a bottle of booze. Books, well, they'd stay dry in the Ural. Who steals books? That's what I figured.

AntMan climbed into the driver's seat of the Ford. There was almost enough room for both of us. "We have to make a few stops. Pick up some supplies."

"Another bottle of Tequila would help," I said.

"We got to use Rayzah for babysitting. Bobbie got called in for work."

"Too many bodies."

"You guessed it."

I was glad Joe wasn't alive to hear about us having to find a babysitter before we could bust a car thief and recover the Judge's secret envelope.

Ant was shifting into reverse when I remembered, "Hey, stop, we forgot something." But when I turned around, Pig-Dog was already sleeping in the back of the pickup, using Ant's Desert Storm duffel bag as a pillow. "Never mind. Drive."

With the six-pack cooler between us, life was good. AntMan had the radio tuned to 97.1, the time-machine station that played hits from before the year 2000. That was the cutoff. Someone named Amy Grant was in the middle of "Baby, Baby" when the DJ interrupted to say the police had found a body on Stainback Highway. Old news, but me and Ant couldn't help glancing at each other.

Foot on the gas and two hands on the steering wheel, AntMan kept us pointed deep into Puna. We were headed toward his place out past Hawaiian Paradise Park and Hawaiian Beaches. "A lot of bodies these days," he said, shifting into overdrive.

"No more than usual." That's what I said.

He had a theory about bodies. On Maui, they were always dumped in cane fields. On Oahu they were always left in dumpsters behind strip bars. And on the Big Island, they were always dumped by the side of the road. "Think about it," he said.

I tried not to. He'd make a good cop thinking like he did.

"Our killers are either too lazy or too stupid," he said.

I scratched my head. I didn't know much about murderers. That was the Judge's specialty. She had locked plenty of them behind bars, made a few enemies along the way.

We were quiet as the miles rushed by, Pig-Dog sleeping, the light fading. It felt like we could drive right off the end of the world and be lost forever. I wasn't worried. AntMan couldn't kill us. He had kids.

We were carried along by a stream of cars driven by hungry people heading home after 16-hour shifts at Sears or Target or Pizza Hut, or some other mind dumbing, brightly lit hell hole where good people go to work so they can feed their kids. I'm not going to tell you the name of the roads because I don't want tourists getting the idea they should drive out there for a look. Believe me, where we were headed isn't a must see. It's a best-left-unseen destination.

We drove through old lava flows, by cheap lots and cheaper houses with water catchment and septic tanks. Some even had hook-up to an electric pole. No phones, no cable. No city noise. The good life.

We drove until the asphalt turned to gravel, then to cinder, then to plain dirt. We reached the ocean and drove along the coast. The lava rock cliffs dropped down to choppy blue water. On my side, walls of Albizia and Palmetto blocked my view.

"Why are you two living way out here?" I asked, looking behind me to check on Pig-Dog. He was lying on his back, feet in the air, staring up at the sky and snoring.

"Bobbie liked the price. And the location. She likes the quiet."

I could hear the waves breaking on the cliffs. The truck hopped, landed, and hopped again before finding its footing.

"Where else can you get a lot for $3,500?" he asked.

I could get a lot for $3,500 but it wasn't land. We passed a wood cross stuck in a pile of lava rock. AntMan slowed down and crossed himself, saying, "Po ting."

"Who?"

"They left her body there."

I didn't ask or look back.

"The family flew out and took her home. If you're lucky, your family will take you home when it's time, Manny."

I doubted Steamer the cat knew the way or how to get there. "If she's not buried there, why the cross?"

"Keeps the ghosts away." That's what he said. "Sometimes they start walking."

I reached for the .22. I'm not saying I believe in ghosts, and I'm not saying they had anything to do with what happened later, just letting you know how we were getting fired up. I was still holding the .22 when Ant swung the wheel right and turned into a cinder driveway. It ended at a babysitter sitting in a silver Nissan Sentra. When she saw us, she started the engine and drove straight at us, playing chicken long enough to yell out the window as she swerved to get by us, "They're inside. I'm late for work."

The car disappeared in a cloud of red dirt and cinder. We parked next to an inflatable pool. A school of plastic ducks floated in the clear water. AntMan told me cellphones didn't work out here, and the road washed out when it rained, but it was a good place to raise kids.

"Why's that?"

"Quality of life."

"Sure," I said, and stuffed the .22 under the seat, just far enough so I could reach it without having to stretch.

The house was one of those HPM jobs, a prefab rectangle with a kitchen at one end, living room in the middle, and three small bedrooms and a shared bathroom at the other end. It was built on an 8,000-square-foot lot, the county minimum for a single-family dwelling. To save more money they had skipped a concrete slab and gone post-and-pier style with a tin roof. Lucky for AntMan and his cop bride, no one else had seen the benefits of living in the boonies with ghosts. His mansion was nestled in the middle of a hundred vacant lots overgrown with jungle.

Pig-Dog was on his feet, keeping his eyes on the road while AntMan worked a key into the front door. "It's the ocean air," he said, jiggling the key. "Salt rots everything."

I walked across the road, stood at the edge of the cliff and looked down a cliff that dropped fifty feet to the blue water. There was a narrow trail for fisherman and opihi pickers, and when the Ant's kids were old enough they'd be able to hop and skip and fall down to blue water. Maybe even see the spot where a woman had been left to die.

I walked back and found AntMan in the tiny living room. The two kids were wadded up on the couch, snoozing in soft blue and pink blankets.

"Maybe we should wait on this adventure," I said, watching him pick up the blue boy, hug him to his chest, and do the same with the pink squirmer.

"No way." He handed me the pink bundle. Something was moving in there. Hands with tiny fingers tentacled my thumb. I needed a drink.

Antman grabbed a couple of bulging shopping bags. "Supplies," he said. "Diapers. Check. Chow. Check. More blankets. Check."

"We can't take this gal on a stakeout."

"They're tough," he said. "Tough cop kids."

"I hear you're not supposed to drop them."

"Not on their heads. Don't want to do that."

Pig-Dog jumped up, resting his front feet on my waist, so he could sniff the goods. Was he smiling? Another guy who wanted kids? He didn't look the type.

AntMan threw their supplies in the back of the truck, added the six-pack cooler, making room in the cab for two car seats. The sleeping kids fit in there real nice, strapped in like miniature astronauts. Pig-Dog jumped into the cab so he could lick their faces. I let him keep my seat, and I stretched out in the back, watching the sky go by as AntMan backed us out of the driveway and onto the road, bouncing and braking and lurching out of the wilderness and toward town.

The two bundles slept like good cops all the way to Rayzah's place. When Ant twisted a sharp turn into her driveway, Pig-Dog barked twice. Teresa tore open the truck's door, shoved Pig-Dog out of the way, and scooped them up into her tattooed arms. They squawked and cooed and waved their arms, what AntMan claimed was their way of showing excitement.

Me, I thought it meant someone had to change their diapers.

"My little babies," Rayzah said, hugging them to her chest, which both of them seemed to enjoy. There was plenty there for them to enjoy. "You better take care of Antony," Rayzah told me, while holding a baby in each arm.

In the old days, when Ant was a kid, Rayzah spent a lot of time taking care of him. It was a mother-kid kinda thing without the real mother part. They were related somehow, someway, the way everyone in Hilo is related to everyone else, so she took care of him. "He's your responsibility now," she said to me. The kids dug their tiny fingers into her Pele tattoos and gave me baby stink-eye.

"Don't let anything happen to him," she said. "He's a father."

"What about me?"

"Jeez, Manny. Think about it."

Yeah, no kids were going to miss me.

"Remember, you still owe me," she said.

"For what?"

"For my shotgun."

"I gave it to Twyla."

Rayzah shook her head. "Never saw the girl. Never saw my shotgun. Twyla said she lost it."

AntMan handed me a bag of baby supplies, saying, "We won't need these." I handed the bag to Teresa. Waitresses know how to hold lots of stuff. I tossed the baby-safety seats into the back of the truck.

"We'll be back," AntMan yelled at Teresa.

"If I'm not here, I'm at Reuben's." She waved goodbye with her arms full of babies and baby supplies.

I slammed the door and AntMan gunned the engine. As he backed into the darkness, he punched the CD player. Patti Griffin broke open the night, singing her brassy version of "Please don't let me die in Florida."

We felt something heavy land in the back of the truck. When we looked back, Pig-Dog was sitting there, braced against the wheel well and tearing into a bag of Blanes shoyu chicken and roast pork.

"Where the hell did he get that?" Ant said.

"He's a hunter."

Pig-Dog, his mouth full of chicken and pork, howled a bugle call at the sky. Ant stepped on the gas and we rushed toward Hilo. "I got baseball bats in the duffel bag," he said. "Hand cuffs. Bobbie's extra set and mines. Mace. My dive knife is around here somewhere. And a flare gun."

"A flare gun?"

"I'm on parole."

"Right."

"I don't want to hurt anybody, just make an arrest." He pointed at the glove compartment. "Check in there."

I pressed the black button, lifted out a red shopping bag from Island UnNaturals, the place where Joe used to buy all his beer and wine. They had good sales on Fridays, even if you had to bring your own bag and listen to a mob preach about vitamins and the evils of gluten. Inside the bag, there was a jumbo-sized first-aid kit.

"Just in case."

A first aid kit and a flare gun. We were in business.

We followed the road into town and turned up the mountain. It was dark, so I can't give you the exact location but somewhere on that road AntMan turned off the headlights, slowed to a crawl, and made a looping right turn, saying, "It's a dead end. I think this is it. We got them trapped."

The truck bucked and rattled. We were driving through the agricultural lots above Hilo, a mixture of old plantation-style homes on tiny lots, sprawling ranch-style custom homes on 20-acre spreads, and all kines rolling hills. They were spotted with grazing cows, angry goats, snooty horses, beehives, sheep, and screaming chickens that looked like screaming chickens.

"There," he said, pointing into the darkness on the left. "I can smell them."

I didn't smell anything but stinky feet.

He drove the truck onto the road's slippery muddy shoulder, turned off the engine, and rolled down the window. I pulled my hoodie over my head and hunkered down to stay out of the cold wind.

I heard them before I saw them. Roosters. The truth is I hate roosters almost as much as I hate car thieves. Pig-Dog barked three times. As my eyes adjusted to the darkness, rows of rooster condos appeared out of the night. Their A-frames were made from corrugated tin, with a fat rooster staked in front of each condo so it could screech out its frustrations 24-hours a day. As dark as it was, I guess my hatred gave me night vision.

"Frickin chickens," I said, reaching for the .22. "I should've known."

"Forget them. Look over there. Up there." AntMan pointed at headlights moving along a driveway, winding their way into the shadows before reappearing in front of a sprawling one-story ranch house. All the windows were lit up, and we could see that the headlights belonged to a pick-up truck towing something on a small trailer. There was a barn to the left, and one of those American steel Quonset huts in the back.

"Let's go." AntMan climbed out of the truck.

I stayed put. "Can't we free a few roosters first? Send them to the promised land?" For once, the .22 felt good.

"You want Joe's truck, don't you?"

He walked around to the passenger side, opened the door and reached into the glove compartment. He tossed the first-aid kit on the floor and pulled out his dive knife, a folding

Dacor model, made in Japan, with a six-inch blade in a leather case. I had seen it in action before, when it was cutting the head off a Maui pineapple, one of the sweet white ones.

"Always be prepared," he said. "Isn't that what the Cub Scouts taught you?"

I was never in the Scouts, the little Nutzis, but I did spend a couple years trying to get out of the army. They were smart enough to keep me away from anything sharp.

I took a swig of tequila, grabbed the .22, and climbed out of the truck. I was checking the .22 for bullets when AntMan tried to hand me a flashlight. I waved it off. So far, flashlights hadn't done much good for me. He gave up and stuck it in my kangaroo pocket. "Be careful, the battery's low, use it as a last resort."

"Sure."

He moved into the darkness, flare gun in hand. Me, I had the .22 in one hand, the tequila in the other. Out there, in the dark, we were a long way from the Empire. I had eight bullets and a bottle for company.

It was tough going. We climbed a hogwire fence and dropped down into thick clumps of pasture grass, the kind that had the bad habit of dropping suddenly into a sinkhole. The flashlight would've helped but AntMan wanted to go commando style. He went on his hands and knees, moving like he could see in the dark. I got down with him, and we crawled our way up the mountain. We were gliding through something that smelled and felt like pig guts covered in chicken shit when he stopped and raised his fist, just like in the movies. We were at the edge of a concrete driveway.

Dragging that trailer, the tow truck was driving into the barn. I took a swig of tequila. A few minutes later, three men came out of the barn and walked toward the house. One of them was short, heavy set, mostly belly. He took the lead. Silhouetted against the house lights, they climbed the steps to the porch. Three more men were waiting up there, sitting at a table and drinking beer from cans.

"The hideout," AntMan said.

The sprawling house looked like it had ten bedrooms, all lit up. If the hideout was supposed to be inconspicuous, all the lights and weren't helping.

"Who knows how many rats are here," AntMan said. Those were his exact words. Rats. It made me look at him. Either he was smiling or grinding his teeth, like one of those poor doughboys ready to charge out of the trenches, go over the top in war movies. "You check the barn," he whispered, pointing to the left. "Watch out for the dogs."

Five dogs were chained in front of the house, a couple more by the barn. Rottweilers. Big ones, double the size of Pig-Dog. I was wondering where he was, when I smelled blood. He crawled up on bent knees while he chewed through the neck of a rooster. I drank more tequila and wondered if there was such a thing as a small Rottweiler.

AntMan stuck his mouth close to my ear. "I'll take the Quonset hut." He was smart enough to be a cop, which wasn't saying much, but he wasn't smart enough to see a suicide mission. Five years of living with Bobbie Marta had made him desperate.

"Then what?"

Something in that big head of his clicked and sparked. "Check it out, see what you find, and we'll meet back here."

"That's the plan?"

"That's it."

Pig-Dog looked from me to AntMan, then back again. The first mosquito of the night buzzed my ear, and I handed Antony the gun. "Take it," I whispered. "You need it more than me." He handed me the flare gun, slipped the knife off his belt, and handed it to me. "Be careful out there," he said. I think that was a cop line from a TV show.

He had to find a way around the house and into a steel Quonset house. My main concern was being eaten by Rottweilers or lighting myself on fire with the flare gun. I slipped the knife in my back pocket, finished the tequila. The flare gun I kept in my hand. It had a nice feel.

Flashing a two-finger peace sign at me, AntMan crawled toward the driveway. One of the Rottweilers barked, then all of them joined in, like they had practiced the drill all their lives. Dogs like to talk. The men on the porch stood up. One of them reached behind him and pulled out what could have been a shotgun or hunting rifle. Something with a long barrel.

Lucky for us, Pig-Dog had the brains in the family. He was already half way to the front door, barking and snarling and circling the dogs.

"What the fuck is that?" a woman yelled. A man appeared in the lighted doorway. "Jeez, what the hell is that?" he shouted. "Who has the shotgun?"

From the porch, a shotgun blast lit up the night. A Rot squealed, like it had absorbed buckshot. Pig-Dog kept barking and running and swooping in to snap at the Rots. It was a dog riot.

"Let the dogs loose!"

"I'm not going out there," a squealer shouted.

As I crouched low and headed for the barn, a shotgun blast ripped through the night.

"What the hell is that thing?" Another shotgun blast. A dog yelped and kept yelping. It didn't sound like the Pig. "Jeeesus!" a woman screamed. Another shot. More squealing. I thought I heard something being ripped apart.

I ran left, into the shadows and past the two big Rots staked in front of the barn. They were bigger up close, about the size of ponies, and when they saw me they focused their barking at me, feeding their noise into the mangled mess of roosters crowing, dog's howling and the occasional shotgun blasting.

The barn doors, big enough to drive a semi-truck through, were locked together with a thick chain, so I ran around back and felt along the weathered wood until I found a loose board. I stuck the flare gun in my pouch, and pried the wood back with my fingers. Did the same for its neighbor, making a space big enough to crawl through leg first, then hip, shoulder, and head.

Moonlight fell through a thousand small cracks in the roof and walls, enough light to see rows of cars on blocks. Some of them were broken apart, like chickens at a banquet. It was a nice old-timey chop shop. I used the flashlight, just for a second, long enough to see that it was worthless, barely bright enough to see my feet. I turned it off and put my hand in front of me so I could feel my way through the lines of cars, until I smelled something familiar. I stopped, sniffed again. A hint of shoyu chicken and potato salad. Joe's favorite. I found Joe's pickup truck up front, near the double doors. The tow truck was parked next to it. I had to look twice to believe what was in its trailer: Joe's Ural.

Those car thieves were busy little buggahs.

I heard a shotgun blast. Then another. The dogs managed to bark louder, the chickens to crow louder. I ducked behind Joe's truck and yanked open the driver's door, reached under the seat, grabbed the manila envelope, and tucked it into my pants.

"Shut the fuck up," someone yelled. Whoever he was, he was at the front of the barn. His flashlight beam slipped through the cracks. A chain clanked to the ground.

I slipped over to the Ural and dug around until I felt my stack of books. The doors swung open. I dropped my flashlight in the Ural, grabbed my library books, and ran. Behind me, it looked like Shortie dah Big-Gut was leading the way, waving at his minions to keep pace. I fumbled my way to the back wall and felt for my escape hatch. A flashlight beam swept the barn. A couple of Rots leaped over cars, snapping and snarling. I gripped the books tight, hunched down, aimed my shoulder at the narrow opening in the wall and smashed through, like the first person in a buffet line. I landed in the mud and tried to get to my feet. A Rot crashed through the rotting wood, aiming for my neck. I held the books up like a shield just in time to see Pig-Dog fly through the air and catch that Rot by the neck.

He dug his teeth and tusks into that dog's throat, and I ran, trying not to hear the growling, whining, and whimpering. When I looked back, a shotgun blast lit up a tableau of Pig-Dog leaping over a fallen Rot and aiming for a gigantic stomach pointing a shotgun. A pack of Rots came charging around the corner of the barn. I fell backward into the mud, stood up and ran.

The shotgun tore open the night. I kept going, hands full of books, listening for the patter-patter of Rottweiler feet as the flare gun slapped me in the stomach. If those Rots had been human, I would've lit them up, but they were only dogs doing their job. They were closing on me. I was reaching for the flare gun when I heard Joe's .22 go pop, pop, pop. It sounded like a baby crying in a barroom brawl.

Entry 14: BORN TO STUMBLE

I'm a big guy, but I'm fast on my feet. The night I ran from the Rottweilers with shotguns, I must've run off course. I never found AntMan's truck, not even the road where we parked it. Maybe I was running with my eyes closed. It sure felt like it. Sucking in cold air and sinking knee-deep in pasture grass, I didn't care where I was going as long as I was going, staying ahead of gun-totting Rots who were barking, snapping, circling, egged on by their twisted, two-legged owners.

The truth is, I stumbled more than I ran, but I kept going, staying low, crashing my way through guinea grass taller than me, wild guava branches, wild sugar cane, and the occasional fence post. I don't know why, but I kept a death grip on my books. Later, when a flashlight beam caught me, I slid face first into an irrigation ditch filled with muddy water but still managed to keep my books dry.

Papa Joe would've known what to do. Me, I was shivering like someone gone crazy on Ecstasy and techno-trance music. Staying low, on hands and knees I crawled away from the lights, struggled to my feet and ran through pastures, dodging cows and goats until I stumbled into a ravine thick with Albizia and nasty lava rock. It took a few minutes to catch my breath.

Then I climbed up a narrow trail, over a fence, and down a slippery ledge to wet asphalt and headlights coming my way.

The music in my head kept pounding. Some thing played on a tuba. Too tired to run, I stood my ground, books wedged under one arm, flare gun in the other, pointed at oncoming traffic. "For the Ant," I shouted, about to pull the trigger. Believe me, I was going to shoot, but something big flew out of the air behind me, grabbed my hoodie and dragged me backwards, out of the road and into the shadows. The ground gave way, and I crashed down a hundred slippery steps. The stars disappeared. In their place, tree roots were growing out of a lava rock. They reached for me as I was dragged into cool darkness.

I heard screeching brakes, men shouting, and doors slamming. A familiar stink seeped into my nose. Pig stink mixed with chicken breath. I rolled over and let myself ooze into a crevice, squeezing in tight against the rotting roots and wet rock. Pig-Dog crawled in on top of me, covering me like a big stinking bloody blanket.

Flashlight beams swept the mouth of the cave, then a couple of Rots scrambled halfway down the stairs before stopping, sniffing, whimpering, and turning tail back up the stairs, like they had seen a ghost. That must've been me. The sound of truck engines faded up the mountain.

Pig-Dog sighed and closed his eyes. I was still in one piece, except for a few scrapes and bruises and a missing flare gun. I stuck my books under my head. They did a good imitation of a pillowcase filled with rocks. I rubbed Pig-Dog with two hands, calling him my good buddy and telling him we could be good friends when he learned how to shower and shave. Maybe use some Old Spice. My hands came away sticky with warm blood. The bullet holes were high up, spread over his chest and ribs, too many to count. He must've charged right into a shotgun blast. The blood kept coming, warming my hands.

I pushed him off me, stripped off my hoodie and tried to rip it into strips. Nothing worked until Pig-Dog nuzzled my pants pocket. That buggah had common sense. I dug out AntMan's knife and cut Joe's hoodie into strips, wrapped them tight around Pig-Dog chest and gut until he looked like a four-legged mummy. He took it like a human, keeping his mouth shut. To patch the last few holes, I cut my t-shirt into bandages and put the finishing touches to Pig's mummy look.

I was shivering. The Judge's envelope was poking me in the gonads. I thought about lighting it on fire to stay warm. Instead, I leaned back and let myself sink into the damp crevice, dragging Pig-Dog with me. "We'll rest here a moment," I whispered, patting him on the head.

The two of us peered into the darkness. Pig-Dog's bloody warmth was making me sleepy. I was thinking about lighting my emergency joint, when the Madonna showed up, late as usual.

Lucky for us she came in low, with her running lights dimmed just enough to guide her through the trees and down the stairs without attracting any attention from stray trucks. She sat beside us, at the edge of our lava-rock bed, wearing a UH Rainbows hoodie, jeans and cowboy boots. Pig-Dog closed his eyes.

"Manny, I have to warn you."

"About Rotweillers with guns? You're a little late."

"You can't stay here," she said.

"It's nice and warm here."

"They'll be back for you."

"Pig-Dog is no mood to travel."

"He'll die here."

Heck, I didn't need a Madonna to tell me that. His bandages were soaked through with blood. He couldn't have much left in him, maybe half a pint. The world doesn't take kindly to hybrids, unless they're orchids, and Pig-Dog was no orchid. He was a nasty ass part-pig thing who liked to scrap with Rots.

The Madonna reached down and brushed dirt off my forehead. I wanted her hand to stay there. It felt warm, almost warm enough to be real. Her face was glowing, enough for me to warn her about bright lights attracting the wrong crowd.

She touched Pig-Dog's bandage. "He seems to have taken a liking to you."

"He's a fighter," I said.

"Po ting. He's always getting into trouble." She took her hand away from Pig-Dog's bandage. "I'm worried about him." Her fingertips were glowing sticky red. That didn't stop her from reaching down and hugging him tight, like he was more than a dirty, stinky hairball. He didn't open his eyes. She said, "He's not what he used to be."

That made sense. You get a couple dozen holes in you, you're bound to lose a step. He laid his head in my hand. His breath brushed over my wrist.

"He used to be part of a family." She looked up, pointing at the cave's ceiling. "They drove him out."

That's what she said, really. When I looked up, all I saw was rock. Pig-Dog dug his nose into my armpit and started snoring.

"Everyone needs help, Manny."

"So it seems."

She turned her back to us and faked like she was walking up the stairs, but her feet never touched the ground. "Take him home, Manny."

"Can I borrow your hoodie?"

She pulled it over her head and tossed it to me. As I was burying my head in its celestial folds, it evaporated and went back to being worn by the Madonna.

Pig-dog growled in his sleep.

"Take him down the mountain," she said.

"How? He must weight three hundred pounds."

"Didn't you tell me that Joe left you in charge?"

"Sure." The truth is I didn't remember. I would've said anything to stay in place and not move.

"Drape him around your shoulder, like a scarf," she said. "You know the fireman's carry, right?"

She wasn't always around when you needed her, but she kept her eyes open.

"Sure, I know it."

"Pick him up and start walking," she said. "One foot in front of the other, keep going, and stay off the main road."

She was always good for suggestions. "He'll bleed out," I said. "He's got enough holes in him to strain noodles."

"It could be worse." She shrugged. "Things can always get worse."

Nice attitude for a Golden Madonna. She started her fade-out routine, floating up, generating flickering light, and waving a beauty queen's wave, heading out of darkness and back to the stars. "Get moving, Manny."

"Hey, come back here and give me a hand!"

She gave me one last wave. Then Pig-Dog and me were back to being alone. I pulled his warmth close to me. I was finished running. The night closed in around me, and I felt too sleepy to move. Most people don't realize that it gets cold in Hawaii. And it gets colder the higher up you go, especially at night, until you hit snow and freezing winds. Me, usually I like the cold. It's good for sleeping, especially if I'm under a blanket next to an open window, with a space heater and a bottle of alcohol.

I'm ashamed to say, the thought of alcohol made me dig into my pocket for my lighter and the emergency joint. The flame made me think that I could burn my books for warmth. To start the party, I could use the Judge's envelope as a torch. A few puffs later I was sitting up with Pig-Dog on my lap. The weed was making me think. Before me and Pig floated off to the Madonna's frickin idea of heaven, some sinkhole at the end of the universe, I wanted to know what was in that envelope.

By the light of Joe's Zippo, I dug out a page and started reading. It was tough going, not just because of the weak light. The ink was fading and the lines were packed too close together. Someone must've used an old typewriter, a real spool and carriage-return model, to do the job. The first line was whited out. Its replacement was typed through the sticky white stuff. I hadn't seen that since my school days. But I could read the words.

February 15, 1993

Your honor,

138

This will be our last contact with you. Although we are saddened by our daughter's death, we look to the future with the hope that we can at last put this behind us.

I wish there was more that I could tell you. We loved her as our daughter and while she was in our home, we treated her with respect and kindness. At no time was there a sign of what was to come later. She was a bright young woman with a very strong work ethic. When she decided to leave home to attend college in Santa Cruz, we were concerned, but we knew she had the tools to succeed. It came as no surprise to us when she graduated with honors and was accepted into graduate school. By then we had lost direct contact with her, but we were all very proud of her accomplishments. Now, we are struggling to understand why it ended this way.

That's as far as I got before the lighter blinked out.

I stuffed the envelope back in my pants, and crawled out from under Pig-Dog. He was lying there still as Papa Joe. In the dark, I saw his eyes open, look at me, and close. His breathing sounded rough, like a drunk passed out on cheap wine. Maybe he could last until I got back. That's what I was thinking. I turned and climbed the first few steps out of the cave. I remembered him warm against me and his heart beating against mine.

I came back to him, dropped to my knees and hefted him onto my shoulders. Holding his legs tight against my chest, balancing his weight on my shoulders and neck, I stood up. I climbed the stairs, putting one foot in front of the other. My knees wobbled. I slipped, straightened up, and kept going.

We reached the top of the stairs and saw the stars. His heartbeat grew stronger against my neck. It seemed to be pumping through him to me, propelling me down the mountain toward the sea, like I was being carried along by his weight.

Entry 15: SUSPICIOUS MIRACLES

I woke up naked on the Empire's roof. Blood and dirt were running off me into a rusty drainpipe. I was standing under Joe's rainforest shower. He claimed it made him feel like he was swimming naked in a velvety mist. To me it felt like being pelted by BBs.

It took me most of the night to get there, ducking behind trees and rubbish cans to hide from passing cars, waiting to see if the chicken rancher and his Rots would come back for a second try. By the time I passed the 7-11, the jail and the high school, I was ready to drop. When the early bird retirees at Blanes saw me stumble to the counter, with Pig-Dog on my back, my eyes on the sky, my tongue hanging out of a crazy smile, clothes covered in Pig-Dog blood, and mumbling about the power of Portuguese sausage and tequila, they must've thought I was either crazy or a pig hunter looking for his truck. I stunk so bad the gals behind the counter wouldn't sell me any food or let me sit down, which is saying something, considering it was outside seating.

When I finally made it to the Empire, the sun was an orange threat on the horizon. I laid Pig-Dog on the ground, like a wounded sack of rice, and checked his bandages. As far as I could tell from the crusty reddish-brown stain on his shredded bandage, the bleeding had stopped. When I put my head to his nose, warm breath tickled my ear hairs. His heart was still pumping, and if his heart was pumping, the Doc could fix him. I asked Pig-Dog to give her a call.

A few minutes and a climb up the fire escape later, I was scrubbing my sore spots with a scratchy bar of military-grade soap under a BB blizzard. An ambulance turned into the alley. Lights flashing, siren going, it accelerated to Joe's driveway, braked, turned, and stopped an inch from Pig-Dog.

Doc Trina stepped out of the driver's seat, looked up and waved at me. "Manny! Hey, Manny." She was wearing her black, Viet Cong pajamas and big mushy orange Crocs, the imitation shoe kind. "Get your ass down here. I've been looking all over for you."

I turned off the water, stepped from behind the bamboo slats, and climbed halfway down the fire escape before she held up her hands. "Go back! I've seen enough."

Like I said, Doc Trina was smart, the brains of any operation, but sometimes she sent mixed signals. "Which is it?" I shouted at her, a cool breeze fluffing my leg hairs. "Down or up?"

"Put your clothes on," she said, acting all innocent, like she had never seen me in the nude, off duty or on. I didn't blame her. She was trying to stay focused, keep her mind on business.

I climbed back up and found a "Got Margarita's?" t-shirt and a pair of Joe's jeans left hanging on a rusty nail. With the shirt tucked into the faded jeans and the belt pulled extra tight, I figured I had covered up enough to look almost decent, even to the Doc.

She was on her knees, checking Pig-Dog, unwrapping his bandages. While she did the important work, I rolled up Joe's pants to keep them from dragging on the wet asphalt. "Jeez, Manny, what happened to this dog? You have him wrapped up like a mummy."

"That's what I thought." As the Doc peeled off the last piece of bloody t-shirt, I told her that we needed to get up the mountain. Then I filled her in about AntMan and me finding the guys who had stolen Joe's truck and motorcycle, and how AntMan got lost in the shuffle.

"Shuffle? That's what you call it?"

Friggin words. They never did their job. "Can you fix the Pig?"

Digging her fingers into Pig-Dog's hair, she said, "I'm a doctor, not a vet."

"Dogs are easier than people."

"Bullshit. They're more complicated. They have four legs and they can't talk."

Pig-Dog smiled as the Doc felt him up, running her hands over the hard-to-get-at spots. "What did you say happened to him?"

"He got shot."

"By what?"

"Something that made lots of noise and holes." I didn't mention Joe's .22. The Doc didn't like that gun.

"These are old wounds. Scabbed over. It looks like he tore them open, maybe from running." She stood up and nudged Pig-Dog with her foot. "Get up."

Pig-Dog jumped to his feet. Apparently the night of sleeping on my neck had done wonders for his recovery. He licked the Doc's hand, lumbered over to the hose, sat down, and waited for me to turn on the water. The Doc beat me to it, turning the knob as she said, "He stinks."

"He always stinks. He was bleeding last time I looked."

"You're imagining things."

"Me?"

"You're an irresponsible pet owner."

"He's not my pet."

"A pet owner who smokes too much weed and talks to imaginary friends."

Did I tell you that the Doc doesn't believe in miracles? She says she's seen enough dead people to know better. I told her that I had seen blood pouring out of him, that I had just scraped a ton of it off me.

"You're sick," she said, turning the hose on and holding it to his mouth, pumping him full of water. "Your dog thing was thirsty. That's all."

Pig-Dog was on his feet, looking around for a snack. What could I say? That the Madonna had given me a self-healing model? If I did, the Doc would lock me up for another thirty days. She didn't believe in Madonnas. Me, I thought it was better to be labeled lazy than crazy.

She dug in her pockets and pulled out a Tootsie Roll, one of those mega-long models that looked like a Cuban cigar. Before she could unwrap it, Pig-Dog snatched it from her hand, bit through the wrapper, and inhaled. The cheroot and wrapper disappeared down his gullet.

"Good boy," the Doc said. "He's cold and hungry. That's all. "He's fine."

I figured a doc shouldn't feed a dog candy, but she wasn't a vet, and he wasn't all dog. The pigs I knew could eat anything, even each other, so maybe candy would help cure him. Pig-Dog sure thought so. He spit the wrapper onto the asphalt and looked up at her while baring his teeth. Bits of Tootsie Roll were stuck between his canines and his tusks. That was his way of saying thank you. I had seen him do it after eating red dogs. I dug my fingers through his wiry hair, searching for wounds. Except for a few sneaky bugs I was hoping were only fleas the size of cockroaches, there was nothing.

"You have to stop exaggerating," the Doc said, pushing me away. She sprayed Pig-Dog with cold hose-water. "There's nothing there that hasn't been there for a long time. Old battle scars."

"Sure," I said. But for purposes of this report, I confirm that as those heeling preachers say on the radio, it was a "Friggin miracle." I was opening my mouth to tell her so when she reached up, pinched my lips shut, and told me that Teresa had called. The kids were at Reubens and she was working the breakfast shift. According to the Doc, we had two hours to find AntMan before Marta got off work. If we didn't, Teresa would kill me, then Marta would kill me again. "Then I'll finish the job," the Doc said.

It felt good to hear that people still cared enough about me to threaten my life. I said, "Didn't Pig-Dog call you?"

"What are you talking about?"

Words again, screwing with me.

"Don't worry," she said. "We'll find him."

I liked the "we" part. The Doc had resources. She grabbed my arm and pulled me to the ambulance. "Ride in the back," she said. "In case we run into anyone." If she was driving I was sure we'd run into someone. The Doc always felt the need for speed. She snapped her fingers and Pig-Dog ran over to her, dripping wet. "Him too." She jerked the back door open. "Get in and pretend you're casualties."

"Have you seen Professor Twyla?" I asked.

"Never mind her. She's at the hospital keeping an eye on Ms. Song. She has enough problems. She'll call if she needs us. We have work to do." The Doc looked down at the asphalt where Joe had died. She shook her head, and asked, "Is this where it happened?"

I didn't say anything.

"At least he was at home." She looked around the alley, then up at the sky, like she was looking for symptoms of life. "You know what I mean, Manny?"

"Sure." I didn't, but like I told you, the Doc was the smart one. She knew how to think. A light clicked on in my head. "Wait." I climbed up the fire escape and found the Judge's blood-splattered envelope on the wet roof, right where I had left it.

"Let's go," the Doc shouted up at me.

I climbed down and tried to hand her the envelope. "I found this at the Judge's house."

She shoved it back at me. "I'll look at it later. AntMan first. Get moving."

I climbed in and sat down on a steel bench attached to the wall. Pig-Dog jumped in behind me, and the Doc slammed the door. Across from me a familiar looking body was snoring on a metal gurney. Pig-Dog nudged my knee with his snout and dropped Joe's zippo lighter in my hand. Where Pig found it, I don't know. Like him, it had been healed. It lit up on the first try. "Thanks," I told him, snapping it shut. He found a soft spot on the floor and curled up to sleep. I slid the envelope under my butt as Doc Trina climbed into the driver's seat. "That's Miles," she said. "Never mind him."

Miles was lying on his back with his knees bent and his toes pointed at the door. Wearing sunglasses, a blue scrub shirt, black jeans, and red high-top tennis shoes, he looked like a casualty. The Doc backed us down the driveway, talking over shoulder. "He had a hard night." She swung the wheel to point the ambulance up the alley. "He owes me a favor, so we're borrowing his ride." She looked at me through the rearview mirror. "Spray some disinfectant on your face. On those scratches. There, on the top shelf. Spray the dog-thing, too. Just in case."

Miles groaned, rolled onto his side, popped open one eye, pointed it at me then Pig-Dog. He groaned again and kept rolling, turning his back to us. I sprayed down Pig-Dog, head to foot. By the time we reached the main road, he was sparkling with disinfectant. I didn't spray any on me. I let nature do its work while Miles snored loud enough to make hearing Doc Trina a challenge.

"Which way?" she shouted.

"Up the mountain."

She stepped on the gas, and the ambulance shot into traffic. A green thermos, a fancy hydro bottle that cost a hundred bucks, rolled out from under the gurney. I picked it up, unscrewed the lid and sniffed coffee and some kine alcohol. I sniffed again. The fumes helped me not to think about the Doc working the steering wheel, finger-pecking her phone, and telling me that she didn't want dispatch to know where we were but she did want them to know how to reach us in case of an emergency.

I sipped the coffee cocktail, and couldn't tell if the coffee or the alcohol was burning my throat. Three big gulps didn't help.

"I smell coffee," the Doc shouted. "Don't drink Miles's hangover remedy."

I swallowed twice before tucking the thermos between my legs, where it felt warm even through the thick jeans.

"Damn," she shouted, tossing her phone at the passenger seat. "I hope no one gets sick."

Like I said, the Doc was different. I told her we should go back to Reubens. "Let's see if Rayzah wants to come. We need reinforcements. There must be twenty guys up there. And plenty dogs."

"Don't exaggerate."

The Doc knew her diseases but she wasn't good with numbers. Even if we could wake up the snoring hangover called Miles, counting Pig-Dog that made four of us. As far as I could see, we were way short on firepower. In fact, we didn't have any. "How about Frankie?" I asked. "He knows his way around. Spends a lot of time drinking and working outside."

"He's too old for this."

We passed Blanes, then Kosmic Cones and the library, cruising like the Doc had an actual driver's license, not one bought on the Internet. Her real license got jerked years ago for too many speeding tickets. I'm only reporting that because, really, she shouldn't be allowed on the road. But that was the Doc's only crime, no matter what people say. And Rayzah, too, the only crime she committed was feeding kids too much cheese. Anything else you can pretty much throw out the window.

The Doc braked as we passed the jail, braked again as the road split. "Directions!" she shouted. I buckled my seat belt before I gave her the route. We hit a rough stretch, and I gripped the bench, braced my feet against the rumbling metal, and looked around for anything that could be used as weapon.

The ambulance was a sharp, new ultra-fast model made slim for long runs on narrow country roads. There were cabinets filled with syringes, bandages and tape. There were some nasty looking scissors that could poke out an eye or two, and some super flexible hoses for strangling people. Under the cot filled with Miles, there was a Betty Boop lunch box, with a ham sandwich, an apple and a bag of Fritos inside. I was tearing open the package of Fritos when Doc Trina shouted, "There's the turn! Up there. Right?"

Before I could say anything, she yanked the steering wheel hard right, throwing the bag of Fritos out of my hands and into Pig-Dog's mouth. Then she flicked on the siren and the flashing lights. It felt like Christmas. I closed my eyes and fell asleep, waiting for her to shout, "Rise and shine. Time to open your presents."

*** (Writer's Union rest break) ***

"There!" She pointed up the road.

Maybe I was still groggy from sleeping. The place looked different. The sprawling house, the barn, and the storage shed were quiet and still. Deserted. A few trucks were parked next to the porch, but no people or Rots.

"Not much action," the Doc said. "You sure this is the place?"

Pig-Dog barked twice, struggled to his feet, launched himself at the back door, and ricocheted into Miles.

"Must be," I said.

The Doc managed to find a few more potholes and crack in the road before she took her foot off the gas, and swung into the driveway.

"Wait!" I said, grabbing at her shoulder. "What are you doing?"

"Finding Antony!"

We were flying now. The ambulance rocketed by huge roosters chained to tin-roof condos and crowing loud enough to challenge our siren. Miles rolled onto his back, licked his lips, and asked "Are we there yet?"

"Almost," I said, looking out the front window as the Doc hit the brakes. We slid over gravel, almost stopped, kept going, splashing through muddy water, and crushing a kid's bike, a white chicken and a red wheelbarrow. When we finally stopped, the Doc jumped out, shouting, "Anybody home?"

With the lights flashing and siren blasting, she ran up the stairs and banged on the front door. "Open up!" She shook the doorknob. Shoved her shoulder at the door. Kicked it. No response, except a single dog barking somewhere in the house. She was lifting her hand to knock again, when the door opened and an old gal in black shorts, rubber boots and a baggy t-shirt stuck her head out, then the rest of her, and shouted, "What? I don't want to buy nothing. Go away."

I think that's what she said. It was hard to hear over the roosters and the siren. I flicked switches, trying to find the siren. Miles reached over, found the switch next to the radio, and turned off the siren. He took a quick look at the situation, laid back down, and said, "Wake me when you need me."

Pig-Dog was chewing at the passenger-side door, trying to get into the fight. "We're not selling anything," the Doc shouted, pointing at the ambulance. "We're responding to an emergency call."

"What emergency? Go away."

"Automobile accident. A man wandered off. Disappeared. An Alzheimer's patient. We received a report this morning that he was seen wandering along this road."

"Where? What man? No man here."

The Doc pointed over her shoulder. "Down there. On the road. A big fellow, six foot maybe six two, about 250 pounds, maybe 300, wandering around, looking confused. Dresses like a missionary."

"No missionary here." The old babe had a barbed-wire hair to go with her shoe-leather skin.

Pig-Dog was barking and the rosters were screeching as the Doc and the old gal went at it. They shook their heads, waved their arms, and snapped at each other until the Doc spun around and ran down the steps, shouted through the ambulance window, "Miles, get this thing turned around. Manny, come with me."

From the dead, Miles sat up and blinked. Seeing him up close, I noticed he had thin lips, a flat nose, eyes set close together, and scraggly black hair that made him look like an exclamation point. At least that's what he looked like to me. Other people say I got his description all wrong. Enough said.

No matter. Whether he looked like Ms. Song's least favorite punctuation mark or a model for skinny jeans, he grabbed the thermos from between my knees, twisted off the cap, and gulped three times before wiping his mouth with the back of his hand, snapping to attention, and shouting. "You got it, Doc!"

"Professor Manny, right?" he said to me, offering his hand and the thermos. I gulped two shots while he rubbed Pig-Dog's head, like they were old pals. "Remember me?" he asked. "Me and my partner hauled away the Nutty Professor from your classroom?" He tilted his head, turned it so I could see the back. "I got a haircut."

"Sure." That's what I said.

He straightened up and finished off the last of the coffee. "Cures the common cold," he said, and wiped his lips again. "Got to go. Doctors orders." He handed me the thermos, squeezed by me, and climbed into the driver's seat. The thermos was empty. His drinking abilities inspired confidence, so I gave him a second look. Maybe he was five foot or five two, 140 pounds, with a new haircut, wide shoulders and biceps the size of footballs. He looked capable of moving large objects.

The Doc opened the back door. Pig-Dog jumped out and ran for the barn.

"Grab the first-aid kid," the Doc said, pointing at a metal box the size of a small suitcase. "Look official."

I grabbed it, jumped out, and followed her as she shouted at the woman on the porch, "We'll take a look around."

"No, no, not here," the woman shouted from the porch. She was holding her cellphone. "I call the police."

"Good," shouted Trina, heading for the barn. "I'm sure they'll be of assistance."

We tried the barn. The front doors were chained shut, so we walked around to the back. "I'll show you where," I told her. A second later we saw shiny new nails in the old wood. We stared through the cracks. "Nothing," the Doc said. I stared too. The barn was empty.

"They're quick," I said.

Miles shouted from the ambulance, "Ready to go!" He had it pointed at the road, with the engine running. Still a long way off but coming fast from where there wasn't supposed to be a road, two pickup trucks were churning up red dust. Where that chop-shop-farm road let out, I'm still not sure. Lots of roads in Hilo are like that

"Where's Pig-Dog?" I said, following the Doc. She went past the porch and around back to the Quonset hut.

"Hurry," Miles shouted at us.

We looked through the windows of the Quonset hut as my feet sunk ankle deep in mud. The first aid kit weighed a ton.

"A couple of tractors," the Doc said. "No cars, no motorcycle, no trucks, no dogs." We turned and ran back toward the ambulance, watching the two pickup trucks. They had slowed down to a crawl, bumping up and over a rough stretch of road. We could still escape if we hurried.

"Where's Pig-Dog?" I said, looking around.

"Crap," the Doc said.

"Move!" Miles shouted.

"Come on, Doc." The trucks were picking up speed. Miles was edging the ambulance away from the house. I grabbed her arm and ran toward the ambulance, trying to catch up. The passenger door swung open. "Never mind Pig," I shouted. "He knows his way around."

The Doc played her part, yanked her arm free, and stopped to shout at the woman on the porch. "Thank you. We'll check down the road."

"Doc!" Miles called.

I jumped in, crawled in back, and threw open the door. The Doc stepped in, gracefully, as if she were boarding a cruise ship bound for Tahiti.

"Go!" she said, moving up front while I yanked the door shut. "Use the siren."

The good thing about working with the Doc, she always had a plan. Miles flicked on the siren and pressed his foot on the gas. As we skidded over the red cinder, the crazy porch-lady disappeared inside the house and reappeared a second later with what looked like a broom. "A broom?" the Doc said. "Is that what shot your dog pal?"

"Look!" I pointed out the back window. Pig-Dog was zigzagging through the rooster condos, a fat red chicken clenched between his jaws. "Hungry," I said. "He missed breakfast."

"I gave him a whole candy bar."

Miles shook his head, "That's one nasty looking dog."

"A fast runner," the Doc said, settling into the passenger seat. She tapped Miles on the shoulder. "Slow down, give him a chance."

Miles took his foot off the gas. The speedometer dropped from 40 to 30. Pig-Dog was fifty yards uphill from us, running parallel to the road but keeping pace. The two pickup trucks turned into the driveway.

A shot ripped over the tops of chicken condos. Two of the feathery residents who had made the mistake of scrambling onto their roofs for a better view were knocked off their perches into a cloud of blood and feathers. As the ambulance accelerated up a small rise and dropped down behind it, I lost sight of the house.

"That didn't sound like a broom," I told the Doc.

"Open the back door," she shouted.

The safety latch was tricky. I had to kick it before the door swung open. We sailed by Cali grass, wild sugar cane and hog-wire fences under bright patches of blue sky. "Slower," the Doc said. "I'd hate to lose a good patient."

Pig was burrowing a pig trail through the Cali grass. "He's coming!" I shouted.

Miles hit the brakes, and Pig-Dog leapt out of the grass, flew over the flood ditch that separated the field from the road, touched down on the asphalt and ricocheted into the back of the ambulance. With the rooster still in his mouth. Its sagging neck suggested that his crowing days were over. As we bounced into and out of a pothole the size of a small car, Pig-Dog flipped the rooster into the air, caught it by the neck, and bit it in two. The head fell to the floor, the neck stayed in Pig-Dog's mouth.

We bounced up again, and I saw the pickups reach the house. As Pig-Dog chewed and swallowed, the two trucks turned around and headed back to the road. I'm sad to report that I didn't feel a sense of urgency or disappointment. All I felt was hunger. Maybe it was those two chicken feet sticking out of Pig-Dog's mouth, but all I could think about was a plate of Blanes chicken katsu.

"Floor it!" the Doc shouted.

Miles hit the gas. "No problem."

Except, the back door swung open. I reached for it, caught it, and swung it back into place. Serious, I thought it was slammed tight, and I'm pretty sure we could have outrun those trucks. From what I saw since then, Miles was an even crazier driver than the Doc, but Pig-Dog had other plans. He spit the chicken feet on the floor, leapt at the door, hit it, and bounced back.

"What the heck!" the Doc shouted. "Stop him."

I tackled him around the chest. It was like holding onto a greased lawn-tractor. The ambulance hit a rock, jumped up, and the back door flew open. That's when Pig-Dog shot out, carrying me along with him.

*** (Hand cramp, rest break) ***

We hit the ground, rolling and bouncing, and landing in the mud. The ambulance stopped, backed up, spraying more mud on me. The Doc jumped out as Pig-Dog shot up a narrow trail that disappeared into a dense wall of wild guava. It was the crappy kind that didn't grow fruit, just more branches.

The Doc helped me to my feet, then yelled at Miles, "Go to the hospital."

"Forget that," Miles shouted back, edging the ambulance forward. "Get in, all of you."

"We'll be okay." The Doc waved him off, moving toward the trail. "Make sure they're not following, then come back for us. Meet us here. Get going."

The ambulance pulled out, siren and lights blazing as we squeezed into a tightly packed wall of wire guava. It was everywhere, busy covering the island with a cable-thick cobweb of useless tree trunks and branches.

Hidden behind the mess, we crouched down, watching the two pickups skid to a stop at the intersection. The first one, a black beat-up Ford F150 turned left toward the ocean. The second, another Ford, this one rust colored, with huge mud tires, turned right, showing us the bullet holes in its side and disappearing up the mountain.

The Doc headed uphill, shoving guava out of her way, calling for Pig-Dog. To stay up with her and not lose an eye, I kept one hand in front of my face while the other fought off branches. Breathing hard, I grabbed her shoulder, told her to stop. "He'll be okay," I said. "He's one of the Madonna's."

The Doc pulled me close to her, so she could dig her fangs into my wrist, the way she did with her patients. She slapped me hard across the jaw. "Snap out of it." I think she learned that line from a movie. Something with Cher in it. "Now!" she said. "We're looking for Antony."

I sucked in the mountain air. It tasted of blood and chicken shit. I told her the story as close as I could remember, this time without the Madonna.

"The caves? Manny? What caves? Which way?"

I looked around. Everything looked familiar, and nothing looked familiar until Pig-Dog stuck his head out of a thick cobweb of branches, grunted twice, and disappeared the way he had come. We followed him, ducking under barbed-wire branches, stepping over fallen trunks, and slipping on mossy rocks until we broke free into a clearing. Pig-Dog ran down steps carved into lava rock.

There was a road, and on the other side of it, a small parking lot. Both were empty. I guess it was still too early for tourists. They didn't swarm from their hotel rooms until after lunch, what they called breakfast. "Is this where you were last night?" The Doc was already headed for the stairs that led underground.

"Maybe." I knew where I had been, but I didn't want to go down there. Something was telling me to stay above ground where I could see the sky.

"It was dark. It could have been."

We heard Pig-Dog barking. He popped back up. Barked at us to keep going. The Doc reached the stairs first, ran half way down and stopped. She held her hand out to stop me, like I had planned to keep going past her. The Doc's hand was steady. Mine were shaking as I looked down at Pig-Dog. He was sniffing a body at the bottom of the stairs. He circled it a couple of times, stopped and looked up at us.

Taking the stairs two at a time, the Doc reached the body first. She bent down to listen for breathing, feel for a heart beat. I was looking at desert boots and camouflage pants. "It's Antony," she said, brushing dirt and mud off his face. "He's breathing. Barely. No bullet holes, but he's beat up pretty bad."

While the Doc was busy playing with her phone, I reached down, picked up Joe's .22 and turned my back to her. The .22 was covered with mud and dirt. It had survival instincts. I checked for bullets. A light tap sent empty copper casings into my hand.

"Damn! No signal." The Doc shouted at her phone as she ran up the stairs. Me, I didn't like the dark but I wasn't leaving the AntMan alone. Pig-Dog was grunting deeper in the shadows. I stepped over AntMan, felt around in the dark with my foot until I hit something. Joe's zippo worked on the first try. There was enough light to see a body lying face-up, with a neat little bullet hole in its forehead, a neat little hole that looked like it came from a .22. When I heard the Doc yell from the top of the stairs, I snapped the lighter shut and tucked Joe's .22 into my pants.

"Manny, what are you doing down there?"

The truth is I was pulling the Judge's body further into the cave, but I didn't tell her that. When I was sure the Judge was far enough in, that's when I heard the siren.

Entry 16: KEEPING SECRETS

When Miles saw the hospital, he turned off the siren and eased off the gas. The ambulance slipped past the Emergency Room, glided through the parking lot, and came to a professional stop behind a dumpster.

The Doc told him to leave the engine running with the AC on. She strapped Antony to the gurney, and we muscled him out the back, careful not to step on a sleeping Pig-Dog. "Stay here," the Doc told me. "Keep out of sight."

I figured that would be easy work as long as the police didn't show up. As long as I could forget I was trapped in a metal box with Joe's .22. As long as I didn't have to look at the Judge rotting in a cave.

Miles closed the doors in my face, telling me not to worry, that he'd report her out for repairs.

The Judge needed more than repairs. But there was no point in dragging Miles and the Doc and AntMan into that mess. They had enough to worry about.

Through the tinted window, I watched the Doc and Miles playing push-me-pull-me with the gurney. While they zigg-zagged AntMan into a straight line that led to the back door of the hospital, I was wondering who had put a hole in the Judge. She had plenty of enemies, me included. Would the cops be crazy enough to believe that AntMan had something to do with her murder?

Sure. No problem. They believed lots of crazy stuff. It's part of their job description: Willingness to believe the impossible. That's what I told myself. And if they found me with the .22, they'd believe it was their job to lock me away until Hawaii could legalize the death penalty.

I tried to remember the last time I had eaten. If the cops were going to arrest me, or an old lady was going to shoot me with a broom, I wanted it to happen on a full stomach. Maybe a stomach stuffed with fried rice and Spam. I checked the Betty Boop lunch box. Empty. How and when he did it, I wasn't certain but looking down at Pig-Dog I knew who had eaten my ham sandwich. I checked the refrigerator and found a withered banana hidden in a paper bag behind the vials of rescue drugs. I checked under the driver's seat, searched the closest, and sat down, still hungry. Pig-Dog shifted his weight, lifted his rear end, and two thermoses, one red, one blue, rolled out from under him.

I stuck the blue one back under Pig. I needed red power. Twisting the cap, I saw the manila envelope peaking out from under Pig-Dog's head. My fingers touched bloody shoe prints that were hiding Joe's name. Doc Trina must have stepped on it while fighting to keep AntMan alive.

With the envelope safely on my lap, I finished working the cap off the thermos. The insides smelled of optimism and tasted like vodka and orange juice. Two quick gulps gave me the strength to look out the back window. All quiet on the western front. Two more gulps helped me peel back the clasp on the envelope and slide out the letter I had started reading the night before. In better light now, I skimmed down the first page to make sure I hadn't missed anything. Another two quick gulps from the thermos made the second page appear.

> *Only later did we learn from a close friend that there were rumors of a child. This is an avenue we do not wish to pursue.*

For eighteen years we did our best for her, and her death has hurt us deeply. There is nothing you or I could have done to change things. We mourn her passing, and hope you find the peace that we have found in prayer. At least now she is at rest.

The signature line and return address had been crossed out with a heavy black pen. Pig-Dog and me sat staring at each other, sifting through our memories until Twyla kicked the door. She was standing out back in her skinny jeans, "I hate New York" t-shirt, and Joe's leather jacket. "Open up!" she mouthed at me through the thick glass.

Miles had left a thin polyester uniform jacket hanging in the corner. I stuffed the manila envelope in its waist pocket and turned the jacket around so the envelope faced the wall. The .22 fit in the refrigerator, in the paper bag with the dead banana. More health food.

When I opened the back door, Twyla handed me a can of warm coke and a cheese sandwich made of white bread. There was a piece of lettuce and a slice of something yellow stuck between the slices of bread. Twyla couldn't stop talking. According to her, Doc Trina had AntMan in a private room on the third floor. He looked terrible. If we had found him any later, he would have died. The Doc was waiting for him to stabilize so she could operate. Twyla said he was going to be okay. She was sure of it. She wiped something wet from her eye, and told me that Ms. Song was sleeping, and the Doc wasn't allowing any visitors. I was supposed to stay in the ambulance until the Doc could figure out what to tell the police.

"About what?"

"She said you'd understand."

Keeping a tight grip on the sandwich, I tossed the coke into the parking lot. It hit the asphalt, spitting foam and flames as it rolled under the dumpster. "Soda can kill you," I said. "Come in and keep me company." She climbed in, and I pulled the door shut.

"Po ting," she said, bending over Pig-Dog and rubbing his sleeping head.

She must've picked up that phrase from her students or Ms. Song or the Doc. Hilo people used the abbreviated version of "Poor thing" to describe everything from a kid crying for candy (Po ting) to an old man in a crosswalk hit by a beer truck (Po ting).

I ripped the cellophane off the sandwich, bit into a chunk of stiff white bread and hard cheese. Cheddar? Maybe. Hospital food. Who could tell? The withered lettuce was a treat. On the second bite, a strip of cheese stuck to the top of my mouth. I needed to start drinking again. Too bad the red thermos had been sucked dry during my reading assignment. I reached under Pig-Dog and dug out the blue backup.

It smelled safe. Tequila and lime juice. But when I poured it down my throat, the high-test tequila and syrupy lime juice scraped the skin off my teeth and burned my throat. Luckily, it took the sticky cheese with it. There's a silver lining to every tequila cloud.

Twyla closed her eyes and laid her head on Pig-Dog's chest.

She was too innocent for her own good. Looking at her made me think of those small green birds that crashed into Joe's front window. They'd knock themselves out trying to fly through the old glass, and if they were lucky and there were no cats round, sometimes after a few minutes they'd pop back up and fly away. Most times they just stayed there on the concrete.

I ripped off another bite of fake-cheese sandwich. "I got a question for you," I said, trying to swallow.

"Ask me anything, Manny."

"Do you have any drugs?"

"I'm surprised. Don't you have one of your emergency joints?"

I shook my head. "Used it during the last emergency."

"Don't steal any from the ambulance. They're for sick people."

I was sick, but I didn't tell her because I was too busy wondering what kind of official emergency would require a joint. Another shot of tequila helped my mouth find a few stray words. "You ever been to Monterey? Maybe Santa Cruz?"

"What?"

Through the window I saw the door to the hospital swing open and Bobbie Marta step into the sunshine. She was wearing her dress blues and carrying a Marta kid under each arm. Before she could look our way, I pulled the curtain shut. The truth is I wanted to kick the door open and run. It didn't matter where. Anywhere to escape. Only the tequila kept me in place.

Twyla reached over my shoulder and peeked out the window. "The police person," she said. "I saw Doctor Trina talking to her."

"Does she know we're in here?"

Twyla shook her head. "I don't think so."

While I drank, she kept an eye on Bobbie.

"I think she's praying." She pointed out the window. Bobbie was standing in the middle of the parking lot, looking up at the sky, hugging her babies to her chest.

"Must be talking to the Madonna."

"The singer?"

"A friend of mines."

"From inside that thermos?"

"Could be. She's the one with the drinking problem. But I don't think she likes kids."

Twyla backed away from the window. "Here she comes."

Bobbie was on the move, marching toward us. I chewed faster and swallowed the last of my sandwich, something that took plenty work. No telling how long I'd be in custody, and the Big Island jail wasn't known for its snack bar.

Officer Marta kicked the door twice. "Anybody in there?" Another kick.

Twyla whispered in my ear. "Maybe we should talk to her, tell her the truth." Her breath felt warm and tender. Po ting, she was too young to know better.

The knocking stopped and Twyla peeked out. "She's leaving. It's Miles. He's coming this way. Wait. They're talking."

"Get away from the window."

Twyla covered my mouth with her hand. Her fingers smelled of hospital soap and jasmine. "Quiet." She looked again. "She's walking back to the hospital. Miles is coming this way."

I stashed the thermos under Pig-Dog.

"She's inside," Twyla said, and pushed open the door. She jumped down to the asphalt, slapped Miles on the shoulder like he was an old pal, and ran to the hospital. Miles watched her all the way to the door. "Get in here," I told him.

After he climbed in, I pulled the door shut. He told me the bad news about Ms. Song. The Doc didn't think she would make it. I wasn't supposed to tell Ms. Twyla. "I need a drink," he said. "Ms. Song was my English teacher back in the day."

I was beginning to think everyone in Hilo had conjugated verbs with Ms. Song.

"If not for her," he said. "I would've never made it out of school. Sucking English. I hate it."

While he was busy hating the common enemy, I figured it was a good time to break the bad news. "Sorry, I drank your stuff, Miles."

"What stuff?"

"The stuff in the red thermos. And the blue thermos."

He shook his head. "Not mine." He dug behind the fire extinguisher and pulled out a stainless steel hip flask, about the size of a fat wallet, and waved it at me. "Miss something?" He laughed, gulped, and screwed down the cap. He was tucking the flask into his scrubs when he asked, "Tell me, Manny, what do you know about Ms. Twyla?"

"I know she's a professor."

"She's a good looking woman."

"I didn't notice."

"A very good looking woman."

"She knows how to ride a motorcycle."

"No kidding?" He gazed out the window like he was hearing music from the clouds. "I like motorcycles. Does she have any family here?"

Good question. I was about to tell him how she could carry a shotgun under her arm and a pregnant girl on her back, when he kicked me in the shin.

"Doc's coming," he said. As he jumped from the ambulance, he waved good-bye. "Stay cool." The Doc came next, wearing her black scrubs. I was still thinking about the Judge, the real Judge, not her body in the cave, wondering if she had been on her way to tell Joe a family secret when her old enemies caught up with her. Maybe they were up in the clouds now, together. Or just gone? Nothing, forever.

The Doc yanked open the back door. Pig-Dog was sleeping, but he had his priorities. He lifted his head, smiled for the Doc, and went back to sleep. The Doc rubbed his head with her foot. I figured she needed to keep her hands clean. "Twyla told me you didn't look good." She studied me for a moment. "Manny, did you hear me?"

I tried to sit up straight.

"We have to tell the police," she said.

"Tell them what?"

"About Antony. Someone nearly killed him."

I slumped forward, digging my elbows into my knees and resting my chin in my hands. The tequila was playing with me, making me wonder if the police would look in the right places, and what the Doc knew about the Judge and Papa Joe back in the day when they were young and limber enough to wrestle.

The Doc lifted my chin, tried to see inside me. Maybe she did. Her and the Madonna could do that, see inside people. "Twyla was right," she said. "You don't look good, not that you ever did."

What did she expect? No one looks good in the back of an ambulance. Three days without sleep or food, surviving on weed, tequila and fake cheese is a prefect recipe for not looking good.

163

I handed her the manila envelope and asked her to read the letter. While she scanned, I closed my eyes and inhaled the clean plastic smell of ambulance machinery. Maybe Pig-Dog had it right. Sleep was a good place to hide. I closed my eyes.

The Doc shook me awake and handed back the envelope, saying, "So what?" You didn't know?"

"Know what?" People told her everything. They never told me anything.

"Talk to Frankie. I don't have time for this."

When she slammed the door, Pig-Dog woke up. His tongue was hanging out and his eyes were glazed from too much dreaming. I busted open a packet of saline solution and squeezed it at his mouth. Most of it landed inside, some of it smacked him in the nose.

The truth is, I don't remember much after that. The police called it "a kidnapping." Me, I only wanted to get out of that parking lot. The sooner, the better. The next thing I know, I was sitting in the driver's seat turning the key in the ignition, driving to the end of the parking lot, then stopping at the exit. That's when the passenger door opened and Twyla jumped in, still wearing Joe's jacket. "Going somewhere?" she asked.

"The Doc told me to run an errand."

"No, she didn't."

"Get out."

"Not until you turn off the engine." She locked her door.

"Go away. I'll be back."

"No, you won't. Where are you going?"

There were only two choices. Right to go up the mountain. Left to go down to the sea. It's like that on the Big Island. Up or down. The Judge never did like the cold. She was a surfer girl, so I turned right, headed for the caves.

I didn't tell Twyla where we were going, and when she told me to stop, I kept driving, so it's true that I didn't give her a choice. It was a kidnapping.

Entry 17: HOLY MOLE FIGHT

The truth is, Twyla didn't see the body until I carried the Judge up from the cave. She was playing lookout in the ambulance.

But after she helped me load the Judge in the back, she kept telling me to drive straight to the police station or the hospital. I told her the Judge didn't need a doctor or a cop.

When I took the back roads, the Judge didn't mind. She was in no hurry. Twyla was the troublemaker. Kneeling in the back of the ambulance, looking down at the Judge, she said, "The police will know what to do."

"Sure," I said, glancing over my shoulder. She had stopped zipping up the body bag and was giving the Judge a long look. I turned my eyes back to the road. Twyla was tougher than me. I had seen enough of the Judge while hauling her up from the darkness. Now we were close friends.

"She must've been beautiful," Twyla said.

In the rearview mirror, I saw her touch the Judge's cheek and leave her hand there, as if she was trying to comfort her. "Sure," I said. What else could I say? There was no point in saying that beautiful and judge were two words I would never use in the same sentence, especially now, after she had spent the night in a cave. But a little exaggeration couldn't hurt anyone, especially not the Judge, so I lifted the thermos in the air, and said, "To a tough old gal!" And followed the toast with a double gulp of Mexico's best.

Twyla bent over saying stuff to the Judge that I didn't hear because Pig-Dog barked three times and started licking the Judge's face. I guess he thought he could cure anything with that tongue. It's not something you want to see, a dog-ting licking a dead person. Even if he was trying to make her feel better, she deserved better than a hole in the head and a lick from one of the Madonna's friends.

"Where's the closest police station?" Twyla asked.

I tossed the empty thermos at Pig-Dog's head. It bounced off his skull, and he stopped administering first aid. Marta and her crew can charge me with that, too. Animal cruelty. Or interfering with a good Samaritan. If I had left him alone, he might have worked a miracle like he did with his gunshot wound. Back then I was more interested in the miraculous appearance of another thermos.

Twyla finished zipping up the body bag. When we crossed the main road, she climbed into the passenger seat, saying, "Stop at the jail. They'll know what to do."

I jacked the AC to high to keep the Judge happy. Twyla zipped up Joe's jacket and crossed her arms in front of her. According to the nametag under her right chest bump her name was Miles. She didn't look anything like Miles. When I told her so, she said that it was a souvenir.

"One stop first." I tapped the brake, just a little test, and turned left taking the back road to the Judge's house. "Buckle up. The brakes feel a little mushy."

"Let me see." Twyla stretched her leg over, pushed my foot out of the way, and pressed down on the gas. Her leg rubbed against my mine as we rushed downhill. The road, barely wide enough for a motorcycle, dropped down a steep stretch lined with parked cars. I figured it was best navigated at a crawl. Twyla kept her foot on the gas until we hit fifty.

I pushed her away and tapped the brake.

"The brakes are fine." She poked me in the ribs. "Leave them alone."

In neutral, we coasted toward the Judge's house. The day was turning dark blue, shifting to night. Before dark, I wanted another look at the Judge's garage. If I could get rid of Twyla and snatch my boat, I could take care of the Judge and Joe in one trip. The road looked clear. But I wasn't sure. I stopped three houses up from the Judge's house.

There were a couple of pickups parked along the street but no blue-and-whites sedans. That didn't mean anything. Half the cops in Hilo drove their own cars as part of a deal with the County. That's why there were so many Mustangs and Pathfinders with funky portable red-and-blue lights strapped to the roofs.

I was shifting into drive when a slick looking stud stepped out of the shadows and tapped his knuckles on my window. Even in his baggy blue uniform he looked more like a model than a cop. His bright white teeth and slick haircut belonged in a magazine, not in a cheap house with a wife and two kids cutting into his prep time. Pig-Dog barked once in his sleep, too late to be considered a warning.

Twyla leaned across me and rolled down the window. "Good afternoon," she said with a smile, her shoulder pressed into my chest. "Do you happen to know the quickest way to the police station?"

He tipped his hat. No kidding, that's what he did, like he was back in a 1950s TV show. "She's new," I said. "I'm showing her all the short cuts."

He climbed up on the running board and tried to see inside. He smelled of citrus and gun oil. A couple inches over six feet with a face that launched a thousand skirts there was something about him, even back then, that made me wonder. Most of those Hilo cops, even the fat ones, tailored their uniforms to skin tight. This guy's hung on him like a cheap hooker. "You," he said, squinting at me. "Do I know you?"

Twyla flashed a smile. "He's lost but won't admit it."

"I need to take a look in the back," he said, tugging at my arm and trying to pry the door open and me out at the same time. I've been stopped by a lot of cops, but before this guy never one who tried to do more than one thing at a time. They like to work by the numbers, first this, then that, like when they're tying their shoes.

Twyla seemed unconcerned. She pointed at his wrist and said, "That's a distinctive tattoo."

A bracelet of little black apples, each with a bite missing, circled his wrist. That's when I was certain he wasn't a cop. Cops in Hawaii can have tattoos but no cop could survive with an apple-bracelet tattoo. I was about to give him cracks, when Pig-Dog climbed over Twyla, and snapped at his fake cop's face. Scamboy let go of my hand and stepped back. "What the hell is that?"

Pig-Dog licked his dog lips and sniffed the air with his pig nose.

"He's our service dog," Twyla said.

Scamboy reached for his gun. The muscles in his neck looked like spastic snakes, maybe the ones who had bitten into all those apples. I pressed the gas pedal, edging the ambulance downhill as Pig-Dog barked and Twyla waved goodbye.

Scamboy grabbed the door handle. I stepped on the gas. His fake cop's face turned red and his eyes bulged as he tried to make his legs go 30 mph. He jumped onto the running board and stuck his head through the window.

Pig-Dog lunged. His piggy feet dug into my lap. His piggy breath clouded my vision, and his heavy pig body pressed against my chest, making it hard to steer or see the road.

"Pull over," the fake cop yelled, hanging tight with one hand while reaching for his gun.

Twyla smiled, flicked on the siren, and shouted, "Sorry, we have a call." She slipped her leg over mine and pressed my foot into the gas pedal. Scamboy held tight, like an opihi. We were going 45 with his face stuck through the window when Twyla shifted her foot to the brake. The ambulance jerked to a stop. The fake cop flew forward, bounced off the hood, and hit the ground rolling. Back on the gas, we blasted down the road, missed his legs by an inch, and rattled over the wooden bridge.

Smiling and pushing Pig-Dog off me, I inhaled hot tar and wild ginger.

"Persistent," Twyla said. We stopped at the intersection, checked both directions. "And the tattoo. Weird." She checked the rearview mirror. "Am I right?"

"Too pretty for a cop." That's what I said.

Pig-Dog growled.

Anyway, that's how we met the fake cop with the apple tattoo. If I had known then what I know now, I would have backed up and driven over his legs, then backed up and tried the tires on his chest. One thing for certain, he wasn't from Hilo or anywhere on the Big Island. Even the Car Rancher could've done a better job of faking a cop.

We turned left and drove by the give-away-food church, cruised by Blanes, going slow enough to check for Rayzah. When I didn't see her, I turned the ambulance right, then left. Blue-and-whites were crawling all over town. So were Mustangs and Pathfinders. One was parked in front of the Palace, another in the alley behind the Empire. Our little run-in with Scamboy had made Twyla hesitant about asking any of them for directions.

We rode the ambulance down the one-way alley that led to the back end of Reuben's. No sign of blue-and-whites back there. It was too scary for them, especially this close to sundown. I aimed the ambulance at a narrow space between a pickup truck overloaded with ginger root and a rusting VW bus with four flat tires. The brakes worked like a prayer, which was not at all, until Twyla stepped hard on my foot. That stopped us in place.

"You have to work them," she said. "What's here?"

Pig-Dog sniffed the air.

"Mexican food, margaritas, and companionship." Rayzah's motorcycle was parked next to a row of rubbish cans, their tops pressed down on mounds of garbage that smelled of rotting fish and stale beer. To Pig-Dog they looked like rubbish muffins. He threw himself at the back door until it gave way.

169

For a moment we stood in the alley looking at the peeling backside of the two-story building. Its flakey paint was trying to cover rotting wood held together by a tin roof. A 25,000-megawatt air-conditioner the size of a bank vault was chained to the wall, spilling a stream of stinky water into the alley.

"A chain?" Twyla said. "A thief would have to be pretty desperate to steal an air-conditioner."

College professors, right? They live sheltered lives.

Pig-Dog sniffed his way across the alley to a row of rubbish cans. He found one worthy of his undivided attention. Bracing his front paws against the top of the can, he leaned against it until it toppled over, spilling a buffet of flies, smelly pork, and petrified beans onto cracked asphalt.

We stood there watching him swallow chunks of mysterious stuff without bothering to chew, which made Twyla say, "I need a drink."

I followed her toward the screen door and the sound of banging plates. Most people go through the front door of Reuben's. Not me, not since they remodeled the front end. Those days it looked too nice. The new tile on the floor, the new tables, the new paint, the new chairs, the flat screen TVs, and the velvet paintings of Fernando Lamas and Frida Kahlo were fine for eating. But for drinking, I liked cracks in the floor, a neon glow behind long shelves of tequila bottles, and moldy piñatas hanging from the ceiling since 1984, so covered in dust and mold that they look like bloated dirigibles filled with flammable gas.

When I came in the back way, I could avoid all the niceties and see who was doing the cooking. If it was the old man, I ordered the chile verde or anything else with pig in it. He knew the secret to cooking pig. Long and slow. But if his subs were working, I stuck with the cheese quesadilla. It's hard to burn cheese to a point it no longer tastes like cheese.

As we stepped into the steaming, smoking kitchen, Twyla said, "Nice."

Two young guys in shorts, t-shirts and hairnets were working over steaming sinks. The Old Man was popping a plate of rice into the microwave, tending three cast-iron frying pans on two stoves, and telling his workers to pull a tray of roast pork out of the oven.

Twyla nodded her head at the stainless steel freezer doors and said, "Don't get any ideas."

"Ideas?" Rayzah came through the swinging doors that led to the dining room. "Him? Not likely!" She picked up three plates with one hand and waved at us to follow her into the dinning room. "Not unless the idea has something to do with food or drinking."

Before I stepped in, I looked through the safety windows cut into the swinging doors. They were there to keep the wait help from smashing into each other. I used them to spy. Good, cheap margaritas are hard to find in a world crawling with tourists who are willing to pay anything for alcohol. Drives the price up. But Reuben's served the best margaritas on the island and kept the price down. Add good, cheap food to the equation and you're talking plenty people in all shapes and sizes, mostly extra-large. So it's a good idea to keep an eye out for malcontents in the lineup.

The inside was hopping, every table full, and Reuben's wife was shoving pitchers of margarita's across the bar as fast as the two waitresses could haul them away. None of the clientele looked familiar, except for a few of the regulars at the bar, who were already so full of margaritas they were leaning forward, looking like ink blots.

Rayzah pointed at the desk behind the prep counter. "Sit there," she said. She was a smart gal that Rayzah. With the waitresses so busy picking up their orders and keeping an eye on the cash register, no one would see us behind the busy counter. I took the soft chair facing the desk and Twyla plopped down in the folding chair next to the cash register. "Two plates of Chilly Rellenos," I said, "with beans and rice." A second later Rayzah was pouring us margaritas with no salt, on the rocks into tall glasses. She left the pitcher. Me and Twyla tried shouting at each other over the roar of banging plates, exploding laughter, and the relentless, crunching of salty tortilla chips. I gave up and gulped down two glasses of tequila before Rayzah came back with a sizzling plate of pork nachos, left them for Twyla and tugged me into the men's room.

"Tell me what's going on," she said, locking the door behind her. I sat down on the toilet, still holding my glass. She leaned against the sink. Between sips I gave her the particulars about AntMan's and mine's adventure, except for the part about the Judge.

"Holy mole." That's what she said. Joe used to say that all the time. I didn't find out until later that him and her weren't talking about the same mole. Her mole was a menu item, a chicken dish with chocolate sauce that cleansed your soul and your intestines at the same time. Papa Joe's mole had something to do with WW II and a gal named Mary. I think.

She jabbed my shoulder. "Manny, wake up. What now?"

Someone banged on the door. Neither of us paid any attention.

"I need your help," I said.

"What?" She punched me in the chest, grabbed the glass from my hand, and downed what was left in one gulp. That's the good thing about drinking on the rocks. There's no danger of ice-cream headache.

I figured a compliment would ease the way. She was wearing her black uniform shirt that sported two pitchers of margaritas bumping heads. Across her chest pink lettering screamed, "Drink more tequila." Her hair was pulled back in a bun and her jeans were spotted with grease, beans and kernels of rice. There's nothing more exciting than a woman dressed for hauling Mexican food and margaritas, so I said, "Nice outfit."

"Screw you, Manny." She handed me the empty glass and used the neck of her t-shirt to wipe her mouth. "Who you trying to kill now?"

That was kinda mean since I hadn't tried to kill anyone yet, but I figured she was still hurting from Joe disappearing, so I didn't waste any more time on compliments or other bullshit.

"Pop the door," I told her. "Just a sliver."

She opened it, and we saw Twyla sitting at the desk, Joe's jacket wrapped around her mini-frame. The neon glow of a waterfall sign for Stella-Artois was backing her up. On the wall next to it, a frowning Frida Kahlo on black velvet gave us a dose of stink-eye. Twyla had already made a friend.

"She's a good kid," I said.

"She's no kid. And you still owe me a shotgun."

"Not me. Do me a favor. Keep her here while I slip out the back."

"Where you going?"

"Places."

Maybe she thought about what would happen to Twyla if she kept hanging with me. Or maybe she was thinking about that leather jacket. Anyway, finally she said, "I need a drink. Lock the door after me." She shoved her way into the noise. As I tried to pull the door shut, a thick hand grabbed it and tugged in the opposite direction. "Let me in!" a drunken bass shouted. I snapped the door shut, catching fat fingers, gave it slack and watched the fingers disappear. "Hey!" A fist slammed against the door.

"Occupado," I shouted.

"You suck!" The door shook under the shout and another blow.

I was thinking about kicking some ass, but Doc Trina always told me I should count to ten backward before doing anything drastic, so I was busy counting down from five when I heard Rayzah shouting for me to open the door. She came in holding a pitcher of Reuben's best, yelling at the crowd to "Get back! Get back!"

I locked the door behind her.

"Hey," a fist slammed into the door.

Rayzah sat on the sink, drinking from the pitcher. She wiped her chin with the neck of her t-shirt and exhaled a cloud of Sauza Silver. It smelled better than the rest of the room, which had the delicate reek of airline disinfectant, Ajax cleanser, and dried pee. She handed me the pitcher. Life got better with each swallow. I said, "You know anything about the Judge and Papa Joe?"

"Everybody knew about them."

"Not me."

"You have a big mouth. No one tells you anything."

"Me?"

"You can't keep a secret."

"Me? It's my business to keep a secret."

"How much weed you been smoking today?"

I tried to count, digging into the cloud of bathroom stink and extra-strength margaritas for a memory, but nothing surfaced. "I been busy."

"While Joe's on vacation?"

That threw me. "Sure," I said, trying to remember my story. "He's traveling." Lucky for me, a fist banged on the door and a familiar, nasty voice shouted, "Open the friggin door."

Rayzah shook her head. "At least you're keeping one secret. Okay, this is the last time, Manny, and only because that girl isn't safe with you. I'll keep her busy while you slip out the back. In this crazy crowd, she won't see you."

"Open the door!" someone shouted.

"Shut up." Rayzah kicked the door, which produced more pounding, barking, and then a man's voice screamed," Shit! Get that frickin dog out of here!" More barking. Then more people yelling and screaming. "Shit! Shit! Shit!"

Rayzah yanked open the door, and we stepped into tequila-fueled chaos.

Reuben's son was hanging onto the neck of big guy who kept screaming, "I gotta pee. I gotta pee!" They were dancing the mariachi, swinging in circles, surrounded by shouting customers and shrieking waiters and a knife-wielding cook. Pig-Dog was dancing with them, snapping at butts and heels. Twyla was guarding the cash register, kicking anybody who got close enough to smell money. She pointed at the front door, as I heard Rayzah shout, "That's a good looking cop."

Scamboy was standing outside with his hands on his hips, trying to see over the crowd of drunks throwing plates of enchiladas at each other.

"He's not a cop."

"Even better."

"You wouldn't like him. He has an apple tattoo. Here." I made a circle around my wrist. "And he tried to shoot me."

"Can't blame him for that. The shooting, I mean. There's no excuse for the tattoo." She pushed me toward the kitchen. "Frankie knows about the Judge. Ask him." She pushed the hair off her forehead and charged into the chaos. "Follow me! Crap. This doesn't look good."

Twyla was swinging a plate at a big guy with a skanky ponytail. He reached for her neck. The plate connected with his head and he went spinning away.

I can't guarantee the accuracy of this section of the report. It's always hard to remember exactly what happened in a food fight, especially one involving Mexican food and tequila. As Ms. Song would say, things get a little fuzzy in a barroom brawl. But I knew I couldn't leave Twyla, not there.

I grabbed her arm, and we punched, kicked and gouged our way to the kitchen, past the freezer. I grabbed a bottle of stray Sauza on the way. Pig-Dog and Rayzah covered our retreat, snapping and biting and barking at the revelers. Music was blasting, food was flying. People were kicking and screaming, plates were flying like Frisbees. Time was standing still, then it was running forward. We threw our shoulders at the back door, busted through, and landed safely in the stinky quiet of the alley.

We slipped on the wet asphalt. Twyla caught me, and we managed to stop our fall and turn around as Pig-Dog flew out the door, followed by Rayzah. She slammed the door and pushed a dumpster in front of it to hold back the human tsunami. Pig-Dog howled at the stars. Twyla and Rayzah howled with him. They weren't saying much but they had plenty volume. Pig-Dog broke the spell by stopping to check the rubbish cans for snacks. We watched him knock down an overstuffed rubbish can. It rolled toward Rayzah's motorcycle. She kicked it back at him, and climbed on her bike.

"Where you going?" I said, wiping blood off my forehead. Maybe someone had hit me with a margarita glass. Ms. Song would've called that ironic.

"My shifts over. I'm going home."

Twyla stood next to me as Rayzah kick-started her motorcycle.

"Take Twyla with you," I said.

Twyla slipped her hand into mine, and whispered, "No way. I'm staying with you."

Rayzah gave us a long look. She twisted the gas, jumped the bike a few feet, pulled in the clutch and stopped next to us. She reached over, lifted Twyla's chin, and studied her face. "What do you say, girl?"

Twyla threw her arms around her and kissed her cheek. While they played sisters, Pig-Dog, aka "The Cannibal," dragged a pig-butt bone the size of a truck axle toward me. Like I told you, Hilo is a tough town.

Twyla stepped back to me.

As she revved the engine, Rayzah yelled, "Take care of that jacket. Papa Joe was a good man."

She popped the clutch, and the three of us watched her disappear down the alley in a cloud of exhaust.

Entry 18: FRANK PARANOIA

Back in the 90s, Frankie cashed in his county retirement plan and bought an acre on the Hamakua Coast. The sugar cane plantations had gone out of business and were selling off chunks of overworked soil to anyone who didn't mind buying land that had been irrigated with pesticides and decorated with workers' camps and the occasional big white house.

Frankie owned one of those big white houses. North of town on the ocean side of the highway, his place was hidden beyond a cemetery that was overgrown with weeds and balanced at the edge of a steep cliff. Frankie didn't trust visitors. To keep them away, he let the road that branched off the main highway rot in the rain until it was a strip of dirt made of basketball-size boulders, gravel and sinkholes. It was a private road, and he refused to do any repairs, which meant that when it rained, usually from September to July, if you wanted to get to Frankie's house, you had to have a four-wheel drive.

Once a week, Papa Joe used to drive the Ural out there for coffee and cake. The rough ride didn't matter to him. He said that the view from the cemetery, out there at the edge of the world, was as close as he would ever get to paradise. He said it made him want to leap into the blue between the ocean and the sky. Frankie told him to take the dead people with him. Me, I didn't like bad roads or cemeteries.

Frankie didn't care what I thought. He liked his old road because from his front porch he could see anyone on it long before they could see him. He called it "RoadBlock Avenue." Whatever it was, stoned was the only way I could drive it.

I hadn't been to Frankie's place in years, so it took me a couple of hours to find the right turn. I drove over shaky bridges, down narrow roads lined with camp houses built on postage-stamp lots sitting shoulder-to-shoulder, their roofs almost touching. After two U-turns, I skidded into a muddy swamp that Twyla said looked like a road. I was hoping the dark clouds were only passing. If it started to rain, we'd have to get out and swim. The two-ton ambulance was made to carry everything from a baby to a sumo wrestler, but it wasn't a boat. It was dead weight, with or without the Judge.

We felt our way over the bumps, me gripping the steering wheel and Twyla leaning forward, hands on the dash, straining to see, like a couple of wanna-believers staring at a Ouija board. Flashes of lightning helped light the way. Through a cloud of rotting bananas, chicken crap, and exploding rubbish cans, we pressed forward, inhaling recycled air pumped through a moldy AC.

"It's freezing in here," Twyla said. "I'm opening the window."

She had a blanket wrapped around her legs, I had a towel around my neck, and we were sipping anti-freeze borrowed from Reuben's. As we inched our way along the muddy road, she found the right button, and salty, warm ocean air rushed in through her open window. Pig-Dog went crazy, howling and spinning in circles. No matter what we said or did, he wouldn't stop bouncing off the walls. I figured he was pissed because we had him in the back, keeping the Judge company. Twyla had better eyes than me. She pointed into the darkness. "A cemetery."

She was pointing at Papa Joe's favorite place for a picnic. The graves were overgrown with a towering blend of stinkweeds and rampaging grasses, including the celebrated Guinea and Cali brands. Only the tiptops of the gravestones were visible. Prime oceanfront real estate.

"Nice view," I said. "Good spot for whale watching."

"What about the dead people?"

"Joe didn't mind. He used to go there for lunch."

"I want to see it."

When she reached for the wheel, Pig-Dog jumped up front and barked first at me then her. He didn't stop until we passed the turn and headed for a tiny light at the end of the road. The moon came out from the clouds, and the light turned into Frankie's house. Twyla grabbed her chest, "It's right out of Poe!"

I stepped on the gas. I didn't know anything about Poe, except he had something to do with a football team from Baltimore. But I knew Frankie had weed at his place. I stepped harder on the gas. The wheels spun for a second. Then we shot forward. Frankie's two-story house grew bigger and bigger until we saw Frankie standing on his porch waving a storm lantern.

We parked next to his Ford F-100 loaded with lawn gear. I left the engine running, and left the AC on super high to keep the Judge happy.

"The Doc is looking for you," Frankie shouted at us. "Something about you stealing an ambulance."

While Twyla sloshed through the mud, I slipped the Judge's envelope from its hiding place and stuck it in my back pocket. Pig-Dog was already sitting next to Frankie, looking up at him like he was his long-lost master.

"What exactly is this?" Frankie asked, holding the lantern closer to Pig-Dog.

"We're not sure," I said. "He's a friend. I think."

"Is it a pig or a dog?"

"Both. I think." I tossed Twyla my scarf-towel and she used it to rub down Pig-Dog until it was almost possible to discern the outline of his true identity. Pig kept his eyes on the road. Frankie rubbed his chin the way he did to generate ideas. When it didn't work, he shifted the lantern closer to Twyla and smiled. "Well, a young lady." He took a step closer to her. "You must be..."

"Twyla." She held out her had.

"A beautiful name." He looked behind him to see if Pig-Dog had made a move, then turned back to shake her hand, saying, "Franklin to my mother and Manny. Frankie to my friends."

The two of them did the hugging-kissing thing. I remember because Frankie made it more of a bear hug than one of those European touch-and-goes that pass for hello. Twyla didn't seem to mind. She hugged backed, making her biceps bulge, and followed that with plenty of chatter about Pig-Dog's exploits. Frankie returned the favor by telling her all about his career in law, his successful retirement, and finished with, "Time to celebrate. A beautiful woman has come to visit in an ambulance." He checked to see if Pig-Dog had moved. Frankie didn't trust animals anymore than he did people.

Pig-Dog didn't mind. He was too busy watching the road.

"I like that." Frankie used two fingers to pet him on the head. "I can always use a guard dog. If it is a dog? My last one ran off. Didn't like the cemetery. Can't say I blame him." He looked at Twyla. "Dealing with dead people isn't easy. But they keep away the paparazzi. Who's in the ambulance?"

I didn't know anything about paparazzi in Hilo, so I started talking about our visit to the chicken-ranch and finding AntMan beat-up at the caves. While I filled in the details, Frankie spent the time glancing at Twyla and Pig-Dog and the ambulance. When I was through, he said, "The Doc told me all about that. Have you seen the Judge?"

Twyla looked at me, and I said, "Hey, Frankie, you got anything to drink?"

"Follow me. We shouldn't be standing out here like targets." Frankie had his priorities. Hide first, then questions. He was stepping through the front door when he said, "By the way, my neighbor is trying to kill me."

I figured he was just being Frankie, what Ms. Song called being overly dramatic, what the Doc called being a paranoid psycho. "What neighbor?" I asked. "You don't have any neighbors."

He held the door open for Twyla. "Oh, I have neighbors, all right. You've been wandering around in your own little world being Manny the pothead while I'm out here on the frontlines."

"Frontlines?" If anyone was on the frontlines, it wasn't a guy in a house with an ocean view. I had a .22 in the refrigerator, Joe's body in my freezer, the Judge in a body bag, and a frigging pet that looked like it belonged in a horror movie. That was the frontlines.

Frankie told us to leave our shoes in the hallway. Most people left them outside, but Frankie didn't like people stealing his shoes or counting flip-flops to see how many people were hiding inside. Hiding being what Frankie thought people did at home. He patted Twyla on the shoulder. "You, my dear, will understand. I have a feeling you can sense these things. Am I right?"

"Certainly."

Either she was a good actor or she actually believed him.

"Good. Good. I'll show you. Follow me."

His place had been built in the 30s, a craftsman style bulging bungalow with high ceilings, wood floors, double-hung windows, and colonial columns. There was a dinning room on the left, a living room on the right, and a staircase in the middle. Frankie paused at the first step to say, "Lock the door!" Then he headed up the stairs to the second floor, holding Twyla's hand and using his lantern to light the way.

Frankie didn't like paying for electricity, especially if it involved the need for new wiring. The house was full of useless wiring left over from the days when fuses were as big as carrots and wiring caught fire every other Friday. Nowadays, his electrical system consisted of three kerosene lanterns that Joe had given him along with a warning about fire risks. Frankie wasn't afraid of fire. He had let the paint peel away to reveal raw wood, then let rainwater and ocean spray soak in until the house turned into part sponge. Frankie figured it would take fifty gallons of gasoline to catch his place on fire.

Even though he could have hooked up to the county water system for a few cents a day, he collected rain from the roof and piped it into a 500-gallon catchment tank. Cheaper that way, and the pipes doubled as his escape route if he ever needed to slide down from the second story. For toilets he had a couple of porta-potties stolen from a construction site in Kona. For decoration, he had tacked up a few surfing posters.

He was standing next to one of them at the top of the stairs, waving his lantern like a torch in a dark cave. "Come, come," he called. Pig-Dog and me made the stairs sag, creak and groan as we huffed and puffed toward the flickering light. "Did that pig-thing wipe his feet?" Frankie asked.

"He's very clean," Twyla said. "And his name is Pig-Dog, not pig-thing."

Frankie blocked Pig-Dog with his knee, and said, "Show me your feet."

Pig-Dog hung his head but didn't lift his feet.

"He's a big pecker. Where'd you get him?"

"A present," I said.

"From the Madonna?"

"How'd you know?"

"He looks the part. Like a Trojan horse."

"He's a dog," Twyla said, and whistled softly. "Come here, baby."

Pig-dog swiveled in behind her, peeking around her smooth corners to eye Frankie. Even pig-dogs know better than to mess with lawyers, especially paranoid ones like Frankie who smoked enough weed to make a goat crazy.

"Well, if he's a friend of yours, Twyla, fine. Tell him to come along." Keeping his eyes on Twyla and Pig-Dog, Frankie led us down the hall to his room. It was as big as a basketball court, but the only furniture was a canvas cot with a punctured mosquito net. On the far side, double doors led to the lanai.

Frankie opened the doors, stepped outside, and motioned for us to follow. There were two canvas director's chairs, a blue and white cooler, and a brass telescope pointed across the river. "Sit here, my dear," he said, his hand on the back of the director's chair nearest the railing. "Sorry, I don't believe in wasting money on furniture. Manny, drag the cooler over here and you can sit on it."

In his double-thick socks, faded Levis, and a hoodie with a UH Rainbows logo across the chest, he looked almost normal. Almost.

My butt rested on the cooler for a couple of seconds before he made me stand up. The breeze off the ocean blew cool air up my pants legs, as he reached in the cooler and dug out three aluminum cans of Maui Bikini Blond. Frankie didn't have money for chairs but he had plenty for imported beer.

"Help yourself." He tossed a can to Twyla. I snagged a Blondie and popped it open. A fat tortoiseshell cat appeared out of the shadows, took one look at Pig-Dog, and jumped onto the railing. Like a stone, he dropped two flights down, bounced off the catchment tank, and disappeared into the shoulder-high grass.

A slippery trail led through the grass and down the cliff. At the bottom, slippery rocks were covered with fat opihi and crashing surf. Frankie sat down in the free chair and set his beers between his legs. With his hand resting on the professional-grade telescope, he stuck his bloodshot eye to the eyepiece and searched the darkness across the river. Way off in the beyond, pinpricks of light looked like twinkling stars.

I was working my way to the bottom of my first can of Maui's best when Frankie, still eyeing the scope, said that he had stopped at the hospital on his way home. "The Doc is worried about you, Manny."

Twyla dug at her back pocket. "I'll call her."

"Sorry, young lady, no reception out here." He was still eyeballing the scope.

"What are you looking at?" I asked.

"My evil neighbor." He motioned for me to take a look. I tried to see through the tiny eyepiece. Everything looked fuzzy and black, while he said, "A realtor from Honolulu made an offer for my place, a very good offer from a buyer who wished to remain anonymous." He pointed across the river. "I think it's them."

"I don't see anything."

He pushed me out of the way and looked through the lens, made a few adjustments. "Don't touch anything, just look. Put your hands in your pockets."

Twyla pushed me and him out of the way and peered through the lens. "I see it. There's a double-wide trailer. Storage sheds, two big warehouses, all of them lit up."

Frankie was glowing. Maybe it was the lantern, but both his beers were empty. "We'll see more in the morning," he said. "He's building a metropolis over there. Night and day. He's a busy little developer."

He said developer the same way some people say crack-head. I figured he was tripping mad because someone dared to move in and block part of his view.

"A week ago they came back with a second offer. This one was lower than the first. The realtor, even for someone from Honolulu, sounded embarrassed, even nervous."

Like I said, Frankie had spent too many years prosecuting people. No more bright side of life for him. I didn't blame him. Heck, I knew plenty of crazy people in Hilo who deserved to be suspects in a lineup. Me, for instance. Burying the evidence so my pal wouldn't get framed had to be jail worthy. But if a guy wants to buy land, build a few hundred houses that no one can afford, and make a gross profit, that's the American way, right?

Frankie didn't think so. He dove deeper into his paranoia pool. "Now that the Judge is missing," he said, "I guess I'm next."

"What does the Judge have to do with this?" Twyla asked.

"I'll show you. Stay here."

He walked inside. Twyla and me shrugged at each other. I drank one of his beers, tossed the empty over the rail, and snagged another one just in time to see Frankie walk in with his bolt-action .22 rifle, a box of 200 shells, and a bag of weed. Not a good combination. "There comes a time in a lawyer's life when taking care of lawns isn't enough." He looked down at Pig-Dog. "Let loose the pigs of wars, right, fella?"

Pig-Dog showed some tusks. Maybe it was a smile.

"Don't smoke and play with a gun," Twyla said, pointing at the bag of weed Frankie was holding to his nose.

I wasn't worried. Sober or stoned, Frankie couldn't hit anything. When he bought the Marlin on sale for $119 from a grocery store near Volcano, the box of .22 shells were a promotional item. Me and him had tested a few dozen shots at a stray rooster. Every other round was a dud. They must've been sitting on the shelf long enough to soak up the Big Island's atmosphere. We had given up after Frankie accidentally shot out the back tire of his lawn tractor. No roosters had been hurt during filming.

"Frankie shoots better when he's stoned," I said, hoping he'd roll one.

He sat down with the gun and weed in his lap. "Where's my beers?"

I shrugged.

He set the shells on the railing and picked a beer out of the cooler. An owl flew along the tops of the trees. Friggin owls. Twyla didn't see it. She had her eyes closed with Pig-Dog curled up at her feet. Frankie was too busy sipping beer and rolling a fat one on the stock of his bargain-basement bolt-action to see any owls. When he stuck the fat boy in his mouth, I did the honors, lighting the end with my Zippo. It was good tasting weed, a mild Sativa that reminded me of cinnamon toast. I blew the exhaust at Pig-Dog. Frankie did the same. Twyla sniffed the air, woke up, and kicked at us. "Stop that," she said. "He already has enough problems."

Pig-Dog kept sleeping the sleep of smoky innocence.

"I miss the Judge already," Frankie said. "She'd know what to do about my neighbors."

Twyla looked at me, like I was supposed to say something, so I said, "Joe would know."

Twyla kicked my shin, and said, "If you start shooting at every flakey real estate developer in Hawaii, you won't have time for much else."

"I got plenty of time." He pretended to spit on the ground. "For him and his friends."

"He has friends?" I said.

"Plenty. I'll show you in the morning."

"If someone has friends, he can't be all bad." It was stupid but I said it. I don't know why. Maybe the weed was too good. I was feeling like the world made sense, a whole lot of smoky sense. When Frankie tossed the roach over the rail, I half expected it to fly back into my fingers. That's how good life felt.

Twyla opened her eyes and asked for the bathroom. Frankie pointed at a portable in the back yard. "Plumbing problems at the moment."

As her footsteps faded down the stairs, he said, "A good looking woman."

"Sure."

"I like her name. And the jacket. That's Joe's jacket, right? How'd she get it?"

"She's sneaky." Keeping an eye on the door, I dug the envelope out of my jeans. "Take a look at this." Frankie held it by two fingers, like he was trying not to get germs from the blood stains.

"Hurry, before she gets back, read the letter." I told him how I found it the day he helped me mow my way to the Judge's house. He gave it a look, and while he tried to remember how to read, I took his baggie and rolled another joint with his extra-long Bob Marley papers. He was still staring at the letter when I lit the joint and inhaled. So far I was getting the better part of the trade.

Frankie drank more beer.

"What does it mean?" I asked him between inhales.

"It means the Judge and Joe had a daughter, they gave her up for adoption. They went their separate ways, the Judge to

186

college, Joe in the Army, and in '93 the Judge got this letter from the adopted parents but she didn't tell Joe."

"How do you know that?"

"Because the date's on the letter, and because I wrote Joe's will. You're in there and so is his daughter, and he never asked me to change it. For some reason, who knows why..." he rubbed his chin and gave me a quick look. "Maybe she was trying to protect Joe. He was a big guy but he wasn't as tough as he looked. Maybe she knew there was nothing the two of them could do. It wasn't their life anymore. As far as I know they never saw or met the kid. Then out of nowhere the Judge changed her mind. She must've been trying to get to him the night she disappeared. I guess."

Maybe he used different words but that's the way I remember him telling it. I understood most of it, even the part about Joe and the Judge having a baby. I couldn't picture them but I could understand it. The part I didn't understand was the part about me being in a will.

Frankie killed his beer, tossed the can, and held out his hand. "Give me another blondie." I dug into the cooler and tossed him two, feeling like a nurse handing a patient his medicine. He opened one with his thumb, stuck the other can between his knees. "The Judge will explain it all."

"Sure," I said.

"Once we find the Judge."

"Yep. The Judge will know."

Frankie handed me the papers, took the fatty from my fingers and tried to smoke it to death. Between puffs, he said, "If my neighbors didn't already get her."

Twyla's footsteps came running up the stairs and down the hall, giving me just enough time to fold the evidence and stick it back in my pocket. By then the envelope was looking pretty beat, like something I would hand into Ms. Song for a grade.

Frankie contemplated the smoke drifting from the end of his joint. "Is this weed as good as I think it is?"

I guessed it was. Twyla was standing over me, moving her lips with no sound coming out. I was thinking that the Judge must've looked a lot different in the old days, when the Judge was young and mobile, flexible enough to hit the dance floor. Maybe even, if she was lucky, she looked a little like the young woman standing over me.

Twyla said, "This pot smells like a day-old donut."

"I'm all for day-old donuts," Frankie said, "especially apple fritters, the ones that look like cow pies."

"I had some good malasadas at the academic sensation meeting."

"Academic Senate," Twyla said. "I wish I had some chocolate milk. I love donuts and chocolate milk."

"Joe liked donuts," Frankie said.

We watched the moon duck into the clouds. After a few more tokes, Frankie said, "Donuts won't hunt you down and shoot you for locking up their relatives." Then he oozed to the floor and curled up, one hand on the telescope's tripod, the other on his .22 bolt-action rifle, with his head resting on Pig-Dog, using his gut for a pillow. A few seconds later, both of them were snoring.

"Will he be okay, Manny?" With the starry night behind her, Twyla looked like a saint on a holy card, or a missing person on a flier at the post office. She kicked my shin, and whispered, "Will he?"

"Let's go. I want to check something." I was too stoned to understand families, but I knew where there were plenty of graves, and I needed two of them.

Entry 19: HEADSTONERS

We barefooted down the stairs, borrowed an oversized hurricane lamp, and climbed into the ambulance. Twyla handled the steering while I gazed out the window. She was looking for "Driver's Training." I was looking for ghosts.

As we headed away from Frankie's place, our headlights caught a pack of skinny dogs crossing the road. I reached over and pressed the horn. Twyla stepped on the gas, and the dogs disappeared into the shadows. She looked at me and said, "We should have brought Pig-Dog."

"Frankie needs him more than we do."

"For what?"

"A sleeping pal. He sleeps alone too much." I had both hands on the dash. Twyla was a good driver but the road was crap. I buckled my seat belt.

"I like to sleep alone," she said, and flicked on the brights.

I watched the California grass brush against my window, like scratchy sandpaper tentacles. It could crawl for miles and then pop up to 10 feet. Poison kept it quiet for a few weeks. Cutting made it grow back thicker. Frankie says it came to the Mainland on the slave ships from Africa and spread across the continent. He said it was history's way of reminding us of history.

Only Guinea grass was worse. I don't know where it came from, but it grows in thick, round razor sharp patches that even goats wouldn't eat. Burning only singes the tips. The rest of the plant is made of asbestos. Poison makes it grow taller. And driving through it will scrape the paint off your truck or ambulance.

"How about you, Manny?" Twyla asked. "Do you like sleeping alone?"

I saw an opening in the Cali. "Turn!"

Twyla jerked the wheel left, and we went sloshing through the mud, widening the road as we plowed back the walls of grass. She shifted into low gear and tried steering with one hand. Her arm muscles bulged but she kept us on track, even in the muddy parts, which was pretty much the whole way. The engine was whining and the tires spitting mud. I rolled down the window, leaned out, and inhaled ocean smell. "Water ahead."

The Cali slapped me back inside as a rock wall popped up in front of us. Before I could reach for the parking brake, Twyla took her foot off the gas and we sank to a stop.

"We're here." She turned off the engine and managed to slide the key into the front pocket of her skinny jeans. "I could get used to driving an ambulance," she said. "It's better than teaching." She climbed out, tried to squeeze between the ambulance and the rock wall, gave up halfway in, and climbed onto the wall.

It was an old wall, handmade without concrete. Rocks, some as big as watermelons, some as small as softballs had been placed carefully together to form a three-foot wall at the edge of a cliff. When I climbed up next to her, I could see a couple hundred feet down. Moonlight glistened as waves broke against jagged rocks.

"Life starts here," she said, standing at the edge, arms out like she was going to fly, "and goes on forever."

Lately, I hadn't seen much proof of forever. I was certain the people buried behind us would agree. "Let's find the cemetery."

She jumped down and squeezed into the ambulance. "Wait a minute," she yelled out the window. That gave me time to search my pockets for the joint I had borrowed from Frankie's stash. I lit up as she backed the ambulance into a fifteen-point U-turn. When the front end was pointed at the main road, she dug out the lantern, and turned it up as high as it would go. Back on the wall, she held the lantern over her head and took the lead, saying, "Just in case."

We picked our way along the rocks to a spot where a chunk of the cliff had taken the wall with it and fallen into ocean. I imagined bones sticking out of the cliff face. That happens. On Maui, the next island over, the island that looks like Malibu, they have plenty bones sticking out of the earth. A group of grade-school kids found a hand with three fingers that pointed to a burial site. The dead have a way of popping up. I guess that's what Twyla meant about life going on forever.

From where we were standing, we could see three rows of graves. They looked like heads of swimmers bobbing in a grassy sea. I put out the joint and looked up at the sky. The truth is, I was looking for the Madonna, wondering when she would show up. This was her kind of territory.

"We could see more," Twyla said, "if someone had mowed the weeds in the last couple of years."

"Maybe they don't want to be seen."

"Who?"

"The dead people."

She jumped down and made her way through the weeds to the first tombstone. Looking down, she said, "I want to be cremated."

That came out of nowhere but it sounded reasonable for someone who was a long way from her seventy-second birthday. I wondered what the Judge wanted. To be dropped in the sea with Joe? To go up in smoke or buried under ground? She wasn't talking. It was still too early for her to stop keeping secrets.

While Twyla bent over trying to read the writing on a tombstone, I finished working on the joint. When she gave up and took the lantern with her, I followed the light. Not even I

191

was dumb enough to be caught without light in a graveyard. Each step I took, those dead people whispered, Get off me.

"Cremation," Twyla said, opening a tiny gate. No more than a foot tall, it was connected to a matching fence that formed a rough square around four graves. Parts of it had been smashed flat. "Cremation is simple," Twyla said. "Any mortuary can do cremation."

Obviously, she hadn't been living in Hawaii long. Nothing is simple here. She left out the part about showing up at the mortuary with a body on the missing person's list. I stood beside her at the edge of a semi-circle of gravestones. We were looking at three generations: A grandmother and grandfather who died in 1893, a daughter in 1917, and a granddaughter in 1959. I didn't write them down but they were something like that.

She rested her hand on my shoulder. "Why just a daughter and granddaughter? What about their husbands? Brothers? The fathers?"

The truth is, I've always had trouble keeping track of family ties. Once people get past mother and father into grandparents on two sides, aunts and uncles, cousins, nephews and nieces, I stop listening. It's too confusing. Locals swear by it, who your parents were and who their parents were, and where they all came from. They remember all of it, especially where they were born and where they went to high school. Me, I was born in Manila but I didn't stay there long enough to remember it or get anywhere near a school.

She held the lantern close to my face. "What about you, Manny?"

"About me?"

"Your body. When it's over."

"They can leave me where I drop."

"They?"

"People. I'll drop, hit the pavement, and pretty soon people will get tired of walking around me, or stepping over me. Sooner or later one of them will sweep me up. Toss me in the rubbish. It doesn't matter." That's what I said, and I still believe it.

I bent down and dug my fingers into the dirt. It was dark and clammy and crawling with worms. Not exactly what Joe requested. Twyla touched my head, and when I looked up, she was ringed in spooky moonlight. "Don't worry," she said. "I'll take care of you."

That's when we heard the engine noise. We climbed onto the wall and saw three sets of high beams bouncing along the muddy road, aimed at Frankie's second-story light. As they passed the cemetery, Twyla pulled me down with her, but I caught a glimpse of a pickup truck, jacked up on fat tires and transformer suspensions, before we landed behind a tombstone.

Twyla was digging her phone out of her tight jeans, asking, "What's Frankie's number?"

It was in my head, somewhere.

"Shit," she said. "Never mind. No reception. We have to move."

I grabbed her arm. "I'm driving."

She jerked her arm free, jumped onto the rock wall and ran for the ambulance. The trucks were closing fast on Frankie's place. The house went dark.

"Hurry!" Twyla called back to me. She was already in the driver's seat, and the engine was running. That girl could move. When I heard the first shot, I was jumping into the passenger seat. As I pulled my door shut, she stepped on the gas. Our tires spun in the mud.

"Ease off the gas, girl."

Twyla had two speeds. Stop and go. She hit the brakes, and I jumped out, ran around back, gripped the door handles, and climbed onto the bumper. "Now! Give it gas. Easy!"

She floored it, and the wheels spun, spitting mud. She braked. Floored it, dug us deeper. "Hold it!" I jumped down and let some air out of the back tires, jumped back on and yelled. "Go!"

She floored it and we squished our way to hard ground, slipping and sliding, spraying my back with mud as we turned onto Frankie's road. We were going too fast for me to jump. I heard a shotgun blast.

The ambulance lurched forward, picking up speed, then hit a bump and bounced. "Stop!" I banged on the door. She hit a pothole, then the brakes, and I flew off, falling back and landing on my ass. It hurt, I can tell you, even in the mud. And it didn't help to be sprayed with more mud as she drove away. It was beginning to feel a lot like my first night with Twyla, minus the pigs. Not counting the ones shooting at Frankie.

From my seat on the ground I had a good view of Twyla's brake lights. Always the spectator, never the hero, I stood up as the brakes lights flashed red. The ambulance was reversing at me, spitting mud. I stepped off the road. The ambulance went by me, stopped, and the passenger door flew open. "You okay?" Twyla shouted.

"I thought you forgot me."

"Never." We heard Frankie's .22, two sharp cracks, answered by a flurry of pistol fire, shotgun blasts and glass breaking. "Sorry. Get in. Sorry. I was excited."

One thing I could say about that girl, she was always polite. As I climbed in, she flicked on the siren and running lights. Spinning circles of red and white swept through the cab as she stepped on the gas. I saw the flames. Frankie's truck was on fire. The flames jumped to his house, climbed the walls to the second story, and the night turned bright red. We saw the flashes before we heard the shots. From the backs of trucks they were shooting in the air as he popped off .22 rounds from a second-story window.

The trucks backed up, turned, and pointed their headlights straight at us. I gripped the dash as they came at us in a flying wedge. Twyla pressed hard on the gas and shouted, "Buckle up."

Believe me, I had already strapped in. The two trucks in back spread out, giving us three targets. Twyla drove straight, right down the middle of road rage. I was wishing I had one last joint, or at least some shells for Joe's .22. A shot pinged off our windshield, leaving a spider-web as a reminder.

Twyla screamed, no words, just a wide-open scream, muscles in her neck and arms tense and tight in the bloody glow of headlights and fire.

"Ramming speed," I whispered, and closed my eyes, wishing for one last joint. I heard gunshots and horns blaring and screeching brakes, felt myself lifted into the air. When I opened my eyes, we were flying off the road, jumping over a ditch, scraping over a discarded porcelain tub, touching down, and sliding through a sea of sticky grass. We were frozen, with our mouths open, like in a buddy movie, waiting for a drop off the cliff into the final credits. Instead, we hit Frankie's shed. The engine was smoking. The house was on fire. Frankie's truck was burning down to scrap metal. But we were still breathing. Not counting the Judge. And the shed was still standing, minus a few boards.

Pig-Dog was waiting for us, standing at the front door, barking at the pickup trucks as their taillights faded into the night. One of them was crashing through the cemetery, trying to get back on course. Twyla grabbed two fire extinguishers out of the back and ran at the blazing house. She blasted the flames with foam. Somehow the cemetery buster managed to find its way back to the road so it could chase after the gang's taillights.

Pig-Dog was barking at the front door. I followed his instructions, kicked it in, and followed him up the stairs through the smoke. Frankie's door was locked. I kicked it open and found him face down on the lanai, one hand on his rifle the other on his gonads. Pig-Dog bit into his elbow and started dragging him toward the door.

I grabbed Frankie by the armpits and helped drag him across the floor. The smoke was getting thicker but it didn't bother me. I guess it was my years of training. Don't let people tell you that smoking weed isn't good for you. You have to cough to get off, and I was doing plenty of it. Pig-Dog arched his back and used his tough pig legs to tug as I pulled. The two of us managed to drag Frankie to the stairs. The flames were reaching through the windows but Twyla was in the hallway, hitting them with short bursts of foam, like a fighter pilot in an old movie working her machine gun, conserving rounds, but still tearing holes in the enemy.

"Get him outside," she yelled over breaking glass.

Pig-Dog shifted his grip, bit into Frankie's shorts. I did my part, keeping Frankie's shoulders and head up, backing my way down the stairs, dragging Frankie with me, feeling for the next step. We were leaving a trail of blood, but Twyla had stopped the flames, replaced them with clouds of poisonous flame retardant.

"Keep moving," she yelled as she tossed the fire extinguisher. She kicked away Pig-Dog and grabbed Frankie's ankles, straightened up, and we lifted his ass off the ground so we could carry him across the floor and out the door.

We kept going until we reached the ambulance. When she dropped his feet, I saw blood soaking through Frankie's jeans, high up on his thigh. "He's out," she said. "Put him down." I sat him down in the grass and slowly lowered his head.

We were beat, all of us breathing hard, sucking in air. But Twyla was stronger than she looked. She ripped open Frankie's belt and tugged off his jeans. The hole in his leg was pumping blood. Pig-Dog tried to lick it. I pushed him out of the way and pressed my hand directly on the gusher while Twyla jumped into the ambulance and came back with surgical cord, gauze and tape. She was getting to know that ambulance pretty good. She wrapped the surgical cord around his thigh, above the bullet hole, and tied it with a knot that looked like the bow on a birthday gift.

She lifted my hand off the wound, stuck a wad of gauze into the blood, and handed me the tape. I wrapped it around his leg, looping it over and over again until the tape ran out. "Now what?" I asked.

"Let's move the Judge."

While I grabbed the feet-end of her body bag, Twyla climbed in and pushed at the Judge's shoulders. When the Judge was about to drop, Twyla jumped down and supported the body bag long enough for the Judge to make a graceful landing in the mud. Twyla was already using the armpit method to drag Frankie toward the ambulance. I grabbed his feet. For a lawyer he was heavy, and Pig-Dog wasn't much help. He barked once and ran off as we struggled Frankie into the back of the ambulance. We were about to close the door when Pig-Dog came running back carrying a can of Bikini Blonde between slobbery teeth. Frankie's arm was hanging off the gurney, and Pig-Dog dropped the can into his bloody fingers.

Frankie eyes opened slowly, looked at me and Twyla, then down at his hand. It took some effort but he managed to lift the can, pop the top (all with one hand), and say, "Good dog." When he tilted the can toward his pie hole, Twyla realized what was happening, snatched the can, and passed it to me. "We're taking him to the hospital."

Frankie refused to go anywhere until he shot his neighbor. "Get me my rifle, Pig-Dog."

"Don't!" Twyla shouted. She kicked Pig-Dog in the ass and out the door. Then she slammed it shut and told Frankie that he'd have a better chance of hitting his target after the Doc had plugged the hole in his leg. That made Frankie think. He reached for the beer. I held it way from him and was about to take a drag when I saw blood on the can and my fingers. I opened the door and tossed the can in the grass

Twyla was already in the driver's seat. From what I had heard, the commandments tell you it's okay to lie in an emergency, so I told her, "You're the better driver. You take him. I'll keep an eye on the place. Take care of things."

Frankie told her he wanted to stay, the bleeding had stopped, and he never felt better. He said he didn't want to go. He hated the hospital. And where was his beer? "Can Pig-Dog come with me?" Then he closed his eyes and passed out.

"Out," Twyla shouted, gunning the engine.

I jumped out and looked at the disaster that used to be Frankie's house. One wall was scorched. His truck was charcoal. The Judge was on her back in the weeds. But not everything was bad. I figured there was still beer in Frankie's cooler. I stepped over to the driver's window. Twyla leaned out, put her arm around my neck, and pulled me in close, where she could press her cheek to mine. Her breath touched me. She had some heat. "Be careful," she said.

I could take care of myself. That's what I was going to tell her, but she didn't give me a chance. The ambulance was already heading toward town.

Entry 20: NOODLES & SPICE PACKETS

I managed to knee-crawl the Judge into the narrow space under Frankie's post-and-pier house. She'd be plenty cool under there until the sun came up. For added protection, I told Pig-Dog to stay with her and bite anyone or anything that came close. He barked once.

Up on Frankie's lanai, I sat in the dark and watched the moonlight on the river. Pig-Dog came up and sat next to me.

"You're supposed to be watching the Judge," I told him.

He laid his head on my bare feet and started snoring. That's another example of why I shouldn't be held responsible for what he did later. He didn't take orders from me. And I never said he did. No matter what the cops tell you, I only said he was a present from the Madonna.

Anyway, listening to Pig-Dog's snoring, a kinda punk-rock lullaby, I dozed off. When I woke up, he was still snoring and the sun was crawling up and over the horizon, like a convict climbing over the barbed-wire fence at the Hilo's Correctional Center. I inhaled fresh morning air with only a hint of burned house, greasy Pig-Dog, and dead Judge. And I started coughing.

The hacking woke up Pig-Dog. He helped me find a package of hamburger in one of Frankie's coolers. It was only a couple weeks past green, so I found Frankie's camp stove, hooked up the propane bottle, and lit a flame. Frankie's military mess kit doubled as a plate and a cooking pot. As soon as the meat was sizzling, Pig-Dog dug his tusks into my ankle. I tossed the burger on the floor before he could rip through to bone.

While he was chewing, I boiled enough water to cook a package of freeze-dried noodles. For half price, Frankie had bought a closet full of the stuff from Papa Joe. The noodles were made by a company called Raunchy Ramen and during my testing that morning proved to be almost flame proof. Only the cellophane wrappers were singed. I made a note to ask Frankie how to get a patent for ramen as insulation in home construction.

When I tried to toss the unopened spice package off the lanai, Pig-Dog caught it in midair. "Don't eat that crap," I said, picking up a military spoon big enough to double as a shovel. "Don't!" I pointed the spoon-shovel at his beady eyes. Without chewing, he swallowed the packet. I tossed another packet over the rail. He leaped, caught it, and swallowed it as he flew over the rail. He landed in the mud. His eyes bugged out. He bounced up, chased his tail, going in circles faster and faster until he spun out and circled the house, snapping at weeds.

Must've been the aluminum, or the mystery spice. Plenty times, I had seen that spice cause serious side effects, like blood pressure spikes high enough to power a 300-pound politician in a marathon. Raunchy Ramen should be required to list the serious side effects on their cheap packaging: "For your safety, keep the noodles but dump the spice packets."

When my noodles were boiling, I used the spoon to hold them down while I drained the hot water over the rail. Only a couple of stray splashes hit Pig-Dog. No problem. His greasy coat was made to handle.

I ate the noodles straight, in one long slurp, tipping the pot toward my mouth and shoveling them in with the spoon. I learned that from the movies. My first balanced meal in a decade went down smooth and sweet. Two more packages minus the spice packets helped steady my stomach nerves enough for me to focus through Frankie's telescope. His neighbor's place looked quiet and peaceful if you liked dual-wide trailers, rusted storage buildings and peeling Quonset huts mixed in with mango and avocado trees and 40-foot-tall explosions of bamboo. The evil compound was surrounded by hog-wire fence and a gate with two guards that didn't dress like missionaries, unless missionaries wore jeans and muscle t-shirts and carried baseball bats. The skanky compound looked more like a base-yard for a construction crew than a home for a real estate developer.

The trailer had a wooden porch attached. A big black SUV and a little red Porsche, a restored coupe from the 60s that looked like a scone on wheels, were parked out front. Beyond the cars, across a wide gravel road bordered with mango trees, there was a storage building as big as a football field that was old and rusty enough to be left over from the plantation days.

The side doors were open and a couple of pick-up trucks were parked inside, with men crossing back and forth, from the shadows to the light. The trucks were off roaders, with heavy-duty suspensions and fat tires. I gave up trying to see the license plates, and watched a funky blue pickup stop at the front gate. Papa Joe's Datsun. Why was I not surprised? The guards did some chatting with the driver, checked the back, before the gate went up. The old Datsun slid across the gravel and stopped at the entrance to the parking garage. As an early Christmas present, the Datsun's door swung open and out stepped the Singing Professor.

I twisted the lens, trying to focus. The Professor was wearing knee-high rubber boots, baggy jeans, a baggy green t-shirt, and his floppy lauhala hat with the bill pulled down over his eyes. He climbed into the back of Joe's truck and must've yelled something at the men inside the parking garage because a couple of them walked out, flipped him a middle finger, and walked back inside. He lit a cigarette, blew smoke at the sunrise. Even from a half mile away, I could see the pasty glow of his nicotine-stained cheeks. Well, maybe not exactly. Maybe I was imagining that glow, but I could see his guitar in the cab.

As I rubbed my eye to bring it back to life, Pig-Dog walked in looking winded and smelling of raw hamburger. He had an unopened package of noodles clamped between his jaws. He sat next to the telescope, no doubt proud of himself for surviving the spice-packet attack. Through the periscope I could see the Singing Professor with his hands cupped around his mouth shouting at the rusty garage. Pig-Dog had better ears than me. He jumped to his feet, and barked twice before twisting his grizzly mouth into a toothy sneer.

Across the river, ten men wearing long pants, t-shirts, and baseball caps, filed out of the storage building. None of them had a guitar. The Singing Professor jumped down and waved them into the back of the truck. He was digging through his pockets when the screen door to the trailer swung open and two men walked out. First came a medium-size thug in khakis and a green polo shirt. A few steps behind him, a tall, thin model in skinny jeans, a green polo shirt, and a red scarf stepped out and let the screen door snap shut. Even without his police uniform he looked familiar. The way Scamboy stood there relaxed and loose, like a manikin in a store window pretending to look down at his phone, made me want to beat him senseless.

As if there weren't enough pickup trucks, another one pulled through the gate. Clean and shiny black with fat tires and chrome rims, some kind of Ram MegaCharger, it kicked up mud and gravel as it passed Joe's Datsun. It parked near the trailer and a beer belly big enough to carry twins stepped out from the driver's side. The back of the truck was filled up with Joe's Ural. Seeing it trapped there made me hiss, "The Car Rancher."

Pig-Dog snarled.

On their way to the trailer, the Singing Professor and the Rancher shook hands. Like buddies, the two of them walked up the steps to the porch, where they did the handshake thing with the plantation boss and his model flunky. All of them were pals. Business partners. The Professor took a wad of something from his pocket and handed it to the flunky. The flunky nodded and handed it to his Boss. After giving it a quick look, the Boss tossed it to the Car Rancher, who stuffed the wad into his back pocket. The Rancher lifted his stomach off his belt, and all four of them looked across the gulch at Frankie's place.

I dropped below the railing. It wasn't much of a hiding place, like trying to hide behind a picket fence. Pig-Dog hunched down next to me, his eyes boring holes across the river.

Well, well. I knew a Ruskie troika when I saw one, and this one was big enough to be a quartet. The Singing Professor was picking up cheap farm labor in a stolen truck. The Car Rancher was collecting his reward for trying to burn down Frankie's place. The Boss was planning to buy more land. And skinny boy was thinking about how tight his pant were. Frankie was right. His new neighbor needed a kick in the ass.

The slow moving river, no wider than a single lane road, twisted through the gulch, crawling around and over exposed rocks. In spots it looked shallow enough to cross, but if it started raining that could change fast. At the mouth of the river, crashing waves covered the small beach. Frankie had told me about a way to cross near a waterfall. I saw the waterfall. It would be a hard climb both ways, down our side and up the bad side, but it would put me close to their HQ, and there would be plenty of cover in the creeping jungle of bamboo, guava and banana trees. I picked up Joe's .22 marlin.

Pig-dog had different ideas. He bolted down the stairs. I followed him out the door, and across the yard to the Frankie's shed. He stopped at the sagging double-doors and waited, looking back at me.

The Ace padlock had a rusty key in it, which didn't say much for Frankie's paranoid-pothead security system. But it did make it easy for me to open the doors. Frankie's VW bus was hiding in there, pressed up against sagging walls under a sagging roof.

I wiped away a few layers of cobwebs. Underneath was a two-tone camper model that needed welding, dent pounding, Bondo slapping, sandblasting, and three or four gallons of paint to hide the graffiti and rust. When I looked inside, Pig-Dog was already sitting in the passenger seat, his head bumping against the roof, his nose pressed against the glass. I had forgotten how small those buses were.

The key was in the ignition. I climbed in, moved the stick shift back and forth, up and down until I found neutral. The steering wheel was new, made of dark wood and chrome, more suitable for a GTO than a VW bus. To keep from hitting my head on the roof, I had to sit hunkered over, hands and elbows resting on the steering wheel, like a bus driver waiting for a customer to find the right change. I pressed down on the clutch and turned the key. The engine backfired once, twice and died. I tried again. Another backfire. On the third try, the engine caught, held, and settled into a rough idle. I pulled the parking brake and went around back to open the hatch. Frankie had dropped in a shiny new rebuilt engine, a tiny four-cylinder with five horsepower. The belts were new. The muffler stock. It looked like the exhaust pipe for a moped. The oil level was good. The tires, ChinaGrips, were sticky with thick rubber. There was a trailer hitch.

I climbed back in and tried the radio. Nothing. Pig-Dog smiled into a growl. He wanted me to drive that underpowered beauty to the neighbor's place and blast away at the bipeds while he tore the heart out of the beer guzzler who had shot him. I could see that in his head.

He barked three times and the Madonna appeared, sitting between us. It was a tight squeeze, but no one seemed to mind. Wearing black-and-white golf shoes, checkered slacks, and a green polo shirt with a polo player charging out of her left breast, she wrapped her arm around my neck and shoulder. "Manny, I need a favor." Her fingers dug into my neck.

"Not now. I'm busy." I was picturing me and PigDog driving the VW into the Developer, watching him and his buddies fly apart in different directions, like bowling pins hit by a slow-moving VW bus. Pig-Dog looked at me from across the Madonna, his thin lips revealing sharp, yellow tusks. He was smiling. That friggin mind reader.

"The man in Joe's truck, the one you call the Singing Professor, I need you to go to his house." That's exactly what she said. Her breath smelled of Southern Comfort. "To pick up a friend of mine."

"You have a friend?"

"If you hurry, you should be able to reach his house before he does. He'll be leaving..." she checked her Timex Weekender. "Soon."

"Any chance we can run over there and shoot the Developer first?"

"This is more important."

Pig-Dog growled a nasty pig grunt. The Madonna told him to hush. She handed me a fat joint. "At least think about it."

The joint between my fingers made it sound better. She produced a lighter, one of those longboys made for lighting BBQ grills. Sorry to say, I didn't hesitate. I stuck the joint between my lips and while she held the flame to some of Puna's best, I inhaled deep enough to stretch my t-shirt a couple sizes.

"You do this for me, Manny, I'll see what I can do for Papa Joe."

"What, bring him back to life?"

"Better."

With the smoking joint between my lips, I said, "How about the Judge?"

"Her too."

I checked with Pig-Dog. He sniffed the air, narrowed his eyes. Like me, he didn't trust her. I took a few more hits before the Madonna disappeared. Then I saw her in the rearview mirror. She was lifting up the engine hatch. "Can't pull anything with this engine," she said. "I can fix that for you."

I jabbed the joint in the ashtray. "Never mind that," I shouted. "Just remember your promise about Joe and the Judge. Buckle up, Pig."

I was edging the old V-dub out of the shed, hoping the Madonna was still back there sucking exhaust, when I heard her yell. "Wait!" We were going so slow I didn't have to hit the brakes. Just taking my foot off the gas made us stop. She opened the side doors and tossed in Frankie's .22 bolt-action and a box of his shells. "Take this," she said. "Don't hurt any pigs! You hear me?"

"Sure." That's what I said, but she was gone before I could tell her that wasn't a promise. What if a pig accidentally stepped in front of the bus? Pig-Dog was reading minds again and he didn't like that image. He gave me a dose of stink-eye. He was right. In that bus, our only protection against the real world was a piece of tin masquerading as a front end. A head-on with pig would not be a pretty sight. Not for us.

Pig-Dog pointed his snout at the road. This time, stepping on the gas made the VW lurch out of the shed and skim over the dirt road. As we passed the cemetery, I kept thinking about those gravestones: grandfather, grandmother, mother, and daughter. Like the Doc says, no one escapes. You can take her word for it. No one escapes.

Entry 21: THE LAST PAY PHONE

We wasted fifteen minutes before I realized that I didn't know where I was going, so I parked across the street from Dinky's, home of the last pay phone on the Big Island.

As soon as I opened my door, Pig-Dog leaped over me and disappeared into traffic. A hand-painted sign on the front window of the tiny mom-and-pop store across the street said Dinky's was selling hot dogs for 50-sense. I stepped out and waited for a hole in the traffic. No truck driven by a singing professor and loaded with a dozen farm workers passed going either way. That was a good sign, the first good sign since the Madonna flew off without giving us the directions to the Singing Professor's house.

As usual, she had been in a hurry, coming and going in a spiritual rush that worked great for revival meetings but was too flashy for day-to-day rescue work.

From a cloud of diesel exhaust, Pig-Dog appeared, dodging cars and trucks, crossing lanes, coming my way. A sputtering moped broke his rhythm but only long enough for a pause. He leaped over the moped and dropped a phonebook at my feet. Across the street, in jeans, t-shirt and white apron, Mr. Dinky was was standing in his doorway, shaking his head and wagging his index finger at me.

The phonebook cover was wet with slobber and teeth marks. I flipped through the pages to the S-section. There was nothing under "Singing Professor."

I shouldn't blame the Madonna for my aimless wandering. The truth is, the wandering was my fault. As the Doc likes to tell me, accepting responsibility will help with my recovery. It was me who had been using the Singing Professor's nickname for so long that I had forgotten his real name. I knew what the Madonna would say about that. Manny, buy a friggin cellphone!

Instead, I tried Pig-Dog. "Show me the way."

He shot into traffic and I followed, dodging between a water truck and a black SUV, a bus and a noisy Harley. The black beauty was bolted to Dinky's outside wall, right next to the doorway where Dinky was standing and giving me stink-eye. Pig-Dog had chewed through the flimsy security cable, so there was no way to re-attach the phonebook. I set the book gently on top of the phone, spine-side up, stuffed between the coin slots and the wall, while Dinky lectured me about the old plantation days when folks had respect for other folk's property.

You mean when folks were property, I wanted to say. That's what the raging professor from Vegas would have said. Instead, since I was representing the Madonna, I went the respectful route. "Sorry, sorry. I apologize." I nodded my head while I dug in my pocket for change. When I realized I didn't have any, I asked for three hot dogs, and Dinky grumbled his way inside, shaking his head. Ethical standards were one thing, selling dogs another. While he stuck red dogs into fluffy white buns, I tried to think. It wasn't easy. Dinky had hulihuli chickens spinning on his roaster. Juicy chicken fumes made me think in circles.

Twyla wasn't an option. When she heard the Singing Professor was involved she'd go crazy and come looking for me so she could lead the charge. Ms. Song was in no shape to answer the phone. The Doc would kill me. That left...

Dinky came back with three steaming torpedoes. They looked well worth the buck fifty price of admission. I tossed two of them at Pig-Dog, stuck one in my mouth, and looked down at my two quarters change. As I chewed, Dinky asked, "Is that dog-thing for sale?"

Pig-Dog inhaled his two dogs and sat down inside the store, near the cash register, looking up at an ancient rotisserie spinning the three juicy chickens.

"Smart, that dog," Dinky said. "I get one daughter at the college. She could use a big dog like that. For protection. You think they let a dog like dat size in the dorms?"

"The university?" I was rifling through the phone book. "Do you know the number?"

"Get yourself one of those cell things," Mr. Dinky said, and pointed to the pay phone. "No one uses dat ting."

"That's what people tell me."

"My daughter has one cell ting. No need for numbers. Use it once, the number stay in there."

Lucky for me, Mr. Dinky decided it was time to feed Pig-Dog a SlimJim, still in the wrapper, which gave me time to slam two and two together while I squinted at a line of miniscule numbers under the UH listings. My friend the librarian answered on the first ring.

We chatted about her motorcycle, and the weather and her catching two students hooking up in the History section. I told her it was so cold down there you needed to huddle close or freeze to death. When I described the Singing Professor and asked if she knew his real name, she said, "That fool." It took her a minute of tapping a keyboard before she said, "Here it is. Professor Notso Cool."

"That's his real name?"

"Don't be silly." She gave me the real name and an address north of town. "That's the address where we've been sending his overdue-book notices. If you see him, tell him he has three books that need to be returned. They're two years overdue."

"I'll do that." Right after I feed him to Pig-Dog.

"Is Ms. Song still in the hospital? Will she be okay?"

I told her not to worry. That's what I tell people when I think they'll start crying if they hear the truth. She couldn't do anything to help Ms. Song so why put her through the sad part? We said our goodbyes. By the time I hung up I had forgotten the professor's name, but I remembered his address.

I said good-bye to the black beauty coin-op. Pig-Dog growled his goodbyes to the roasting chickens, and everyone was happy. Except Mr. Dinky.

"What about that dog?" he asked. You want to sell him? I give you free hot dogs for a month."

I stepped toward the traffic.

"His weight. I'll give you his weight in red dogs." A semi-truck rushed by, and Mr. Dinky tried one last offer. "How bout twenty bucks?"

I was thinking, trying to figure the weight of red dogs as me and Pig-Dog ran to the VW. The math was too tough, so we jumped into the van and headed north toward Honokaa. A couple of times I glanced at Pig-Dog, trying to see him as an outline filled with red dogs. "How much you weigh?" I asked him. He didn't answer. I guess he was more interested in the road.

By keeping the gas pedal pressed to the floor, I could make the VW go 55mph downhill and 25mph uphill. We were on a steady, sluggish rollercoaster ride, with green fields on the left and blue ocean on the right. The Golden Madonna wasn't much of a mechanic but she had worked wonders with the weather. As far as we could see, a bright blue morning was spread across the sky.

On a narrow bridge with two narrow lanes, Papa Joe's truck appeared in my rear view mirror. It came up steady and slow but fast enough to catch us, switch lanes, and rush by like he owned the place. The Mad Professor was leaning back, wearing his lauhala hat, one hand on the wheel, the other holding a red dog. The farm workers were hunkered down in the back. By the time me and Pig reached the end of the bridge, the old truck had climbed a steep hill and disappeared around a sharp curve. I wasn't worried. I knew where he was going.

I dug out the Madonna's joint, stuck it in my mouth and thought about taking the Professor prisoner.

Pig-Dog shook his head.

I inhaled and pictured me kicking the Singing Turd until he spit out the news about who had killed the Judge. Then I remembered Papa Joe telling me that beating people would make me into one of those people who got a charge out of it. I knew the type. I had worked for few. Maybe when it came to the professor, I was one of them.

With the unlit joint between my lips, I slowed to 10 mph, made a left turn without tipping over, and drove uphill past a stretch of rolling green fields spotted with grazing cows. Pig-Dog growled as we passed two modern castles set well back from the road and protected by iron gates and swimming pools. The gates were decorated with jumping bronze dolphins. The castles looked like they had been airlifted from Malibu or an architect's nightmare and dropped in the middle of the old cane land. Now they stood out like counterfeit jewels in a sea of pure green jade.

A few minutes up the road, the mailbox for the Singing Professor's place was almost hidden by high grass and a line of Eucalyptus trees. Pig-Dog saw it first and stuck his face in my ear, barking to test my hearing, loud enough to make the joint fall out of my mouth. I caught it and hit the brakes at the same time. Scraping against tree branches, the van slid off the road.

Either the brakes worked or the mud did. We came to a stop next to a narrow gap in the trees. On the other side of the eucalyptus, a hog wire fence led along the road to a gate made of galvanized steel tubing. The gate was open. A gravel driveway about 200-yards long reached to a single-story house. It was nothing special, a kit-box with a tin roof and a few bedrooms and bathrooms. It was bigger than AntMan's place but not much. Joe's truck was parked in front of the house. Chickens were pecking at the dirt around its tires. To the right, a gravel road led around the house to rolling fields of ginger, grazing cows, and Mac nut trees. To the left in a shallow gulch next to a banana patch, a pigpen held twenty or thirty fat, slow moving pink pigs. Domestics.

Still wearing that silly hat, the Singing Professor was leaning over the fence and jabbing at the pigs with a cattle prod. I knew it was a prod because the pigs squealed and squirmed and jumped after he jabbed them. Me and Pig felt it way up on the road. We jumped with them. I figured that was the Madonna making a point.

The gate was closed and there was nowhere for the pigs to run. Anytime one of them got close to him, the Mad Professor gave it a jolt. He was smiling. I was thinking about Frankie's rifle. Professor Sicko jumped down and walked back to Joe's truck. He climbed in and drove it around the house, up to a hill that overlooked his fields. The Ugly Professor stepped out, still carrying his cattle prod, and surveyed his empire. His aliens were weeding their way down endless rows of ginger. He must've thought it was cotton.

I sat back, stuck the joint in my mouth, and inhaled. The air tasted of weed, eucalyptus and pig shit. Up the road, a pack of wild pigs was working its way along the fence line, moving toward us and the open gate. By the looks of them, they weren't here for the view. The grass along the sick prof's driveway had been dug up pretty bad, rotto-tilled by them or their relatives.

When I opened the door, Pig-Dog bolted over me and ran up the road to meet his friends. There must've been twenty of them, nearly a regiment. I tucked the joint carefully into my shirt pocket and climbed up on the top of the VW where I could get a better look at the Singing Farmer's layout. I wondered if I could drag him into the barn for some useless torture with a pitchfork. As I was dreaming, two kids busted out of the house and ran down the porch steps, kicking at chickens, tossing a Frisbee, and spinning in circles.

They stopped. Pointed at the open gate, and yelled something at the house. The front door opened and a tiny black-and-white goat clattered down the stairs, followed by a woman in jeans and a thick sweater. She was holding a pitcher of milk and what looked like a tray of cookies. When she saw where the kids were pointing, she dropped the tray and the milk, and started running.

Jeez, she could move. I figured the kids kept her in shape. She ran past them and kept going, the kids right behind her. Like their mother, they had some speed. They stayed close. The mini-goat dropped way back, out of sight.

Pig-Dog and his pals had reached the van. They plowed by the tires, sniffing, digging and grunting, and kept moving, aiming for the open gate. In the far away distance, the Singing Professor tapped the cattle prod in his open hand, like a twisted cop on a twisted beat.

I dropped to the ground, opened the side door, pulled out Frankie's .22, and bolted a .22 into the chamber. At the gate, the pigs were waiting, lined up behind Pig-Dog. I stood behind them and watched the woman running at us. She waved. "Close the gate," she yelled. "Please. Close the gate."

Some of the pigs were eyeing the thick black dirt along the driveway. A few of them were looking down into the gulley at the domestic pigs, no doubt hatching a plan for a prison break. Dignified and erect, Pig-Dog stood like a Civil War general (on all fours) ready to lead a charge.

The mom stopped a body-length from the assault troops. As her two children swirled around her, like kids on a merry-go-round, she grabbed each of them by an arm. They came to a stop by dragging their feet.

"Who are you?" she asked.

I stepped through the pigs, and stopped when I was close enough to see her swollen black eye. I set the gun down on the ground, and stretched my hand out to her. "Call me Manny," I told her. "Most people do."

She had thin fingers but a strong grip. The kids looked like they belonged on a cereal box. Clean and cheery, freckled and pink, they dug their tiny fingers into their mother's jean-covered legs. Pig-Dog pressed his shoulder against my hip. I wanted to tell her that the Madonna had sent me, but I figured Frankie's rifle and Pig-Dog had already made me look crazy enough, so I tried, "Professor Song sent me."

She wiped something from her eye. The kids looked up her, at me, at Pig-Dog. Behind them, down the road, the Singing Professor was climbing into Papa Joe's truck.

"My children are coming with me," she said.

Joe's old Datsun was churning up a cloud of dirt and gravel, scattering chickens, cats and goats. "There's plenty of room," I told her. "But we better get moving." I motioned for her to follow me, and Pig-Dog cleared a path for us through his friends. Once we were through, the pigs closed up ranks.

I opened the VW's double side-doors for her and the kids. They climbed in and sat on the back bench, with Mom in the middle and a little squiggler on each side. The one closest to the door, pointed outside and said, "Look! Daddy."

Papa Joe's truck skidded across the gravel and came to a stop. The Singing Professor jumped out, carrying his cattle proud instead of his guitar. He picked up Frankie's .22. If not for the silly hat, he might have looked dangerous. He stopped at the line of wild pigs,

"Where are you going, dear?" He asked, softly, like he was concerned about her. Then he showed his nicotine-stained teeth. The pigs weren't buying it. When he took a step forward, they held firm. He stopped. Maybe he realized they weren't his domestics, maybe he was a chicken shit. His voice changed to mean and nasty. "Leave the kids," he said.

I should've gotten back in the VW and driven away. I didn't want those kids to see their daddy getting the crap beat out of him. But I was thinking about those pigs and that cattle prod, and the Madonna saying she didn't want any pigs hurt in the filming. I stepped through the roadblock of pigs and stopped just out of the professor's reach. Pig-Dog crouched next to me, ready to leap.

"Give me the gun." I held out my hand. "And the prod."

He stuck the prod in his belt, pointed the rifle at me. "Come and take it."

"Bully to the end, right, Professor? Just like in school."

"Do I know you?"

Was I that forgettable?

I didn't have time to ask before he jabbed the gun barrel at me, like he thought it was a spear. I grabbed it, swung it left and up, pointing it at the sky as a shot went off. Pig-Dog lunged and landed on his chest, knocking him backward. The gun came free in my hand. Professor Demento, with Pig-Dog on top of him, hit the ground squealing, one hand holding off Pig, the other one reaching for his prod.

I walked back to the VW. The kids and mom were watching with mouths and eyes wide open. Some writers might describe it as shock. I think they looked more like a family at the circus. Amazed and delighted. Pig-Dog and the Professor were rolling toward the house. Pig-Dog looked like he was enjoying himself. The Singing Professor not so much. He had given up on the cattle prod and was holding Pig-Dog around the neck, trying to keep his snapping pig teeth away from his almost-human neck. It was a circus act, one where the lion broke free and ate one of the clowns.

The herd of pigs ran by them and headed for the pigpen.

In the back of the VW, the mom was holding her kids close, whispering for them to be quiet, not to worry. I hid the gun behind the front seat, climbed in and tried the ignition. Nothing. One of the little squeakers pressed a finger against a window, saying "Doggie. Doggie. Wait for Doggie."

"Don't worry," I shouted over the barking and howling and screaming professor. "He's smarter than he looks. The pig. He can take care of himself."

The kids waved their arms in the air, shouting, "We like pigs. We like pigs." I could see why they were the Madonna's friends.

On the fifth try, the engine started, and after a few minutes of burning the clutch and twisting the steering wheel, I managed a sweeping U-turn. We headed for the main road. In the rearview mirror, three pink domestics busted out of the trees. They were chased us, trying to keep pace with the lumbering bus. Pig-Dog was right behind them, carrying a cattle prod in his mouth and a miniature goat on his back.

215

Entry 22: ABOUT FACING TRUTH

The Hilo Medical Center reeked of air-conditioning too cold to ignore, too sterilized to breathe. The Doc acted like it was a fresh breeze off the ocean. She sucked it in as we climbed the stairs. The Doc was a great believer in exercise. Between big gulps she asked, "Can I trust her?"

"Sure," I said, but the truth is, I wasn't sure about anything. Not even who her was. The truth is I needed a drink, a fat joint and a stomach pump, in reverse order. Dinky's 50-cent hot dog was eating a whole in my stomach. Trying to keep pace with the Doc, I wiped the dirt and sweat off my forehead. My hand came away smelling like hot dog. The good news was the Doc had found a hiding place for the Singing Professor's wife and two kids. The bad news was it was on the top floor and Twyla was up there standing guard. Bernadette was the mom's name, and the kids were named something that sounded like Kid #1 and Kid #2.

We stepped into the hall and Doc Trina pointed at a door marked "Quarantined. No Entry!" She slid a key card through a reader. "Get in."

I was too tired to argue. Whatever she was selling, I was buying, even if I needed a prescription. Inside, AntMan and Frankie were kicking back in hospital beds. Even with bandages wrapped around his head, chest, shoulder, and gut, AntMan managed to hug me with his good arm while whispering, "Take me with you. I can help."

"Don't listen to him," the Doc said. "He's not going anywhere."

Did I tell you the Doc had good ears? She was blocking the door, like a bouncer in black pajamas. "Frankie, too. He's not going anywhere."

"Don't listen to her." Frankie was sitting on the edge of his bed, holding a Koa wood cane with two hands while Pig-Dog tugged at the other end, trying to pull him to the floor. How Pig-Dog had found the room, I wasn't sure. Somehow he had slipped away after the Doc confiscated his cattle prod and midget goat and locked me in a supply closest.

"The Doc worries too much," Frankie said. "My leg works better than an intern right out of law school." He slapped his bad leg. Wrapped in a couple hundred feet of bandages, it didn't look better than anything, except maybe Antman.

"You got a hole in you," I told him.

"Not any more." He rubbed his thigh. "Fifty-two staples. No problem. I'm mobile, baby."

I'm telling you this so you'll see there was no way either of those two goobers could have been blamed for what happened later. Believe me, they talked a good story but they looked like hell, dazed and confused, pale and weak, in hospital-issue pajamas that tied in the back and would show ass if they tried to escape. No bad guy would take them seriously.

"Watch this." Frankie pointed at a wheelchair parked next to the door. "Fetch, Pig-Thing, fetch."

Pig-Dog dropped the cane, spun around, and leaped into the chair. Instead of bringing the wheelchair back to Frankie, he sat there with his tongue hanging out, looking at the Doc for a sign.

"Traitor," Frankie said, shaking his cane at Pig-Dog.

"Neither of you is going anywhere," the Doc said. "If you start bleeding again, you're finished. If the bleeding doesn't kill you, I will. And I'll come after you, Manny, so leave them right where you see them."

217

Did I tell you that the Doc almost had bedside manners?

AntMan fell back deep into his pillow. "I got one good arm and two good legs," he said, and closed his eyes. "I'm kinda sleepy though."

Frankie grunted. "When do I get my phone call?"

The Doc pressed hard against Frankie's bandaged leg until his face went deep red. "Feel anything? Do you?" she asked, resting her 110 pounds on his fifty-two staples.

"Jeezsus, that hurts."

"And you, Antony Marta?" She stepped back and concentrated on poor AntMan. "Maybe you'd like me to call your wife up here?"

Bobbie "the Cop" Marta was downstairs with her two kids, parked out front in a squad car with Rayzah. The Doc had already warned me to stay clear of them. I didn't need the warning. Every minute of every day I lived in fear of Officer Marta busting through the door with a stun gun and an arrest warrant.

AntMan was snoring. To change the subject, I asked Frankie, "How's the medication? Any leftovers?"

"I don't have time for this." The Doc tossed me a laundry bag. "Put your clothes in."

I stripped off my jeans and shirt, giving the Doc plenty of time to see what she had been missing since our last encounter, and tossed them in the bag. When she had her fill of the view, she took the bag and walked out, saying over her shoulder, "Keep an eye on these fools, Pig-Dog."

"Here," Frankie handed me a zip-lock baggie with a joint and two tiny white pills. "My last joint. You look like you need it. Be careful with those sleeping pills. They work fast. Me, I'm tired of sleeping."

I looked around for a place to hide the baggie.

Frankie said, "Pig-Dog told us all about you and him helping that woman and her kids."

"You talked to Pig-Dog?"

"He can carry a tune," AntMan whispered, his eyes still closed.

Pig-Dog was watching us, pointing his nose snout at each new speaker. I tried a few questions on him. "Got any drugs? Are you pig or dog? Will it rain tomorrow?" He kept his mouth shut, except for the part where his tongue was hanging out. I told Frankie, "Maybe it was the Doc you were talking to. I get those two confused."

Before he could say anything, the Doc came back in carrying blue scrubs and a pair of black PF Flyer high tops. "Sorry, no laces." She tossed me the pile and I geared up, slipping the baggie in my waist. My bare feet fit into the doublewides, and looked pretty good, even cool and fresh without laces. I told the Doc she had good taste in shoes.

"They're yours. You left them at the psych ward after your last visit."

"And the laces?"

The Doc shrugged. "Locked up. With your belt."

She must've figured I was still a patient. "Never mind," I told her. There was plenty of tape lying around the hospital.

The Doc took me into the hallway. We peeked into a room a few doors down. Ms. Song was lying in there with her eyes closed. Miles was sitting in a chair next to her, leaning back against the wall with his mouth open and his eyes closed.

"How is she?" I whispered.

The Doc shook her head, and held me back, saying, "Let her rest."

My mind must've been working because I wasn't stupid enough to push my way inside and wake Ms. Song. In the hall, the Doc rubbed her eyes. Air-conditioning will do that, spread allergies and the like by shooting dust, dirt, and the smell of microwaving popcorn into your sockets.

"I need a drink," the Doc whispered, and pointed down the hall. The Madonna and her had a real chemical dependency. You can take my professional word on that. Never mind what they say about my drinking. Or smoking.

The door had her name on it. She pushed me in, and I sat down in the chair facing her metal desk. There was an army cot on the left, a small refrigerator behind her desk, and a bookcase filled with stacks of manila folders on the right. Above my head, the AC duct was stuffed with paper towels and covered with strips of black duct tape. The whole place was no bigger than an interrogation room at the police station. The Doc's idea of comforting surroundings. She slammed the door shut.

I asked her if she had any more tape.

She looked under her laptop. Dug through her desk drawers, until she found a bottle of Jim Beam. "It's cheaper," she said, pouring a shot into a paper cup, and then emptying the rest into a small silver flask. "But it works." After a quick sip from the bottle to make sure no juice had survived, she sat down behind the desk and raised her cup in a toast. "I've been up for 36 hours, patching holes in people. Thanks to you."

"No problem." To tell you the truth, I was already working on a plan to give her more holes to patch. Holes too big even for her skills. "Tell me, Doc, I got to ask you something."

She sipped her Jim, opened her laptop and tapped a few keys, but didn't say anything.

"About the girl," I said.

"Which one?"

"Professor Twyla."

The Doc took another sip. Before she could say anything, the intercom buzzed, and a woman's voice requested her presence in the emergency room. "Wait here." She left me alone with her cup and hip flask. I emptied the cup into me, set it back in place, and wiped my mouth with the sleeve of my scrubs. To keep my mind off the flask, I looked around the office. The piles of files on the shelves were marked from "A" to "Z." Mines was in the "M" stack.

The Doc's handwriting was tough to read, and plenty of the words were out of my vocab range, but I managed to translate the part about my military service and further down a scribbled notation about me and the Madonna, my use of drugs, and my alleged diagnosis, along with an underlined comment: "Patient exhibits symptoms of psychosis."

I sat down in the Doc's chair and typed in a question for her computer, just like the Vegas Professor had shown me. It brought up a definition I could almost understand. According to something called the National Institution of Brain Disorders a psychotic was someone out of touch with reality. I figured that could be anybody. Who wants to get in touch with a dumpster fire?

Further down there was a note about me hearing voices suggesting strange and illogical behavior. Sure, that was obvious. I was living in Hilo. I kept looking for the bad part. It said something about being afraid of people who were listening to my thoughts. Who wouldn't be? Just ask Frankie.

It said something about depression. At least she got that part right.

"What are you doing, Manny? Where's my booze?"

At first I thought I was hearing a voice in my head. It sounded like the Madonna until I spun around and saw the Doc standing in the doorway. "I thought you had an emergency."

"Correct." She grabbed the folder from me. "I only have a few minutes. Give me my flask."

I dug the flask out of my scrubs and gave it to her. While she drank, I felt around for my manila envelope. "What are you looking for?" she asked.

"I had an envelope. With important papers." I was trying to remember where I had left it. It was in my pants. But I didn't have my pants. I had hospital scrubs.

She capped the flask and turned her eyes on me. They must've got a good look because she shook her head. "I'm going to tell you something, Manny. And you're going to listen."

I was listening, kinda, but I was thinking about her and the Judge being friends. No doubt they were working together. That's what I was thinking. Then I got off track because I remembered that my joint and sleeping pills were waiting for me. At least they were safe.

"I'm going to tell you twice," she said, "because it takes two times for anything to sink into that brick you call a brain."

It was almost like she had feelings.

221

"Don't get any crazy ideas." Then she said a bunch of stuff about the Judge and Joe being young and having a kid. I wasn't listening. I was thinking about Twyla. Then the Doc slapped me across the face with my folder, and said, "The world breaks people. That's all you need to know, Manny."

"Makes sense."

After she had another drink, she told me again, to make it sink in. "The world breaks people."

"Sure." I knew that. It was in my file. "What about my kid?

"You don't have a kid."

"What about Twyla?"

She slapped me hard again. This time with her open hand. I guess I was out of touch with reality.

"Sorry," she said, and scratched her head, stretched her neck by twisting it left and right, took a long drink, and stretched again before saying, "None of us is perfect." After the alcohol settled in, she said, "You'll be fine after you get some sleep." She took my hands, squeezed them tight. She didn't have much of a bedside manner, but she had good hands. They reminded me of Ms. Song's hands. "Tell me, when's the last time you saw the Madonna?"

I sat there for a minute, wondering what the Madonna had to do with anything. I was about to ask the Doc, then the intercom called her name again, telling her the lab tests were ready. She stood up, tucked my file under her arm, and disappeared out the door.

Smelling the Doc's antiseptic perfume, I thought about the world being cruel and unusual punishment for some people, and if I ever saw the Madonna again, I'd tell her to make changes, plenty changes.

It must've been the hospital's party atmosphere that was making me feel so happy and gay. To keep my hands from strangling someone, I fingered the edge of my plastic bag.

There was no intercom to call me out, so I walked out on my own, and found the stairwell. The joint felt good in my fingers. It felt even better between my lips. I dug in my pockets for a lighter while I took a quick inventory of my forces. I had forgotten where I put Joe's .22. All my pals were in the hospital. Ms. Song had already done more than her duty. Frankie and Antman weren't even walking wounded. They were flat-on-their-backs wounded. Papa Joe was in a freezer, the Judge hidden under Frankie's house. And I couldn't find my lighter.

I saluted all of them with my joint. That left Pig-Dog, if I could pry him away from hospital food. He wasn't much for chitchat but he could handle an action scene. Me and Pig-Dog against the Singing Professor, a car rancher, and a couple of Fanboys from the Mainland? No problem. We had them outnumbered.

I inhaled Frankie's joint, wishing the weed to ignite. Nothing. Where was the Madonna when I needed her? My feet sloshed around in my lace-free high tops as I climbed the stairs. On the top floor, the door to the maternity ward was open, so I went in and looked at the two rows of little squeakers. It wasn't a pretty site. It looked like a dormitory in a reform school with a bunch of miniature prisoners trapped on their backs and crying for freedom. It should be against the law for kids to start their lives in hospitals. There'd be plenty of time for disinfectants and restraints when they got older. It was almost enough to depress me.

A few doors down, I stopped, glanced behind me. The coast was clear. I knocked twice, counted to five, and knocked three more times. When no one answered, I twisted the stainless steel knob. It was supposed to be locked, but it opened on the first try. The three beds were empty. The professor's wife was gone, so were her two kids and the mini-goat. And no Twyla.

The only thing left was an envelope on the middle bed. The card inside had a picture of a stork carrying a baby in a sling. It looked like a dangerous way to travel. When I opened it, the old photograph of Papa Joe and the Judge slid into my hand. The pink lettering on the card ignored the method of delivery and concentrated on the positives: "Congratulations! It's a girl." The handwriting below it made more sense: "Sorry about the card. Was in a rush. I'm taking Bernadette and the kids to a safe house. Borowing the van. Wait for me. Twyla."

"Sure," I said. The card had a price tag from the gift shop. I was still holding it when I looked out the window. Frankie's VW was gone. The ambulance was still out there.

I stood alone for a while feeling sorry for myself. Then I went into the hallway, found a nurse, and told her I was a nervous father waiting for his wife to wake up after delivery. Did she have a light? She tossed me a red Bic, told me to keep it. Nurses understand the need for nicotine.

In the stairwell, after three puffs, I thought about Twyla. She was thin and small, and I was big and tall. She was a professor, and I was something else.

I tried to picture her mom. She was sitting across from me. We were in a restaurant, a Mexican place in Monterey, near the coast on the way to Big Sur, eating chorizo, eggs, beans and rice after spending the night on the beach. Now it was morning and we were drinking tequila and eating Mexican to help us face reality. With Cal-Mex music playing in the background, glasses clinking behind the bar, and the smell of fried pork in the air, we were saying good-bye.

Remembering made me pinch off the joint and save the roach for later. Right there in the stairwell I burned the card and the picture. I don't remember why. I left the Bic on the fire extinguisher for the next poor devil who was too lazy to cross the street and smoke in the designated area for nicotine fiends. That's what pot did for me. It got my mind working. But if I wanted my body to go along for the ride, I'd have to lay off the smoke and stick to tequila, the original energy drink.

Later on, the cops claimed that there was no way a "drug addled pothead and a trained dog" could have done all the damage alone. Whenever I remember them saying that, I have to laugh. A trained dog? That's funny. I'd like to see someone train Pig-Dog.

But it hurt a little, too, you know. Like I wasn't good enough, even after I told them more than once that I could take care of myself.

Entry 23: ONE HOUSE AND LOT

Here's how it happened. If you don't believe me, ask Miles.

He caught me by the shoulder as I was slipping out the back door of the hospital. "Can I talk to you?" he asked, and followed me into the parking lot. "It's personal."

The truth is I was planning to steal his ambulance, so I kept walking and told him we could talk on the way to Frankie's place if he gave me a ride. I figured he could help with the Judge's body, but something had changed Miles since I last talked to him. Instead of rushing out there to fire up the siren and drink tequila, he told me that the ambulance was for "official business only."

"No one will see us," I told him. "We can take the back road out of town, over the old bridge to Frankie's place. Be back in no time."

He shook his head. "Sorry."

So I told him that Twyla had stolen Frankie's van, and I had to find her before the cops did. Or even worse, the bad guys.

"We can take my car." He held up a key ring heavy enough to anchor my boat. "Ms. Song asked me to keep an eye on Professor Twyla."

Ms. Song was even tougher than I thought, seeing she was passed out in a coma and could still find time to chat with Miles. "For Ms. Song, sure," I told him.

His car was parked next to the ambulance. I liked it, a silver 2001 Honda Civic, the four-door model with an extra-large truck. There were thousands of Civics on the Big Island, most of them white or silver, so his would blend in, even with the oversized muffler and useless airfoil.

I told him about losing my lighter, and he let me in the ambulance to take a look. Checking the refrigerator for a drink, I found Joe's .22 under a 7-11 egg salad sandwich. The sandwich may still be there. The .22 didn't have any bullets but I hid it in the waist of my hospital-issue scrubs and used a roll of surgical tape to secure my high-tops. They gave me a sporty look, kinda, like I was taped up for a rugby game.

Miles was waiting for me in his car. As I ran across the asphalt, I pressed my elbow against the .22 to keep it from dropping down my pants. I had to fold myself up to squeeze into the low-rider. The engine started on the first try and we headed for the exit. "Nice ride," I said as the muffler scraped over a speed hump and the .22 jabbed me in the gonads.

Miles turned onto the main road, punched the gas, quick-shifted, and we were traveling 60 miles per hour with my head pinned against the imitation leather headrest. "It's the Si model," he smiled, "with 127 horsepower." We were going 70, then 80, then he let off the gas, downshifted, and dropped us to 50 as we buzzed by a baseball field. "I was going to lower it another inch," he said, "get one nice set of rims. Now I'm wondering why waste the money. I gotta start thinking about the future."

That was a lot of talking for Miles. I gave him a good look, checking for scars where the Doc might've cut out important parts of his brain. In his white uniform shirt, dark blue pants, and steel-toed boots he looked like Miles, but he didn't act like Miles. When I asked him for alcohol, he shook his head. "Not me. I'm going sober."

I'm telling you this because no matter what you've heard, Miles was no booze crazy hot rodder. The truth is, he was proof that tequila-guzzling kids can become sober men if they're given enough time to realize drinking should be left to guys like me. He was a sober man now, except for his driving. It's hard to give up the need for speed. I guess it's an occupational hazard.

"Why did Twyla go to Frankie's house?" he asked, one hand resting lightly on the steering wheel, one working the stick shift. We reached the ocean and turned north onto the Singing Bridge. The speedometer held at 60 mph as the tires hummed over the metal grids. While I was trying to think of a good answer, he said, "I don't want anyone to get hurt."

Hoping that included me, I watched the speedometer jump to 90 mph. We tore out of town, past the big cemetery and onto the Surf-Spot Bridge, where the surfers way down below looked like bed bugs. He took his hand off the stick to jab me in the arm. "You understand, Manny? Right? I'm serious."

"Keep your eyes on the road." I was all for sobriety as long as it didn't kill me in the process. That car could fly. "If you slow down, maybe we'll live long enough to help her."

"Sorry," he said, I'm used to driving an ambulance." But he didn't ease off the gas. We kept flying, reaching 95, passing cars three at a time, and slipping back into our lane a blink before oncoming traffic swooshed by, heading for Hilo. I gave up and closed my eyes, counted to ten, opened them long enough to check our progress, and closed them again. It was safer in the dark. I peeked out and saw Frankie's turn rushing at us.

"Turn." I thought he'd realize we were going too fast, that we were going to miss it, and we had to make a U-turn. Instead, he tapped the brake, dropped to 65, swung the wheel right, and made a tight drifting turn onto the narrow strip of asphalt that led to Frankie's road.

"Twyla's out here, right?" he asked.

"The road turns to dirt up here," I said. It didn't help. We were going 50 when the Civic flew off the asphalt, hung in the air, and landed on a muddy dirt road aimed at a cliff. "What's she doing out here?" he asked.

"Turn!"

That little Civic handled turns on dirt like it handled turns on asphalt. The front-end dug in, the back end swung around, and Miles punched the gas. We passed the cemetery, which looked miserable compared to its brother back on the main road. The tombstones turned Miles into a philosopher. He said that he wanted to make something of himself, maybe go back to college. As the Cali grass swirled around us, he asked if I had ever dated a woman as smart as Professor Twyla.

I couldn't remember dating, but I used to know a couple of dancers in Honolulu, and they were pretty smart, so I told Miles how doing lots of hand-eye coordination would keep his brain up to par.

"What kind of dancers?" he asked.

Frankie's house rose up, a safety rail that kept Miles from driving off the cliff. He hit the brakes as I pointed at the burned-out hulk of Frankie's truck and said, "Park there."

Miles skidded the Civics over the gravel driveway and stopped between the porch and the truck, where the Civic couldn't be seen from across the gulch. When he killed the engine, I sat there thankful to be watching the rain clouds edge their way along the coast. At least part of the world was moving along at a respectable pace.

Miles reached under his seat, retrieved a pink hydro bottle, and leaned back for a long drink. While he was wiping his mouth with the back of his hand, the sun settled gently behind the volcano, leaving the rain clouds to drift into the night.

Miles offered me the bottle, and I took it, thinking he had finally regained his senses. I was wrong. Clean, crisp and tasteless, Hilo water is better than any water you can buy in a store, but it's still only water, without any of alcohol's benefits.

When he stepped out and closed his door, I slipped the .22 out of my pants and stuck it under the seat. Holding onto the water bottle, I climbed out and closed the door behind me, headed for the house.

"Twyla," Miles shouted. "Twyla!"

I pretended to look shocked. "I thought she'd be here for sure," I said. "Let's check the house."

We walked around the house, looking everywhere, then went inside, checking every room, him and me calling for Twyla, him more than me, before we ended up standing on the lanai. Miles looked through the telescope. "You see anything over there?" I asked him.

"A nice looking Porsche."

He had an eye for speed. "Keep an eye on it," I said, and went down to the kitchen, dug the two pills out of my joint baggie, ground them down with one of Frankie's battle spoons, and brushed the white powder into the water bottle. As I ran up the stairs, I gave it a good shake.

Miles still had his eye on the telescope. "There're some guys moving around over there." I handed him the water, grabbed a beer out of the cooler, and sat down in the folding chair. "Have a seat," I said. "One beer to help me think and then we find her. You can be sure of that. We'll find her."

We sat out there like a couple of buddies watching the night turn black, him drinking drugged water and me drinking beer and wondering what it would be like to face the world sober, especially for longer than a couple of minutes. I figured that Miles was handling it pretty good for a rookie, until he blinked three times and said, "Alcohol will kill you."

Sure. No doubt. That's what it is for. But I didn't want to rain on his revival meeting. He was just a kid, and we should all be more tolerant of sober kids. "You're right," I said. "Tequila, especially. It'll make you see things you don't want to see." Heck, even today I'm still seeing Joe's birthday present.

He stretched his legs while he looked up at the sky. "You got any kids?"

Crazy, huh, that he should ask? It made me dig out Frankie's joint. Holding it made me feel like I was back with

Papa Joe, except Miles was a lot younger and shorter than Joe. I went with my standard: "Not that I know."

"You'd remember a kid."

The joint wasn't lighting itself. I checked the floor, saw a box of Frankie's discount bullets and, right next to it, Joe's Viet Nam Zippo. "How about you?" I said, picking up the lighter and using my foot to slide the bullets closer to me. "You got any kids."

"No, but I got plans."

He rubbed his knee. "Everyone should have kids," he said. "That's what life is for."

I had plans but they didn't have anything to do with kids. I yawned and said, "Plans are good. Man, I'm feelin tired."

He didn't get the clue. "Not me," he said, and drank more water. "I'm wide awake. Alive! Must be sobriety." He offered me the bottle but I dug out a fresh can of beer instead. Yeah, I was thinking, wait until you've had a couple days of sobriety. Right now you're hyped up on good intentions and hormones, but in a few days you'll be begging for booze and sleep and Mexican food.

"If I buy a lot," he said, "maybe an acre if I can find it, my brother will help me build. He's a contractor."

"Nice."

"You gotta have family," he said.

We were back on familiar ground. I sipped the beer, lit the joint, took a puff and offered Miles a hit, hoping it would help close his eyes. He waved it off. "As soon as I can find the right girl," he said, "I'm going to have three kids. Maybe four."

"Maybe, even, get married." Where that came from I'm still not sure, but I said it, like a dad lecturing a kid, like I knew something about biology.

Miles closed his eyes. "Getting married is the easy part. Finding the right woman, that's the hard part. I got some ideas."

His head dipped, and I was leaning forward to check for signs of life when his eyes popped open. "Hey, what do you know about Twyla? Professor Twyla, I mean. She's seems nice."

No bigger compliment in Hilo than being nice. "You look sleepy," I said.

"And pretty." He laughed, rubbed his eyes. "Not me. I don't look pretty. She does. Don't you think?"

I took a long hit off the joint. "Sure," I said, holding my breath, keeping my eyes on his lids. "She's a good looking woman for a small gal. I like the bigger rounder type."

"The professor is the only type," he yawned. "You ever dated a woman that smart?"

He was circling back, hanging to reality by his fingernails. I told him again about my dancing friends in Honolulu who had saved enough to buy a condo in Waikiki, which wasn't easy and took plenty smarts, considering the cost of real estate in Hawaii. Those girls worked some long hours. "Smart girls," I said, "need plenty sleep."

"If you had a daughter would you let her date me?"

"If I had a daughter?"

"Like Twyla. If Twyla was your daughter, would you let her date me?"

"You want to date my daughter?"

"Hypothetically."

"Do I look like her father?"

"Stop joking." He closed his eyes and let his head drop back, pointed at the stars. With his eyes closed, he asked again, "Would you, Manny?"

I had to think about it. He was a good kid, a worker, a reformed alcoholic, and more importantly, he had a brother who was a contractor. You know how hard it is to find a contractor on the Big Island? But was he good enough for my daughter, if I had a daughter? "I don't think that girl is the dating type," I told him. "If she was, I don't think she'd ask me for permission."

"You're right." He opened his eyes.

"She's not the type to stay in one place. That's what I think."

"I'd go with her. Anywhere."

"Anywhere?"

"As long as it's not too far from Hilo."

I gave him a laugh for that one, and gave him a kick in the shin, just for fun. "What if she doesn't want kids?"

"Everyone wants kids."

Romance and sobriety are tough roads to travel on the unpaved gravel of sobriety. "She's from the mainland," I said. "Things are different there. Maybe she wants to wander carefree. Australia maybe."

His face drooped, like someone had stolen his last joint or fed him sleeping pills. So he wouldn't have nightmares, I said, "You could go with her."

"I could do that."

"Leave your brother, your job, and your acre lot. Go with her."

He closed his eyes. I shook his knee. "Miles? I'd let you date her." He smiled in his sleep. "Did you hear me, Miles?" I pushed his shoulder. "Miles?"

Mission accomplished. He was staring at the inside of his eyelids and imagining a world where Twyla loved his island as much as he did. Across the gulch, light appeared in a window of the HQ trailer. The Porsche was still parked out front. I pinched the end of my glowing doobie, dropped the roach in my shirt pocket. There was work to do. I picked up the bullets, stole his car keys, and ran down the stairs.

The box of discount bullets fit under the seat with the .22. They looked good together, like a cover for a news magazine.

On my hands and knees, I ducked under the house. It took me a few minutes in the stuffy, hot, gritty crawlspace to find the Judge. After I dragged her out, I stood up, brushed the dirt off my knees, and looked down at her. Even without unzipping the body bag, I knew she wasn't getting better. I dragged the bag to the back of the Civic, popped the trunk, and somehow managed to lift it, shoulders first then hips, and roll her into the trunk.

Miles was tougher. He was short but compact, all muscle. But I had practice. I lifted him onto my shoulders, and carried him down the stairs to the Civic, the same way I had carried Pig-Dog down from the mountain.

It took the wind out of me. I had to leave him on the hood while I took a smoke break to consider seating arrangements. Two quick puffs brought my lungs back to life. Applying to the Fire Department came to mind. Then my mind really kicked in. I figured the trunk was no place for my son-in-law, so I slid him off the hood and into the passenger seat.

The wind off the ocean felt cool and alive. I looked up at the sky, trying to see something, anything. If the Madonna was up there, she deserved everything she got for watching instead of getting her ass in gear. If you need someone to blame, she's the one you should be investigating. It was her who got the whole mess started. She could've given Papa Joe a hand. And why didn't she help the Judge and Joe when they needed it? And their kid, what did she do for that human being? And Miles? Didn't he deserve her help? Miles certainly needed it, passed out with his pothead father-in-law.

The house across the gulch was sparkling now, every building flooded with light. "Time to go." That's what I said, even though no one was awake to hear it.

We drove back to town, Miles dozing with his head against the window and me playing model citizen, keeping the Civic under the speed limit and in the right lane. At the hospital, I pulled into the parking lot, went around back, and stopped next to the dumpster.

After thanking Miles for the quiet ride, I dragged him behind the dumpster and sat him down. I left him sitting there, sleeping soundly and pain free. They'd find him in the morning. That was all the time I needed.

As I drove slowly through the parking lot, I checked the clock in the Civic: 9:15pm. That really was a nice Honda. How many cars do you know where the clock works? The radio worked, too. The Rolling Stones were singing about "Sympathy for the Devil."

When I stopped at the entrance to the parking lot, Pig-Dog was sitting by the stop sign, waiting for me. I figured he had seen the action from the window in Frankie's room and came down to offer a helping hand, or paw, or pig's foot. I leaned over and pushed open the door. He jumped in. Somehow he managed to close the door after him. Maybe he did it with his tail. Anyway, we sat there for a moment, me staring at the night, Pig-Dog thinking. He must've been thinking because he was the one who pointed his snout up the mountain.

Entry 24: SOMEONE TO BLEED ON

I t took plenty of Pig-Dog barking and a few dozen wrong turns, but we found the road to the Rancher's place.

We parked at the top of a rise and stood on a fallen tree trunk wider and longer than a telephone pole. Looking out across fields of prickly Cali-grass, we saw the sprawl of chicken condos, the Car Rancher's house and its out buildings. Dim porch lights were the only signs of life. No trucks or cars were parked where I could see them. It was Friday night, and the place was dead quiet, not even the chickens were barking. Pig-Dog licked his lips while I inhaled the clean smell of wet grass and cow shit. I needed a few minutes to load the .22 and tuck it back in my waist. The Civic's clock said it was 10:30, so I sat down in the dirt, leaned back and closed my eyes.

When I opened them, Pig-Dog was licking my face. A fat rain drop hit my forehead. I rubbed the sleep out of my eyes and reached for a joint. Down the road, the Rancher's place was still dark except that a pick-up with a cab light was parked at the front gate. The interior light was dim but there was enough of it to see someone sitting behind the wheel. After a few tries, I gave up finding a joint. Pig-Dog was already halfway down the road. I figured he'd scout the place before I did anything drastic.

Raindrops pecked at the back of my neck as I opened the Civic's trunk. The Judge was still in there snuggled up to the tool kit. "Not much longer," I told her, and she didn't argue. The truth is, I was thinking about hauling her down to that pickup and leaving her there, along with the .22, before I called the police to give the Rancher a taste of his own medicine. Instead, I made the mistake of looking at the road, the chickens, and the mountains. It was cold up there, and it wouldn't be any better in the back of truck.

I pried off a magnetic key-box that was stuck to the tool kit. Weren't extra keys supposed to be hidden outside the car where you didn't need a key to find them? That's how quick my mind was working. I picked up the little opihi and slid back the lid. There were no keys inside but there was a fat joint and a book of matches. Miles's recent conversion had not yet reached his emergency supplies. I smoked half the joint, thinking about the Judge. Then I tucked the roach in my shirt pocket. That was my daily good deed. If Miles was ever tempted to return to the smoky side, he'd have me to thank for keeping him sober.

I slammed the trunk shut. The Judge deserved better than the back of truck. Any surfer girl deserved better.

The Civic's clock said it was 11:30. The rain kept pecking at me as I hunkered down and ran along the road toward the truck. The nice thing about the rain, it keeps all the neighborhood dogs under cover. The hundred or so dogs that lived up there in chicken land were motion detectors combined with burglar alarms, but they were passed out for the night, happy to be dry and silent for once. Carrying the .22 in my hand, I spy-walked to the back of the pickup truck. By the time I got there, my scrubs were soaked, so was the .22. Through the truck's back window, I could see a shadowy lump slumped over the steering wheel. It looked dry and comfortable, like a target waiting for a bullet. The driver's window was closed, but Pig-Dog was already standing up, looking inside from the passenger's side.

I ducked down and felt my way along the truck. Even in the rain I could hear the radio playing and the Stones singing,

"Yeah, we all need someone we can bleed on." That's Hilo radio. FM Repetition.

"Please allow me to introduce myself," I whispered and shoved Pig-Dog out of the way. The overhead light was fading, and the Stones weren't loud enough to blot out the snoring. Belly Boy was holding a quart of tequila between his legs, death-gripping it, bent over the steering wheel with his eyes closed, snoring and drooling on his cherished bottle. I didn't blame him. The last thing a thief wants is someone stealing his tequila.

I wrapped my fingers around the door handle, squeezed, waited, and pulled lightly. The door popped open.

The snoring stopped. The lump looked up, trying to see out the front window. He yawned, rubbed his face. I gripped the .22. When he turned to me, his eyes opened wide and his jaw dropped, like a guy in a horror movie. I wish I could say that I leaned in and went to work on him, but Pig-Dog was faster than me.

Climbing over me, he knocked me face-first into the seat. The .22 fell out of my hand as he crawled over my back and lunged for Mr. Beer Belly. The Rancher blocked him with a swinging elbow. Pig-Dog bit into his wrist and slammed him against the door. The Rancher screamed. He reached between his legs, brought his left hand up holding a gut gun. I reached for it but caught Pig-Dog's leg. The cab exploded, like someone had tossed a cherry bomb in my ear.

I fell back, Pig-Dog fell with me, slipping out of my arms. My ears were ringing. I stumbled backward, caught myself, and checked for holes. No holes. No blood. Pig-Dog looked like he barked twice, pointed his snout at the cab. The Rancher was still holding the gun. It was pointed at his leg. His eyes were half open, looking down at the blood pumping out of his thigh.

"Shit." That's what his mouth looked like it said. The ringing in my ears was blotting out everything else.

"So much for gun safety." That's what I said but I didn't hear it. I hope he did.

The rancher looked at me. The gun in his hand, a nasty derringer, was splattered with blood. His mouth moved. Maybe he was trying to tell me that guns didn't kill people. But he ran out of time. The Stones song must've ended because the Rancher closed his eyes and slumped over the steering wheel. The gun dropped to the floor.

In the rearview mirror I saw blood splattered on my face.

I managed to keep Pig-Dog back so I could survey the scene. Even in the half glow, with Pig-Dog trying to squeeze by me to get his licks in, I saw the pool of blood at the Rancher's feet. There was more than enough of it. Just like that, death by self-defense.

I slammed the door. With the end of my scrub shirt, I wiped the blood off my face and the fingerprints off the door handle. Then I left the rancher there to enjoy the night. On the way back to the Civic, Pig-Dog checked the chicken condos for a midnight snack.

*** (Union lunch break) ***

Two hours later, as we drove by the Singing Professor's place, my hearing came back. We parked next to the same line of trees, and I rolled down the window. Pig-Dog jumped over me, out the window, and headed for the front gate.

Funny, but it wasn't until then that I thought of Papa Joe's favorite old TV show. I think it was from the 1930s and called "Sassy." Something like that. In that old sitcom, a Pitbull-Collie mix named Sassy used to help humans pull babies out of fires and solve bank robberies by running away, stopping, and waiting for the humans to follow her to the scene of the crime. Funny, yah, how a hundred years later, there I was living in that sitcom, except that my Sassie was part pig. Later, when I told that to the cops, they told me to shut the frick up.

Oh, well.

Pig-Dog was waiting for me at the gate, so I grabbed my trusty .22, ran too him, and looked over his shoulder, what there was of it. "See anything, Sassie?"

He growled as he pointed his snout at the pigpen. The Singing Professor was standing on the far side, in front of Joe's pickup. Its headlights projected snow cones of yellow light onto two men kneeling with their hands behind their heads. The Singing Professor, or someone who was stupid or desperate enough to steal his silly hat and wear it to a hostage situation, stepped up and kicked one of the men in the back, knocking him into the mud.

The .22 felt cold and useless in my hands. Pig-Dog jumped the gate. Always the show-off, that hybrid. It took me longer. Holding the .22, I climbed the slippery rails, swung my leg over, rolled the other leg over, and held on tight as the gate swung open. I guess I should've checked for a lock first. It wasn't my first mistake.

Pig-Dog used his four hooves to dash for the pigpen.

Bent at the waist and playing army man, I followed him down the trail to the banana patch that hugged our side of the pen. The patch was crawling and hopping with coqui frogs making enough noise to cover the charge of the light brigade. From behind a hanging bunch of bananas as big around as an opera singer, I saw my friend Scamboy step out of the little red Porsche and stand next to the Singing Professor. The scarf around his neck made him standout like a target at a rifle range.

Pig-Dog crawled between the banana trees and dug at the soft ground under the fence. Part backhoe, part bulldozer, in no time he dug a hole deep enough and wide enough for him to squeeze through. After his tail disappeared under the wire, I stuffed my head and shoulders through before rolling onto my back and pulling my butt and legs through. We blended into a platoon of snorting pigs, a couple dozen of them jammed in tight, huffing and puffing, bumping into each other and cursing their fate. With this stinky, stealthy cloak of pigskin wrapped around us, we crawled and shoved our way to the other side of the pen.

Pig-Dog's relatives were very helpful, even if they didn't know it, and I was hoping there'd be a way to reward them for their service to humanity. Maybe a barbeque? Or something like that. Thanks to them only the hog-wire fence and a few feet of mud separated us from the two victims kneeling in front of their worthless scumbag overlords.

"Shut up!" Scamboy shouted. "I'm tired of listening to your whining."

"Wait!" the Mad Professor shouted.

"This is how you do it!" Scamboy lifted his arm. A flash, a gunshot, and the kneeler closest to me went face first into the mud. Without thinking, Pig-Dog leapt over the fence. Without thinking, I fired a shot through the hog wire and watched it miss Scamboy and the Mad Professor. It sailed past Joe's truck, and crashed into the Porsche's front window. A woman screamed. Pig-Dog landed on Scamboy and drove him backward, crashing him into Joe's truck. As I climbed the fence, the surviving kneeler twisted around, grabbed the Mad Professor around the knees, and lifted him into the air, like in TV wrestling.

"Get him off me," the Mad Professor squealed, high in the air and about be body slammed.

Scamboy was too busy to listen. Pinned to Joe's truck, he hammered his gun into Pig-Dog. I dropped to the ground, someone kicked me in the head, and the picture got a little fuzzy.

Pig-Dog was on his side in the mud. Scumboy stepped over him to get to the wrestling match. He stopped behind the New Hulk, raised the pistol, and brought it down hard against the Wrestler's neck. The Wrestler went limp, dropped the Professor, then collapsed on top of him.

I pulled the trigger. Nothing. I jumped at Scamboy. He caught me in midair, whacked my head good with that hammer-gun of his. The jolt knocked me into Papa Joe's truck. The .22 landed next to Pig-Dog and sunk into the mud. I sunk with it.

"I hate dogs," Scamboy said. He kicked Pig-Dog in the gut. Adjusted his scarf. Kicked me in the gut. For kicks, he fired a shot at my head. "Clean up this mess," he yelled at the Professor. "And meet me back at Mr. Stonnard's place."

In the mud, playing dead, I kept digging with my fingers.

"I'll be there," the Mad Professor said. He picked up his hat and slapped it against his knee. In the headlights he looked like a friggin zombie, a friggin pale zombie still wearing bandages under his lauhala hat.

Scamboy climbed into his bloody red Porsche. There was someone in the car with him. Her hands were tied in front of her and her mouth was open, trying to scream. He slapped her hard and when she kept trying, he swung his fist at her. Her head hit the window. He slammed the door and shouted out the window. "Feed them to the pigs."

As the little red car sped for the gate, I saw her again, slumped against the dash.

Digging for the .22, I watched the Mad Professor run up the stairs and disappear inside his house. I didn't find the gun but I found Pig-Dog. His breath stunk, but at least he still had breath. Scamboy had shot off his left ear, but there was no other damage. The hole where his ear used to be looked like a greasy egg, bloody-side up. I shook him a few times, giving him the old, "Wake up! Wake up." When he stayed still, I figured he needed the sleep, so I left him alone and crawled over to the Wrestler. I turned him over. His breath didn't smell any better than Pig-Dog's, but it marked him as one of the living.

I was trying to shake him awake when the Singing Professor came charging out of the house, carrying what looked familiar, a short-barreled shotgun.

I'd liked to say it was a fair fight, that I picked him off with one shot from a kneeling position as he charged me with Rayzah's old gun. But it didn't happen that way. Joe's gun was still lost in the mud. From the porch he fired one barrel. The blast went high. Maybe he hit bananas. A second later it smelled like bananas and I ducked.

Pig-Dog crawled up to me and dropped the .22 at my feet. Then he passed out in the mud. The Mad Professor stopped at the bottom of the stairs, pointed the shotgun at me and fired. A fat slug swooshed by my ear. Behind me, a pig squealed in pain and sent the pack running in circles, crashing along the fence. Something warm was leaking out of my ringing ear. I pointed the .22 at the Bezerk Professor and pulled the trigger. Nothing. Frickin discount duds.

I tried again. A dud. Like I said, guns and me didn't get along. The Professor stepped closer pulling the trigger without reloading. Holding the .22 by the barrel, I lowered my head and charged. He dropped the shotgun, turned to run, and I tackled him around the waist, bear-hugging him and dancing him in circles until I threw both of us into the mud, both of us fighting for the .22. Somehow he managed to grab it, twist it, and dig it into my Adam's apple.

We were on our knees, facing each other. That's how I remember it. The gun barrel dug into my neck while his nicotine breath tried to poison me. I grabbed the barrel. Waited for the blast as the Wrestler flew out of nowhere and knocked the Creepy Professor off me. The gun went off as they fell sideways in the mud. They were rolling around, the Professor's mouth stretched open like he was singing, but I didn't hear anything. I ripped the .22 out of his hand, swung it by the barrel, hammering him in the side of the head. He settled into the mud, ear first, like he was trying to listen to the earth's heartbeat.

I scrambled to my feet. The Wrestler was standing over the Scab Professor, kicking him to make sure he was out. Pig-Dog was on all fours, shaking himself awake. He tried to bark but no sound came out. I had a feeling that sooner or later working for Papa Joe and the Judge was going to screw up my hearing. I felt for my ear. My hand came away covered with blood. A chunk of my right ear was missing. Now me and Pig-Dog were twins, except for him having four legs, no arms, and a leather hide instead of human skin.

Pig-Dog recovered quicker than me. He was already standing next to the Wrestler, licking blood off the poor man's hand. Who knows where that tongue had been. I pushed him out of the way. The Wrestler had one of those weathered faces from working in the sun. Maybe he was 30, maybe 50, with plenty of wrinkles and long hair. After I shook him a couple of times, he started moving his mouth. I heard whispered bits and pieces, mumbles that I figured were "Thank you" and "What the hell?" He pointed at his friend in the mud. Said something. I shook his hand but it didn't improve his volume. He pointed at fields beyond the house and maybe he said "Friends." There was other stuff, but none of it reached my good ear, or maybe it did but I didn't have a good ear. Everything sounded like gurgling in a storm drain.

We bent over his pal. I shook my head, and the Wrestler made the sign of the cross on his chest. It didn't help. Pig-Dog tried licking what was left of his head. That didn't help. Nothing was going to help him. Me and the Wrestler carried him to Joe's truck. We placed him gently on the rusty bed. The Wrestler took my hand and shook it hard, like he wanted my vote.

I would've said a few words, but I was too busy digging my finger in my ear, trying to make it work. I wiped blood on my scrubs and promised myself never to wear headphones with loud music. And no more guns. That's what I promised myself. For the second time that night instead of ears I had wind tunnels. One of them, at least. The other one was just a hole.

The Mad Professor must've moved because Pig-Dog ran over and started snapping at him. I stood over the college boy, wishing I had his cattle prod to help him on his way. That would have been the humane thing to do. Pig-Dog spit blood at him. So did I. Sure, I admit it. I wanted to shoot him. It would have been easy. He was a big target, not too quick on his feet, lying there almost like he was asking for it. With the package of 250 likely dud rounds, I figured I could have stayed up there all night playing Russian Roulette. But I was more interested in that woman in the Porsche, so I stole the bandages off his head and dragged him by the feet to the pigpen. I left him there, propped up against the gate. He wasn't in the best shape, but he was breathing. I kicked him a couple of times to check. His chin dropped to his chest and his hand moved like it was trying to wave me off. Believe me, he was still alive.

I tossed the Professor's shotgun into the back of Joe's truck, and wrapped the bandage around my head, hoping it covered my bad ear. The Wrestler waved to us from the driver's seat. We watched him drive the pickup into the darkness behind the house, toward the ginger fields. Pig-Dog rested his head against my knee. Behind us, his relatives, curious buggahs, were already gathered at the gate, giving the Mad Professor the once over.

I'm pretty sure that gate was locked, but me and Pig-Dog had other things on our mind.

We ran up the driveway and didn't stop until we reached the Civic. Pig-Dog barked twice, turned around, and ran back to the house. I sat behind the wheel, letting a couple puffs of medical marijuana cure my hearing. While I was exhaling, Pig-Dog jumped through the window, over my lap, and landed in the passenger seat. He was getting good at that. I was turning the key in the ignition when he dropped the .22 on the floor.

*** (Union meds break) ***

I was beginning to hate that gun. But the weed and the crusty bandage were helping my ears.

As I drove toward Hilo, I flicked on the windshield wipers and watched the road turn into a river. On the radio, Bon Jovi was singing about going down in a blaze of glory. The ancient music folded me into a video of the Civic crashing through the gates of the hedge-fund manager's plantation, letting loose the Pig-Dog of war, and popping away with Papa Joe's .22 DudMaster.

It sounded good except for the Judge's body in the trunk and Joe's body still in the freezer, and that girl in the car. I wouldn't be much good dead.

Trying to think, I stuck my head out the window and let raindrops slap me in the face. When the Civic passed the turn to the evil banker's compound, Pig-Dog barked twice and growled, which made me keep going straight, pull my head in, and turn off the radio. Besides everything else, the Civic wasn't mine to play with, not even in a blaze of glory.

We needed a precision insertion, a stealthy approach, a focused strike. The rain kept pinging against the windshield. I blinked once, maybe twice. The turn to Frankie's place jumped out of the shadows. The Civic handled the ninety-degree course correction on wet asphalt as if it were on a movie set with Miles at the wheel. We raced by tightly packed houses, over asphalt and mud, and zipped past the cemetery while Pig-Dog howled at ghosts.

The dashboard clock said it was 3:30. A thin strip of yellow on the horizon promised a new day for body hauling and burial. We parked close to the porch, safe from the prying eyes across the river. The Civic's key ring had one of those tiny, emergency flashlights attached, a purple three-inch cylinder. I tore it off and left the keys in the ignition. Its LED light cast a circle of light the size of a dime. Upstairs on the lanai, through Frankie's telescope I could see the lights in the trailer's windows. The Porsche was parked out front. I double knotted the waist strap of my scrubs. Reloaded the .22 with highly possible duds, tucked it into my waist, and followed Pig-Dog to the trail.

The rain stopped.

As long as I held onto Pig-Dog's tail with one hand, the flashlight with the other, I could follow the narrow path that dropped quickly toward the river. Cali and Guinea grass brushed against my face as my feet stumbled from rock to slippery rock. Pig-Dog smashed through the grass and broke free, leaving me in his wake. My foot caught on a banyan-tree root, and I crashed down the last twenty yards, stumbled over a boulder and splashed into freezing water.

Pig-Dog was already half way across the river, flying from rock to rock, like one of those karate mystics who run across the tops of bamboo. I wondered if my PJ Flyers would help me do the same kine skimming.

I tossed the flashlight, held the .22 above my head, and waded deeper into the swollen stream. Up to my knees, the frigid water stunk of mud and mosquitoes. As I crawled to the middle of the rocky rapids, Pig-Dog climbed up the opposite bank. He looked back at me and disappeared up the path to the temple of doom.

Gripping the .22, sucking quick breaths between gulps of rancid water, I told myself I needed to get in shape. Maybe start surfing again. Cut back on the carbs. When I reached the other side, I dug out my last doobie and tossed it in the bushes to celebrate my arrival on dry land. No great loss. It was soaked. At the top of the trail, Pig-Dog was waiting, flat to the ground, eyeing the layout.

When I reached him, I could see the Porsche. Inside the trailer, dark figures crossed lighted windows. Across a muddy crisscrossing of roads, the out buildings were dark. To our left, almost hidden by the trees, a thick sturdy gate protected the compound from the main road. Two guards were parked in folding chairs, with their backs to the house, smoking cigs and watching the road. If a tank showed up, it'd have trouble smashing through the commercial-grade blockade. I gripped the .22. The odds weren't good. Tough luck. We ran across open ground and hid behind the Porsche. It had nice black leather upholstery, and except for the crack in the window, the rest of it was in pretty good shape. Even back then, I liked that car.

Behind us, from the main storage building, a shadowy figure carrying a flashlight stepped into the fading night. We slipped around to the front of the Porsche and watched him pee on the corrugated-tin wall. He stretched his arms over his head, rubbed his eyes, looked down, and zipped up his pants. When he opened the door to go back inside, we heard laughter and music. A group of men were sitting at a picnic table, playing cards, with baseball bats between their legs.

The odds weren't getting any better. Then we heard voices coming out of the trailer, so we slipped back to the other side of the Porsche, and hugged the rear end. Two men came out the front door, dragging a body between them. Scamboy was on the left. The banker, hedge-fund creep, real estate developer was on the right. They dragged the body down the steps. I didn't have to get any closer to know it was a woman. I could see her halo.

Pig-Dog growled. The men stopped. And I stood up. "Going somewhere?" I said, settling into the mud, holding the .22 at my waist like I was in an old cowboy movie, ready to draw.

Scamboy dropped his share of the load and stepped between me and his boss. The creepy banker kept going, dragging the woman toward the cliff. I heard waves breaking against the rocks. Scamboy stepped toward me, his hands raised like a boxer. Really, like a boxer. I almost laughed.

Pig-Dog growled at my side

I was lifting the .22 when headlights flashed across the sky. Shouts and gunshots erupted behind us. I turned to see Papa Joe's Datsun crash through the gate, tear off its hinges, and charge across the mud. It ricocheted off the Porsche and stopped long enough for an army of farm workers to leap out of the back. Armed with pull-saws, machetes, and shovels they charged the storage buildings as the truck's radio blasted "Blaze of Glory" into the night.

Waving baseball bats, a flash mob barreled out of the storage building. The gate guards came running. The three mobs crashed into each other and turned into a rolling, rocking, free-swinging muddy cloud of howling men and flying blood. Pig-Dog couldn't help himself. He turned, ran and dove into the brawl like a swimmer diving into a pool of tequila.

Scamboy grabbed my neck from behind and knocked the .22 from my hand. I was in the perfect position to see Joe's Datsun bust out of the fighting cloud and barrel straight at us. Its rusty grill grew bigger as Scamboy's fingers dug into my neck. Lucky I was a smoker because I could hold my breath for hours. The driver's door flew open and the Wrestler jumped out, hit the ground and rolled, flipped into the he air, and landed on his feet.

I wish I could report that I did some fancy moves. I was too busy watching Joe's truck auto-pilot at me, with Pig-Dog hanging out the back, snapping at the wind.

Scamboy let go of my neck and ran. Instinctively, I reached for a joint. The old Datsun must've recognized the move because it veered right, nicked me on the hip, and kept going, chasing Scamboy toward the cliff. It hit him hard in the back, climbed over him, caught him by the pants, and dragged him to the cliff's edge before the engine died. The rusty grill was hanging over the edge. Scamboy groaned. Probably complaining about being part of the transaxle.

His Boss didn't help. He was too busy dragging the woman to the cliff. I ran at him. He reached the drop-off. Pig-Dog was quicker than either of us. He leaped out of the truck, across the open space, and landed on the Boss's neck, biting down hard. The Boss screamed, stumbled backward, lost his footing. I grabbed the woman's leg, pulled her clear as Pig-Dog rode the Boss like a boogie board over the edge, down the face of the cliff, howling, until they hit the rocks. A wave washed over them, and they were gone.

I checked the woman. She was out but breathing. Someone had knocked her hard on the head. I walked to Joe's truck, gave it a kick in the ass, and watched it nose-dive off the cliff, taking Scamboy along for the ride. I dug the .22 out of the mud and tossed it over the cliff.

A second later the big storage building blew apart, like the Hindenburg, and knocked me to the ground. When I picked myself up from the mud, the world was going nuclear. Trees were on fire, cars and trucks were exploding, people were screaming. Even the ocean was blowing itself into a million pieces, spitting Pig-Dog up the cliff, through the flames and into the sky. I figured he was aiming for the stars.

Anyway, that's when I heard the sirens.

Entry 25: CELL MATES

That's all you need to know, except for the part about the Coast Guard finding me floating in the middle of the Alenuihāhā Channel, halfway between Maui and the Big Island, asleep at the wheel of the Judge's Radon.

The fuel tanks were empty. No cargo. No passengers. Only me passed out in hospital scrubs and Steamer, my cat, chasing imaginary mice. How we got there, I don't know. Where we were going, I don't remember.

The Coasties towed us back to Hilo Harbor, where a couple of detectives asked me all kine questions about Papa Joe and the Judge, so I told them how the Golden Madonna showed up naked with a Pig-Dog that could fly.

"Frickin Manny." That's what the cops said.

When I tried to tell them about the Chicken Rancher, they told me to shut up. They didn't want to hear it. The case was closed. He was a statistic. His death an accident. The gun in his hand, the hole in his leg, and the 20% alcohol in his blood had sealed the deal. The coroner said it took him less than two minutes to bleed to death. When I told the cops it took less than that, they told me to "Shut the frick up."

To show me how much they disliked me talking, they threw me in the back of a police car. I told them about the Singing Professor and how we left him for the pigs to eat, so they drove me out to his farm and introduced me to the Professor's wife. She claimed not to know me, said she had never seen me before, said that her husband ran off to marry a girl he had met while doing research in Thailand. He was writing a book. Sorry, she told me, but they did not raise pigs. They raised miniature goats. She shook my hand and hoped that I would get well soon. She said that her and her two children would pray for me.

Sometimes it amazes me how much time people spend praying in Hilo and still nothing gets better. Weed is still illegal. That's what I told the cops.

"Frickin Manny," they said, and cuffed my hands behind my back. "Where's the Judge? Where's Joe?"

To keep them happy, I tried to tell them about Frankie's freaky neighbor. They duct-taped my mouth shut. Then they slapped me hard. I figured that was to test the tape.

The cops had already put two and three together to figure out that the real estate developer and his administrative assistant had been washed off the cliffs while hunting for opihi. Frankie's report that he had seen the two of them, plenty times, crawling around on the cliffs for opihi had set the cops on the right trail. That same trail led them to discovering that the administrative assistant had been tricked into hiring illegals who had gone berserk, run amok, starting fires, pushing trucks over the cliffs and finally running off, into the hills, never to be seen again. The estate's lawyers agreed. After discussions with their insurance people, they considered the matter settled and promised that a new project manager would arrive from Alaska within the month.

I guess that left me in shock or some other kine syndrome because when the cops asked me about the Judge and Joe, my mind went blank. Had I seen him? I shrugged. Was she with him? A blank. Nothing. The cops shook their heads. Finally, when none of us could find the right words, they charged me with being drunk and disorderly, obstructing an investigation, negligent operation of a watercraft, property destruction, cruelty to my cat Steamer, and stealing the Judge's Radon.

I was looking at hard time just on the drunk and disorderly charge. Every townie had seen me disorderly enough times to know I deserved a couple shifts on the chain gang to change my attitude. They were casting their ballots when the Doc stepped in with my medical file. It looked thicker than the last time I had seen it and smelled of burned cheese and tequila. Pointing out the relevant details to the Prosecutor, she said that I needed help, and now was the time to give it to me.

"Frickin Doc." That's what the cops said.

*** (Cop break) ***

One last thing.

Not long ago, the Madonna came to see me. She was wearing a see-through, summer dress, white with red polka dots. Her blazing red hair was brushed straight back, touching down lightly on her exposed shoulders.

It was visiting day, and we were sitting at a picnic table backed up against the Koolau Cliffs. After surveying my latest brushwork, the Madonna nodded her approval. She liked pictures. She said I was getting better. As a reward, she handed me a block of pot brownies wrapped in silver paper, and a beer hidden inside a soda can. She said that Ms. Song would be pleased. She said that the urn with her ashes was parked in a real nice spot, on a hill above Hilo, in a cemetery with a view of the ocean. It was made of bronze and secured to a block of black marble. The Madonna said it looked like a very secure arrangement, almost permanent, unbreakable...for someone without tools.

I was sipping Bikini Blonde and chewing double-chocolate weed when the she pushed a manila envelope across the table. It was addressed to me. The return address had two names, from somewhere in the Philippines.

"Kids," the Madonna said.

"No kidding." That's what I said, but I say a lot of stuff like that when I'm talking to the Madonna. It wouldn't be much of a conversation if I didn't toss in a noun or two.

We sat there for a long time, me watching the polka dots dance on her dress. Until she whispered, "Any last words?"

The wind brushed across my lips and made the words slip away. The sky turned to black velvet. I guess I was imagining things, just like the Doc says, because I closed my eyes, and when I opened them the Madonna was gone and I was holding Joe's lighter. It felt smooth and new and in perfect working condition. The flame caught on the first try.

In the flickering light, I heard Pig-Dog, somewhere high up on the cliffs, howling at the stars. It sounded better than words.

All Pau (The End)

About the Author

While writing to escape, Lou Zitnik has been paying his share of the bills by teaching at a small college, coaching a swim team, reporting on sports for a daily newspaper, leading Scuba tours, and marrying a pretty attorney. In between gigs, he attended the Writers Workshop at the University of Iowa (MFA) and the University of Hawaii (Ph.D). At the moment, which has lasted nearly forty years, he lives in Hawaii with his attorney and two cats.

Lou has published two other books: *Blues in Paradise*, a collection of his stories, including two selected as first place winners in the Honolulu Magazine Fiction Contest; and *Magic Words in the Palace of Desire*, a novel about two cats and their search for the meaning of love and wasted food in movies.